LENNY

LENNY
First published in 2022 by
New Island Books
Glenshesk House
10 Richview Office Park
Clonskeagh
Dublin D14 V8C4
Republic of Ireland
www.newisland.ie

Print ISBN: 978-1-84840-824-1
eBook ISBN: 978-1-84840-825-8

British Library Cataloguing in Publication Data. A CIP catalogue record
for this book is available from the British Library.

Typeset by JVR Creative India
Edited by Meg Walker
Proofread by Djinn von Noorden
Cover design by Anna Morrison, annamorrison.com
Printed by L&C Printing Group, Poland, lcprinting.eu

New Island received financial assistance from The Arts Council
(An Chomhairle Ealaíon), Dublin, Ireland.

New Island Books is a member of Publishing Ireland.

10 9 8 7 6 4 5 4 3 2 1

LENNY

LAURA McVEIGH

NEW ISLAND

Also by Laura McVeigh

Under the Almond Tree (2017)

To Howard and Riley

The stars in my night sky

With love

'And now here is my secret, a very simple secret: It is only with the heart one can see rightly; what is essential is invisible to the eye.'

Antoine de Saint-Exupéry, *The Little Prince* (1943)

Chapter One

Ubari Sand Sea, Libya, 2011

In the middle of the desert, the boy sat on his young camel, *al mataya*, and looked across the dunes, north to where Ghadamis lay, east across the Ubari Sand Sea, south to the Acacus mountains, but he could see only the haze of the day bubbling on the horizon, heat melting the edges of land and sky.

At first, Izil heard nothing beyond the snort of the beast and a dry, clicking sound from its throat, and the suck of the sand as the animal stepped along the ridge.

When it came, the sound carried high – a whine, insistent and far off, then louder, closer. He looked up and saw the fighter jet as it passed overhead, a dark-grey shadow against the haze of the skies. The jet shot out of view, smaller, higher once more, the sound dwindling. The boy waited. He waited for the sound of dropping bombs, in the distance, with an echo that would shake the valley. He waited for more planes in the sky, but they did not come. His camel, tired of waiting, pulled his head to the side and walked on, following an invisible path back toward the tents.

The boy wondered what it would be like, to pilot such a plane, to fly at speed and altitude, to hold the fortunes of whole villages and valleys under the pressure of your thumb, tensed on a control stick. Out here in the Ubari desert, they had no television, but once when he had travelled with his father to Ghat for a cousin's wedding, he had sat in a row with all the children, while the adults ate and danced and celebrated, and he had sucked on sweet dates while watching *Top Gun* on a large screen. He, along with all the boys, apart from one, had fallen in love with Kelly McGillis. The refusenik was his cousin Hassan, who loved Goose, though he told no one of his feelings, only repeating, 'I feel the need ... the need for speed', over and over, falling about, laughing. His uncle, Ahmed, had beaten Hassan, and offered Izil a job selling mats to tourists in Ghat, if he wanted to stay on in the town, leave behind the desert life as they had chosen to do, but his father would not accept, and they had travelled back to Ubari. He had been sick on reaching his mother, the sugar heavy in his belly, the memory of the movie fresh in his mind.

The noise began again, the low far-off hum, the growl of approach, and for a moment the boy grew fearful. He was alone. The tents were at least an hour away. He feared for his family, even though the planes were meant to protect – that is what they said on the radio. *Sky devils*, his father called them, spitting in the sand.

The boy felt the inescapability of it all – he could not hide, could not run. He would not be able to warn them. So instead he just watched, looking up, his hand over his eyes, the pale cotton of the cloth *cheche* he wore loosely on his head flapping in the light breeze, as it wrapped around his cheeks and over his nose, leaving only his eyes exposed to the wind and light.

The plane flew high above him. For a moment, it paused in the air, then a sound of stuttering and the jet plane began to spiral downward as if it had forgotten how to fly. As it hurtled towards the dunes the boy saw the pilot eject, dangling for a moment in the sky, then dropping, his canopy opening late, the bulk of it dragging him along the dunes.

Further away, the jet plane burst into flames, sending up smoke signals far into the valley.

Izil had watched the man fall from the sky. Others would look for him – the boy was sure of that – but he had never seen one of these sky devils up close and he would not be robbed of the opportunity. So Izil, even though closer now to home, turned and set out for the ridge where the parachute billowed.

The pilot lay twisted in the desert dunes, his body torqued, his breathing faint – lips crusted in sand. Behind him, in the distance, smoked the wreckage of the jet. The man's arms and shoulder blades were pulled back at a sharp angle, weighted by the billowing of the parachute.

He had not had enough time to control his landing, and instead had hit the dunes, dragged along by the heavy rig until it had dropped to the sand, air filling the canopy late, and he had become tangled in it as he tumbled to earth.

The man's head throbbed with pain. His nostrils filled with the acrid smell of burning oil. The earth was still spinning. He remembered ejecting from the Viper, the spring-back of the cord, then free-falling as the desert grew closer too quickly, yanking at the cord, once, twice until it released and the air caught it and he righted, too late, dragging along the top of the dunes at an angle, a reluctant puppet caught up in his own strings. Not a textbook landing, granted, but a landing nonetheless.

He moved slowly, wriggling fingers and toes, bending his knees, checking for signs of damage. He would have liked to have sunk down into the sand, to become one with the earth. But the earth did not want him and so he lay there, the sun burning the back of his head, the parachute canopy rising and falling, sighing in the breeze.

The man waited for death. It did not come. Instead, after a long while, he felt the shadow of what he assumed was the enemy. The sky darkened over his head and looking up through one eye he saw the knobbly knees of the camel, smelt its dung drop to the earth beside him, and sitting on top, a barefoot figure, a small boy dressed in dusty indigo trousers and a faded red long-sleeved *California Dreamin'* T-shirt, an amulet, made of yellow desert glass, tied around his neck, his mother had told him to protect him from *djinns*, a pale *cheche* worn around his head, only the eyes uncovered, watching the man who found he could not speak, his throat parched and his tongue swollen, full of sand and silt.

The boy looked down at him as he lay there – this broken sky king.

Once it became clear that the man posed little immediate threat, Izil decided what must happen next.

Chapter Two

False River, Louisiana, 2012

Lenny slid out of the bald cypress tree, dropping the large cardboard box that swung off the end of his sneakers into the dust below him. Hunkering down beside it, he turned the old Plaquemine orange box over, opening it up, clambering in – ready for flight. His arms were held tense out in front of him as he buried down, his father Jim's pilot cap slipping down low over his eyes as he rocked from side to side.

'*Va-vrooooooom, neaaaaaaaoww ...*'

He tipped a little to the left, steering at a sharp angle.

'*Du-du-du-du-du-du-du.*'

He machine-gunned right, one hand pulling back the controls as his plane shot up into the blue cloudless sky, evading the enemy.

'Ha! You'll never catch me.'

He was the King of the Sky.

Lenny was free, travelling at the speed of light, gone now from the bayou, looking down on the winding silver ribbons and the smiling oxbow gleam of False River, before veering away towards the woodlands further upriver, earth once thick with trees, now yellow and scorched at the edges, dying. A gift to the land, some said, from the chemical companies.

Circling back in the other direction, Lenny flew over the twisting branches and early morning mists of the swampland, swiftly and at altitude, eager to be far from where trapped souls lay in wait, mournful and forgotten. He squeezed the agate stone he held in his fist. His mama Mari-Rose had given it to him – a *gris-gris* to keep him safe (*it'll protect you Lenny – I can't do no more for you, I just can't ...*).

As the sunshine soaked into the morning, he flew over the oak forests to the north, then the marshlands and wetlands that edged the land, circled over the sinkhole as it bubbled in the bayou below, until finally turning back once more he followed the river home – the water a sludgy silver-grey catching in the sunlight – leading him back to Roseville. He imagined he was flying over sand dunes, cutting through a blue cloudless sky. He saw the shadows below.

'Come in, major.'

He held his hand to his mouth, radio control aloft.

'Do you read me?'

Silence crackled down the receiver.

'Looks like it's just you and me then.' Lenny scrunched up in the box that carried the faint scent of sunshine and oranges, leant further forward, the cap slipping down a little, his eyes narrowed, scanning below for the enemy combatants he knew were waiting for him.

He breathed deep and let the air press down on his chest and ribs. It was a late autumn morning, unexpectedly cold and damp, with the trees glowing – russets, golden, reds and greens, and the sky, blue and unbroken. Lenny rubbed his fists on his frayed jeans and his T-shirt worn thin; light summer clothes, which made him shiver in the dappled shade. He tilted Jim's cap back from his forehead so that he could see out. His fingers were still stiff from the damp night before and he pulled the cuffs of the denim jacket down low over his hands as best he could for warmth.

'You'll not get away ... I see you. I see you down there.'

His shout carried on the breeze down to the river's edge and the grass banks below, causing an egret to startle and take flight.

Lenny locked on to the enemy. He punched the air in joy as he pressed down hard with his thumb on the trigger, releasing the missile that followed through the air, down, down, down, locked on the target, imagining the hangars of the chemical companies below, and then a moment later, smoke and white phosphorus flared up from the earth below. *Fire-and-forget.* That's what Jim had called it: fire-and-forget.

Lenny pulled the fighter jet sharply to the left, veering away from the plumes of smoke, looking back over his shoulder to make sure the job was done.

'Major, sir, can you read me?'

Lenny made a *sssssssssh* sound, his tongue clicking as he spoke once more into the radio.

'Coming home, sir. Lockhart is coming home.'

To anyone else passing by False River, and looking down towards the last row of stilted houses that ran down one edge of Roseville, each with their own rickety wooden jetty stepping out into the water, if they happened to spot him there, hidden under the sweep of the willow, by the bald cypress trees that edged the riverbanks, they would have seen a little olive-skinned boy of maybe nine, possibly ten years old, wearing a US Air Force pilot's cap set atop of a mess of white-blond curls (*¡Qué chica eres!* Arturo had told him once, pulling at his hair), peeking out from inside a large cardboard box stamped *Product of Plaquemines Parish* on the side.

And if they didn't see Lenny, they would most likely hear him, for he was full of laughter.

Some children, they just shine, don't they? No matter what.

It didn't seem to bother Lenny that he was out by the river on his own, though, on account of it being a Tuesday morning he really ought to have been at school. They would be wondering where he'd got to – right about now. Lenny gave it a moment's thought. He used to like Miss Avery's class. Now just even thinking about it made the red devil rise in him. Then he thought of his daddy, the sad-eyed look he had given Lenny that morning.

If you missed the bus, it was a walk of almost an hour, bit less if you went by the riverside and were happy to cross at the

Point and didn't mind getting a bit wet, the old swing rope bridge dipping down further each year into the brackish water as it did. He could do that. He considered his options, rubbing the strap of his watch – a frayed strap on a watch that his mother had given him one Christmas.

'So as you can tell what time it is,' she said, smiling at him, helping him loop it around his skinny wrist, the strap hanging loose, not tight to the skin. He had felt it was a momentous gift. He waited for her to teach him how it worked, but she never did.

He'd held on to it all the same, and he'd asked Miss Julie who lived next door if she could help him understand how it worked. Julie Betterdine Valéry was as old as the ancient bald cypress trees.

'Miss Julie's like 150 years old,' said Arturo (Lenny's best friend and one-time neighbour three doors along). 'And she stinks of pee.'

Arturo wrinkled up his nose and passed on calling with Miss Julie, but Lenny liked her. She would always lean over the fence, calling out in her rattlesnake voice, '*Bonjour* Léonard, and how are you today?' when he was out playing next to his mama who knelt in the garden, secateurs in hand, cutting back her own blooms – big blowsy pink and red roses, with a scent and colours to compete with the beautiful white magnolias that threatened to overtake Miss Julie's back yard.

The old lady suffered with arthritis in her bones – early in the day being her worst time. Then, shuffling, all bent over, it could take her half the morning to get from her porch steps down to the fence, so Lenny would be patient and keep an eye on her progress as she worked her way across, slow and careful not to trip.

'Falling's easy,' she'd say, 'it's the getting up that's so damn hard.'

But she didn't like charity, not even the good-mannered sort, and so Lenny would just wait it out until she was there, leaning on the fence, and he'd bring her a cold lemonade from the ice-box if Mari-Rose didn't notice (she was not the sociable type of mother and you wouldn't want to get on the wrong side of her secateurs, just in case). Besides, she didn't like Miss Julie much, calling her 'a world-class meddler' and rolling her eyes from the kitchen window as Lenny would recite chapter and verse to old Julie Valéry on how school was going, what the state of the world was, or discuss the latest advances in space travel, or how his dad might be home by Thanksgiving, or Christmas, or maybe summer, and telling her how his mama would cry at night – but that was a secret. Lenny would keep one eye on Mari-Rose in the kitchen, the other on Miss Julie whose breathing was raspy, and whose hands, with their blue veiny rivers and their splattered sunspots, would rest gently on Lenny's hand as she'd say, '*Merci Léonard* – most refreshing, indeed.'

She'd tip her head to the side a little, and Lenny would feel a warm, happy feeling in the pit of his belly.

He didn't have any actual grandparents of his own on account of Jim's father having died years before and Jim's mother being lost to painkillers in the Californian sunshine some years after, and his mama never spoke of her parents – like she'd come into the world without and it was better not to ask. Lenny liked to imagine Miss Julie was family, and if you saw them sitting together on the steps, their hair touching, smiles wide open to the world, the same lilt to their voices, you'd believe it was true. So, Lenny chose to ignore Arturo, who jeered at him for wasting time sucking up to 'that crazy old witch'.

Arturo was oftentimes of the same school of kindness as Mari-Rose. His dad was an alcoholic who beat his mother, so all Arturo knew of human kindness started from there. Lenny always felt this about him. Even on the day that Arturo beat him black and blue and kicked him in the gut, leaving him lying in the wet grass by the lake, saying, 'Just in case you thought we were still friends,' before turning on his heel, with Lenny wondering, *What the heck was that for?* But he didn't bear a grudge. Lenny reckoned life had made Arturo all kinds of messed up and God had made Lenny kind and forgiving like that. It was all a matter of luck.

'You need to wear it the other way around.'

Miss Julie had taken the watch off his wrist and put it back on carefully, tightening it for him.

'See *sha*, this here's the long hand – that counts minutes. The short one, that's for the hour. Let's start with that, see how you get on.'

And she would test him, with both of them sitting in the sun on their respective back-yard steps, shouting out across the fence. Miss Julie's voice, crackling, 'Léonard, what time is it now?'

Lenny would scrunch up his nose and squint at the lines on the watch face, and give it his best shot, then she'd get him to describe what he saw, and five minutes later she'd ask him again, and again until they tired of shouting at one another over the fence, and so that – over that particular summer when he was almost seven – was how Lenny learnt how to tell the time, while Mari-Rose spent her time indoors on the telephone to the bank, her voice raised, telling them that next month would be time enough to pay.

Time enough. Lenny often thought of his mother saying that, even though the bank didn't call any more.

Now Lenny was almost ten, and the watch didn't work properly. The glass had cracked on the day Arturo beat him up. Miss Julie had given him tape to hold it all together – as a temporary measure – and he'd gotten used to the new arrangement.

Lenny felt his stomach rumble. It was long gone midday and he was still sitting in the damp orange box, which now was a rocket ready for take-off, due for a voyage to Mars. He had been training for this mission for years.

It's not easy to become an astronaut. Not just anyone can do it. For a start, you need to be super-fit.

Lenny worked out every morning in the park – just like he'd watched his daddy do – swinging across the bars, doing press-ups in the dirt, running around the curve of the lake, once, twice, doing star jumps and then raising his knees high, running hard on the spot before collapsing down onto the soft embrace of the grass. Lenny remembered the way Jim would wink at him afterwards, to show he was okay, that he was strong and fine, even though Lenny could make out the thud of his heart through his vest. That was long ago, before Jim had left to 'go fly planes, help some folk needing help', but Lenny still remembered and now he trained too – vital for a future astronaut or a fighter pilot. Jim had warned him, 'G-force messes with your body Lenny, you've got to be ready for it.'

Then apart from the physical training, you needed to obviously know a lot about space and the universe. For this element of his preparation, Lenny spent many hours hunched over the table in the corner of Roseville Library – a little library full in the main of chunky romance novels, a small selection of dictionaries, some shelves of fiction, kids' books, cookery books, a big true-crime section (for everyone loves others' misfortune), and a smaller section still with atlases and an encyclopaedia and a book about space that was like the Bible if you were training to be an astronaut. He supplemented this intensive learning with watching endless reruns of *Star Wars* and *Star Trek* over at Arturo's house (that was before the great 'falling out' – as Miss Julie sadly termed it). So, all in all, Lenny felt pretty much prepared for space travel.

'Ten, nine, eight,' he intoned, frowning, his hands cupping his mouth, rubbing them together for warmth as the breeze off the water came sharper now, the sun slanting lower in the sky.

Lenny looked down at his imagined space suit. Whenever he put it on, he felt like he was protected a bit, or cut off a bit (which was almost the same thing), from the world. It got in the way, though, sometimes. Like if he needed to take a leak – that was hard in space.

Boy, do we take gravity for granted, he thought. Lenny was all about the detail. You get the detail right and then things just fall into place and look after themselves, that's what he felt.

'Seven, six, five ...'

Going to space was pretty complicated really because Lenny had to switch between being in the control tower – the controller was a man he imagined of say thirty-five years old, with a long, foxy face and orange eyebrows – and being Lenny Lockhart, astronaut and space explorer, although that part was easier because he was just playing himself. Some days, though, he played that different ways – like some days he would be really courageous, a no-fear kind of a guy, with some swagger and bounce in his space suit. Other days he would be more mysterious, a kind of sadness behind the glass of his helmet, like he was leaving behind loved ones who would miss him, and he knew this, but we needed someone to go, and Lenny was our guy. Right?

'Four, three, two ...'

'Léonard *sha*, you want some lunch? Jambalaya?'

Miss Julie was standing near the bottom of her garden, by the gap in the fence at the back under the magnolias, peering through.

'Food's getting lonely on the stove. I've made far too much again.'

She sighed.

'Be a good boy, help me out?'

Lenny thought about it for a moment: the hot chicken slipping down his throat, the smell of the meat, peppers, tomatoes and the dollop of gravy she would add in. Space would have to wait.

He clambered out of the box and brought it along with him, flinging it over the fence onto the grass as he slipped through the gap down onto the lawn beside her.

'Well, seeing as you need my help, Miss Julie, I suppose it's okay. But I'll cut the lawn for you this week, tidy it up?' He offered this gesture in return.

She nodded, her lips pursed in pain in a solid line, the lipstick bleeding deep pink into the creases around her mouth. She had once been a great beauty, second-place runner-up in the Queen of False River beauty pageant one year (could have got first place but she wouldn't let the judge feel her up and so she slipped in the rankings – woman has to have some self-respect, she told herself afterwards and she knew she'd been prettier than second place, though of course beauty lies in the eye of the beholder and true beauty, well that's something you can only see with the heart, and that judge was plain short-sighted). Miss Julie knew all this. She'd lived a long time and knew many things by now, so she was pleased Lenny offered to help – though the lawn was starting to look a little bald given how frequently he would mow it. Still, what did grass matter in the greater scheme of things?

Lenny helped her make her way back inside. It took them a good long while for her hips had seized up with all the standing around, but that gave them time to gently navigate around the red-ant trail that criss-crossed east on the garden path, and allowed time to listen to the tapping of a woodpecker that liked to perch on the oak tree by the side of the house, and would keep Miss Julie company often.

'That's Frederik,' she said to Lenny, in a bit of a rasping whisper like it was a secret that she had actual names for birds and frogs and things.

'I know, Miss Julie. You told me before. He's a red-bellied woodpecker. That right?'

'Good work Léonard,' she said, 'fine memory for the detail, that's a real gift, hold on to that now!'

Inside her house in the winter months was cool and damp, when the impossible heat of the summer had ebbed away. Miss Julie didn't believe in indoor heating. No call for it, climate being what it was most of the year. Then there was the cost of having it, and really if you put on an extra cardigan and thick winter socks on those odd cold days and nights when the damp would sink into your bones, you might not look so stylish, but you didn't shiver so much and wasn't that the point really. Miss Julie felt strangely content that she didn't hand over more money for things when it wasn't entirely necessary to do so. Instead, she had a glass jar with a metal screw-top lid on the kitchen countertop and she'd save her spare bills in there, gathering them up for rainy days.

'No point in trusting the bank to mind it for me,' she'd say, 'bunch of crooks these days. Why, I'd just be giving it away and it doing no good in the world.'

Lenny's eyes landed on the dusty glass jar. There was a lot of money in it now – mainly bills, a few coins at the very bottom. He imagined all the things he could buy with a treasure hoard like that. What riches.

The kitchen was warmer than the rest of the house, the stove having been on to slow-cook the jambalaya. Lenny set up the table the way Miss Julie had shown him. Many years ago, she'd worked in a grand hotel over in New Orleans and they had been very particular about the placement of cutlery and the polish to every glass. Miss Julie passed on these preferences to Lenny and he was respectful of the old lady's wishes. Besides, sitting down to eat a meal was such a novelty these days that he liked to take his time over it, liked to make the table pretty too, and he'd wash his hands in the small outhouse to the side of the kitchen, using plenty of hot water and the bar of lavender soap she left out for him, along with a small, fluffy towel that had *Clean hands, closer to God* stitched on the side of it. Then, once cleaned up properly (sometimes even wetting behind his ears and giving his face a splash) he would slide onto the seat opposite her and help serve up lunch.

'This here is my own recipe, hope you like it.'

She spooned brown gravy onto his empty plate, then scooped out the jambalaya, heaping it up on the boy's plate.

'Can't beat home cooking with mystery ingredients,' she smiled.

Lenny laughed. Miss Julie wasn't big on following the rules.

'I added in … can you guess what?'

Lenny breathed in the warm smell of the dish, letting the hot, sweet juices marinate in his senses.

'Sugar and cinnamon?'

'That's right, and a slug of brandy.'

She giggled, her hand over her lips.

'Don't worry, the alcohol will have burnt off.'

In fact, the pot had dried out quite a bit, as they had taken a long time to make their way indoors, but Lenny just turned over the burnt rice, covering it in the gravy and crunched through, making appreciative *num num* sounds as he chewed, savouring the warmth and taste of the food. He no longer shivered, letting go of the chill that had caught hold of him in the night out in the bayou.

She didn't ask him if he shouldn't really be at school and Lenny, having clean forgotten about his earlier plan to walk the distance, let it go from his mind.

'So, where did you travel to this morning, Léonard?' Miss Julie asked him, her expression serious, her eyes sparkling in a face creased with years of laughter and tears (for one often accompanies the other, she found).

'I was in the desert, fighting enemy combatants,' he replied, quite solemn and thoughtful, before scooping up more food from the pot to fill the space he had just cleared on his plate.

Each time he would empty a small piece of plate, he would fill it again, hoping she didn't think him greedy. The ache in his stomach had dulled somewhat and he felt the warmth of the meat slip down his throat, and the gravy juice sticky on his lips.

'And what was the outcome?' She leaned forward, her bony elbows on the tablecloth, keen to hear what he had to tell her.

'Well, it was a fierce battle of wills, but I brought them down in the end, though I'd not much help. They left me to it, you know.'

She nodded.

'And did the other fighters die?' Miss Julie never shied away from the tough questions.

Lenny looked down at the flowery lace tablecloth under which he hid his dirty jeans, marked as they were with soil and grass stains.

'They did.'

'I see. And how do you feel about that?'

Her question surprised Lenny, but he thought about it.

'Sad, I guess. Happy too. It's hard to explain.'

'Oh, murder always is,' she said, disapproving. Miss Julie was very much a pacifist.

'It was either them or me.' Lenny looked up at her, defiant.

'Well, when you put it like that, it's more a matter of self-defence, I suppose.'

She looked thoughtful. Miss Julie's husband, Stanley, had been in the Navy. She had last seen him, one bright spring day, 1952, not long after they'd married when he'd left for war, smart in his uniform, headed to Korea ... He had looked very handsome, she thought, still optimistic, still certain. He had never come back – though she never got a letter, she said, and so she remained hopeful that one day he might just walk back into the house and they'd pick up again like before, though as the years passed this got harder to keep a hold of, love and memory both being slippery to the touch.

She kept a photograph of him in uniform on the hall table and Lenny liked to go talk to him sometimes after lunch, and tell him, 'Stanley, it's about time you came home now. Miss Julie is missing you.'

He would touch the glass as if stroking Stanley's face and the sight of it always made Miss Julie tear up a little, not that she'd let Lenny see that.

'You ever cooked Jamaican food?' Lenny asked.

'What food?'

'Jamaican?'

'Can't say as I have, matter of fact.'

'Just, they have a new book at the library – looks kind of tasty.'

Lenny blushed at the audacity of the suggestion, but Miss Julie kept a steady hand to the conversation.

'Well, that sounds adventurous. Jamaican, you say? And what style of thing they like to eat?'

'Um, mainly saltfish, fried dumplings, roasted breadfruit and I saw something called callaloo fritters, sounded *kind* of interesting.'

'That so?'

Lenny nodded, worried now he had offended her cooking.

'Why don't you take my library card, next time you go, pick it up if it's there. You'll have to help me with ingredients and whatnot – can't be carrying heavy bags, can I?'

Lenny laughed, that deep belly laugh he had when happiest.

'You can help me cook. Always said a man should be able to cook his own food, not be reliant on a woman doing it.'

Lenny thought of his mama and his laughter dried up. Miss Julie didn't seem to notice.

'You want some pecan pie and ice-cream, for afters?'

Lenny nodded, lifting the empty plates to the sink, helping her tidy everything away and then they sat with the bowls and big spoons, a blast of heat coming from the stove as she opened the door again to lift out the pie dish.

Miss Julie's house was the same as Lenny's house. That's to say, both were made in the same design and layout, the same strip of lawn to the fence and path and jetty edging the river at the bottom, the same kitchen windows looking out over the back yard, the fronts looking up towards Main Street. Inside they were entirely different. Miss Julie was keen on flowery wallpaper, the flock kind that you can run your fingers over, and it feels bumpy to the touch. She liked net curtains too, and silk cushions in pastel colours – peach and pink and baby blue. It was not to Lenny's taste, but then it was not his home.

He pushed back his chair, groaning with a full belly, feeling sated and warm and happy, and he did not want to leave.

'Can I help clear away?' He lifted the last remaining dirty dishes and bowls to the sink and she let him, grateful not to have to do it for the sink was a little high these days for her to reach into and she preferred a sink-stopper to save the water from running out.

'People are so wasteful these days,' she'd say, showing Lenny how she liked everything washed and rinsed and left to 'air dry' as she called it.

In the early evening, she would have a bit of a sleep, just sitting up in her chair in front of the TV by the window, a crocheted blanket across her knees. Her niece, Annabelle, had once brought her a gift of one of those soft towelling all-in-one contraptions to wear, like they advertise on television and in the backs of magazines, but it had looked so ridiculous Miss Julie had made her take it straight back home with her.

'Colder winters up where you are,' she said to the girl, 'be much more use to you than me. Don't worry. It's the thought that God sees – he sees your kindness, go on now, take it with you.'

The girl had smiled at her, uncertain, before packing it back up in the plastic it had come in, and putting it back in the car, then kissing the woman goodbye, leaving her alone once more, muttering something about how she should spend the holidays with them – Miss Julie just waving her away.

'There's no blanket can stop you from feeling lonely,' she had sighed to Lenny, who liked the sound of the gift and wished she'd held on to it.

The girl didn't come back and Miss Julie never missed the gift nor the visitor.

'Some folk just passin' through, ain't got what it takes!'

She'd chuckled and switched on the news, which she liked to hear low in the background as she slept.

Lenny tucked the old crocheted blanket around her.

'Who we writing to today, Miss Julie?'

She raised an eyebrow.

'Oh, you want to help with that?'

'Sure.'

'Well, okay then. Today it's the turn of Belly Rae's Grill …'

'What's the issue?'

Lenny chewed the end of the pen, the blue ink squirting into the corners of his mouth and staining his fingertips.

But no answer came for she was already fast asleep in the chair, the blanket hopped up around her.

Lenny settled down with the newspaper to read up on what was happening in the world while the old lady slept, her head tipped back against the headrest, her mouth open, a gentle rhythmic snoring soon filling the room.

To the side, on a low wicker coffee table sat a stack of envelopes ready to go in the mail. She would ask Lenny, usually once a week, to send them off.

'Small acts of protest, love letters to our better angels,' she called them, this bunch of letters complaining about poor customer service, or environmental ills and unseen injustices, often calling for recompense – usually financial. Miss Julie was, in addition to being financially astute, well read and widely read, and she watched more than one channel of news, so she had a range of views on the state of the world and opinions on what was to be done about it.

Lenny had really learnt how to write with her, how to connect the letters up and keep them all in a straight line, practising as she dictated to him, for her own hands had the shakes and most days now if she picked up a pen, the end result, she said, was more like 'One of those heart-monitor machines in the hospital in the middle of heart failure.' Miss Julie laughed for there was nothing else she could do about it.

Outside the air had grown cooler, the day's dust settling on the golden spines of autumn colour. The light had drained from the sky, vivid pinks and oranges being sucked back into the swamp, so Lenny pulled across the net curtains and went to heat up some milk for her on the stove. She had taught him how to light it, and balancing on a chair he could reach up and get cups down, and the milk from the ice-box, and pour a little into a pan, keeping an eye on it and the heat turned down low so that it didn't bubble. His mama had never let him near the stove at home, but Miss Julie thought him sensible enough.

'There's adults not wise enough to use such things,' she'd sigh, 'but Léonard you'll be fine, just be safe!'

He nodded and felt grown-up and trusted and helpful, all at once.

On the television, he watched the news. Helicopters flying over a dusty ochre landscape, buildings with their sides blown out, smiling children, sad children, a soldier smoking a cigarette in the background, the reporter wearing a bullet-proof jacket and talking earnestly into camera, impossible to tell if the words were the first or second take. Miss Julie preferred the volume down low as she rested and so Lenny sat close to make out what was being said. His hand reached up to the screen and traced the glass. He was looking as if behind the soldier. He was looking for something.

Today Miss Julie didn't wake up at her usual time and he let the milk go cold on the small wicker table beside her and the stack of letters. He would soon have to leave – his father would be looking for him, wanting to hear about his day. Lenny looked at the clock on the hall table next to Stanley. Nearly seven o'clock already. If she didn't wake up soon, he'd have to leave without writing the letters and she'd be annoyed at him. Miss Julie could get plenty scratchy. Lenny wondered about what to do. Then he decided to risk it and shook her gently on the shoulder.

'Miss Julie? You still want to write those letters today? Miss Julie?'

The old lady opened her eyes and looked at the little boy a moment, as if unsure who he was, then her face cleared again. 'Oh Léonard, *sha*, you made my milk. You are a treasure.'

He blushed, not used to being fussed over.

'Those letters will keep until tomorrow, not much that can't wait a day or two, right? You'll come see me then? Here, take my library card with you. Why don't you bring me that Jamaican cookery book if it's still there? We can have a look at it together.'

She sat up, looking at the clock.

'There's an old sweater of Stanley's in the cupboard by the stairs, a navy blue one. Full of moth holes, I'm afraid, but otherwise cosy and clean. I took it out for you – noticed you forgot yours today, and it's getting cold, nights out. Take it, if you like?'

She looked at the boy who in turn stared at the swirl of carpet on the floor of the front room, his cheeks reddening, before saying, 'Okay, if you looked it out special. And I'll bring it back.'

'There's a good boy. You can tell your father I said it's okay to keep it ...'

Her voice tapered off, her eyes hovering on the screen now, her mind caught by the newscaster's voice.

Lenny opened the hall cupboard. A dusty golf bag, then a couple of fishing jackets and a solitary orange ski jacket (bought long ago optimistically in a sale, back when she had dreamed of great adventures further afield with Stanley, all the places they would travel to when he would return, kept just in case, but never worn) all fell down on top of him before he found the navy sweater hanging on a hook to the back. It was a warm and cosy sweater, and he pulled it on over his denim jacket, tight up around his ears and cheeks to cut out the bite of the breeze down by the river.

'Thanks Stanley,' he said, saluting the absent husband.

'Thanking you, Miss Julie, see you tomorrow.'

'Bless you, Léonard, good to have your help.'

She always said this – even on the days when he didn't feel like he had been any help at all, even then she thanked him and it made him feel good about the day, and it made the night-time easier to manage.

Chapter Three

Ubari Sand Sea, Libya, 2011

The pilot awoke in the tent a few weeks later. As he opened his eyes, several faces stared back at him and, at the front, sat the young boy who had shaded him from the sun and carried him here on his camel. The voices spoke, a mix of Arabic and another language he did not recognise.

He was alive, but who he was, was lost to him.

At first, the edges of the day blurred around him, faces coming and going, a strong smell that he grew to realise was his own, shame rising in him, trying to turn away to face the goatskin canvas behind him. He could not move.

A woman leant over him, her dark eyes warning him to stay still.

He looked down and saw his arm and shoulder were wrapped and pinned against his side. From the corner of the goatskin tent, a group of women and girls giggled. He tried to sit up but the hollowness in his chest had him flat against the mat on which they had laid him.

'Where am I?' The words, in faltering Arabic, came to him from somewhere he could not remember.

'Safe.' The boy smiled. He leaned towards him, offering water. The man's lips were dry and cracked. He let the water spill down his chin, swallowing in sips, grateful that the boy held the flask steady for him, helped him raise himself up enough to drink.

The boy gesticulated for him – mimicking a sleeping man (snoring, more laughter followed from the far side of the tent), hobbled (to show the damaged leg) and a hand to his head, wincing in pretend pain.

'*Shukran.*'

This feeble thanks was all the man could offer as the darkness claimed him once more, his head hurting behind his eyes as if he had been dropped from a great height, as if the days and nights lost to him waited there behind his eyelids, and he held to them, weighed down and dragged along by them.

In his dreams, he saw the world below; the desert stretching out for miles, the dunes echoing back into the pale pinks of the sky. He felt the thrust, acceleration, G-force, pressure on his abdomen and legs, the jet turning upside down, his mask pressing upon his skin as he shot through the sky. Free. Then the engine catching, something amiss as he had struggled to right the jet, and a feeling of the earth falling away from him. Panic. Just for a second, then he pulled her round and accelerated again – until the blues of the sea in the distance came into view, except it wasn't the sea, it was the sky and the clouds above as he broke through. Free once more.

Below he left behind a dusty clutch of sandstone dwellings, blackened and smoking now in the heat of the day, flames rising into the sky. He did not look back. Fire-and-forget.

The boy let him cry out in his sleep and went outside to play. The caravan of tents was hidden in a *wadi*, in a dip near a large oasis, date palms fringing the water where gazelles and jackals would come to drink, and lizards darted between the rocks.

This was a place they liked to stop, some even arguing they should remain throughout the year, there where the water and shade was plentiful and yet it was far from the towns and cities that skirted the borders of the country. Beyond the *wadi* stretched the dunes, echoing far into the distance – high ridges of sand waves where the children would chase and play in the cool of the evening, running shrieking once, twice, back around the camels that sat now with their legs bent, tethered, watching before the children, exhausted and happy and called back, would return to the lights of the fire by the tents, and watch the dark oasis water catch a hold of the night stars.

But to remain too long, rooted in one place, even one place so beautiful, that was not the Imuhar way – for a man who wanders is free. His home is the desert: the sky, the stars. He is not tethered, neither to place nor possessions, only to the desert sands – that is home and that is what he carries in his heart.

So, when the caravan travelled to the towns, to trade the herds, to buy provisions, to sell the jewellery made, to gather news of the world beyond the edges of the desert, a sense of longing to be back in the sand seas would often come over the travellers – *assouf*, a yearning in the soul. The boy too felt this, how the desert was a part of him, its grains of fine sand buried deep beneath his fingernails.

It was only for the injured guest that they remained there so long, and soon – whether he was ready to move or not – they would need to roll up the mats and tents, pack up and load the camels again, for it would not be long before others came to try and find him.

The man had fallen from the sky and lived. It was a sign. He had been sent to them for a reason, and so he was protected. Protected by Allah, protected by the stars, by the sands other men feared to cross. A pride came to the boy who sat on the edge of the water, his feet circling, his toes cold and wet as he tried to reach out to hook a star, then watched, laughing, as they drifted away from him in ever-widening circles.

He had brought the man: this stranger – a gift from the heavens.

'You've done well,' Izil's father Wararni told him, rubbing his hair with his hand, smiling at his son.

So, he too was protected now.

Chapter Four

Roseville, Louisiana, 2012

Outside, Lenny spotted the outline of his father down at the clump of willow trees that knotted their way around the edge of the lake, for theirs was the very last street before suburbia seeped back into nature.

Roseville was banked on one side by the False River, situated as it was upstream from Alma and Anchor – both now ghost towns, and Roseville too was headed that way. Just a bunch of old bayou towns that drowned long ago when the Mississippi flooded her banks and swallowed them up, or tornadoes and hurricanes struck – lifting whole towns, ripped clear from the earth. Downstream too the parishes had emptied out some when the chemical companies, it was said, poisoned the groundwater and the wells made folk ill. Cancer Alley, they called it. Then the land was swallowed up by the rising waters, drilling offshore in the Gulf damaging the balance of things, and so folk packed up and moved on, further inland or out of state – for what else could you do? You just carried with you what you couldn't bear to leave to the waters.

Each year, more and more of the old places were disappearing, just washed away, huge swathes of the country, plain gone. That was the story all along the riverbanks.

Roseville had clung on – there was a sugar mill working a few miles out of town where nearby at times there was lumberyard work to be found, and tourists still came to visit in the summer, buying up antiques, taking boats out on the lake from the levees, fishing for striped bass or filling up the south flats by Jarreau in duck-hunting season, seeking out Cajun cooking, buying up summer camps on the waterfront, or rooting around the old plantation houses, now open to curious visitors.

Locals were leaving again, though. Roseville was half-empty now, houses shuttered up, the bank signs hammered into the salty lawns, the streets often quiet as few cars ever stopped, always passing by. Ever since the sinkhole had appeared one night, sucking up whole rows of bald cypress, bubbling, a slick dark gleam on its surface and folk had started to get sick – the leaving had begun once more.

At night, Lenny imagined the ghosts coming up out of the swampland and watching the town lights switch off one by one until all was darkness and the only sounds left were the night chorus of the frogs singing, the hoot of the owls, the birr of crickets' wings and the woodpeckers tapping on hollow trunks.

That, and the rising smell of the sinkhole, fetid, poisoning everything it touched.

'Lot of people ill around these parts. Never used to be – it's the chemicals they just let spill into the water' – that's what his mama Mari-Rose had said, soothing Lenny's coughing one night, her hand held flat on his chest.

'Some folk *n'aiment pas* the wild – find it scary to be surrounded by a whole lot of nothing, that too ...' she stroked his forehead, watching Lenny twisting in sinkhole nightmares, imagining the world around him disappearing. At dawn, he woke to find her still there, her hand on his shoulder, a tired look in her eyes, just waiting on the daylight.

Other townsfolk complained as well – mainly Arturo's mother, Beatriz, who dreamed of escaping to the big city lights of Baton Rouge or even further afield and leaving her drunken brute of a husband far behind. She had often shared these daydreams with Mari-Rose over a cup of coffee and pastries, Beatriz widening at the hips from early-onset diabetes, a medical epidemic sweeping the country, with walking looked upon with distrust; and the furthest some folk went in the day was from television to ice-box – some athletic souls even several times in a day, depending on blood sugar requirements, which tended to increase as the cooler bite of autumn, then winter, set in.

'In the city, I'd be a size zero,' she wailed to Lenny's mother, who had looked at her unblinking.

Lenny waved now to his father, and the man raised his arm in return, a dark silhouette against the edge of the tupelo and willow trees.

'Look what Miss Julie gave me!' Lenny showed off the sweater, its sleeves trailing far beyond his hands, the seam down to his knees.

'That so,' his father grunted, barely taking in the boy.

While Lenny was a beautiful-looking kid, with his tawny skin, blondish sun-streaked curls, dark lashes and winning smile, his father Jim was pale-skinned with a look of longing to him. Born in California, yet son to an Irish father from the Glens of Antrim in the north (a man who had been sorely mismatched with his glamorous Californian wife), Jim had been raised as a boy first in the north of Ireland before returning, and he felt himself to be always out of step, neither one thing nor the other – always unsure where to call home, for in truth no one had ever shown him what home could be.

His dark hair, once cropped tight about his skull, had grown long and wavy. A once-handsome man, he now looked like all he wanted to do was to walk away from himself – a man so unlike his son that to see them together, you would find it hard to imagine them linked by blood or temperament.

And Lenny's character and looks had not come either from Mari-Rose, his mother. She was a doe-eyed, full-hipped Louisiana beauty by birth. Once engaged to a childhood sweetheart, a local boy who hung himself one Wednesday in the red barn on the edge of Roseville, Mari-Rose had just stayed put, reckoning, 'I can be as unhappy here as anywhere else.'

There she had stayed, catching Jim's eye at a dance up in Denial one summer – her dancing in a red dress covered in tiny white flowers, her smile a promise.

Jim was drifting, travelling around, trying to decide if a life of combat was a calling to heed or not, if he should return to Texas and his pilot training, or whether he should stay, taking summer work where he could while he figured out his own mind. He had not planned on staying in Roseville, nor had he planned on belonging to anyone – but he found it hard to leave Mari-Rose with her sadness that drew him to her (and harder still when she told him they would be having a child together) and so Jim married her in that red barn (to chase away the demons of the past, she said, though truth be told the owner Man March gave it to them for free, out of sympathy on account of her loss).

The wedding had a band hired in from Red River who did a turn at French music too for the old-timers. It was a good day, could have even been a good beginning, but when the summer lumberyard work dried up and his enthusiasm for Mari-Rose had waned, Jim went back to the base, right back into training and soon was far from Louisiana, and up in the Texan skies, back wrestling with G-force, high above it all – a free man once more. After that, they sent him out to a place in the Mojave Desert they called 'The Box' to learn what to expect – in a place full of fake desert towns, peopled by actors trapped in a war that never stopped.

For a few years, Jim came and went like this, mostly spending his time in Texas or California, or when they needed him to, sent far away to other places where there were wars to be won, or lost.

Lenny – winning child that he was – held only a tenuous claim on Jim's heart (him seeing in the child something of himself that he preferred to forget), and so Jim, a stranger to love and care, found it within him then to leave his wife and son behind for long spells, and go off in search of adventure and glory – or death, whichever would find him first. He allowed himself to get caught up in war, in doing something that took him out of himself. Jim just wanted to feel alive. He wanted to step out of the shadows.

Now, though, he no longer felt alive. War did that to a man.

'How's Miss Julie?'

'She's good. Tired, I think. Fell asleep early and it was hard to wake her.'

'Oh. She give you something to eat?'

Jim asked quiet, as if he didn't much care either way.

'Yep, jambalaya with gravy ...'

Lenny noticed his father's face pinch in a little.

'Sorry Pop, I should have saved some.'

Lenny looked down at his sneakers and the lace on one that had come undone.

'I can fend for myself.'

Jim ruffled the boy's curls.

It had been hard since he'd returned to Roseville. They had warned him about it at the base, how difficult it would be to move from one world back to another, told him to reach out if he needed help. No doubt about that, there were days when he struggled, days too he could see the sunshine of the boy, could feel himself coming slowly back to life, could feel it like a revelation waiting to unfold. Jim flinched, frightened of his own heart, but the boy took his hand, and father and son walked up the track, out into the night, along by the picket fence that ran to the back of the houses of Roseville. On the jetty ahead, the silhouette of an egret leant looking out at the water, craning forward before taking off, gliding gracefully over the river and arcing away towards the grass banks across the water.

Jim turned up the collar on his jacket to keep out the cold night air. On one shoulder, he lugged a heavy canvas bag packed with hammocks and an old tent.

The man walked with his shoulders hunched over, in part to keep out the chill, in part because he didn't notice he did so, for he had grown used to it.

'I went to the desert today, Pop. Killed the enemy.'

Jim looked down as he and Lenny stepped carefully along the wooden boardwalk edged with moss that snaked along the edge of the lake.

'*Da-da-da-da-da*,' Lenny then jumped ahead, zooming now along the path, showing his father how he had shot down the enemy combatants.

'Don't you kids know any different games?' his father asked.

'I nearly went to space too – was in the rocket, all ready to go and everything, but then Miss Julie called for me and I …'

'Space travel. Now there's a career. Need schooling for that, though.'

The man sighed.

'You got to get back to class, Lenny.'

Lenny shifted from foot to foot.

'Your mother wouldn't like to think you're missing out.'

Lenny balled up his fists. 'Don't think she much cares.' He muttered it under his breath.

'What's that, Lenny? Don't disrespect your mother, especially when the woman is not here to defend herself.'

Lenny walked a few steps ahead, his shoulders too hunched up against the cold.

Silence fell between them as the boardwalk petered out and they walked out into the swampland and the trees, the lights of town behind them now.

Lenny heard the howl of a dog far off and the crack of twigs underfoot as he made his way in the dark.

'Watch out for traps, can take the leg off a boy,' his father warned, shining the torchlight ahead of them both until they found a dip in a clearing, surrounded by bald cypress trees, their roots criss-crossing, reaching down into the salty land. There was space between them to light a fire, and Jim set to work.

'When I was your age, I used to love going camping,' he said, rubbing his hands together, trying to gather up sticks dry enough to serve for a fire.

'Grand adventure, life under the stars.'

Lenny shivered in the cold and wandered off to pee beside the trunk of a tree just outside of the circle.

In the darkness, he felt the sway of the trees, and the swamp beyond, alive all around him and he hurried back to his father's side, pushing thoughts of the creatures he imagined out of his mind, trying to focus instead on helping get the flames to dance and warm them both.

'I ever tell you the story of Fionn mac Cumhaill and Bennadonner?' his father asked as the fire settled in and they began to warm by the flames, both sitting on rolled logs. Jim boiled up a tin kettle of water, an enamel mug ready for each of them, a gumbo mix packet in his pocket, lifted from the shelf in the store before anyone noticed.

Lenny smiled. This was one of his favourite stories. He slid closer to Jim on the log that made for a seat by the fire, and he wrapped them both in the blanket from his father's bag, after Jim had slung the two hammocks between the trees next to the glow of the fire and fixed the canvas of the tent hung over them both for shelter.

Jim folded small pieces of paper as he spoke, creating figures to accompany the story he told in the night air. Lenny watched his father and pulled out from his own pockets a folded paper egret, a snake, a fox, a bear and some tiny figures which Jim had already made for him, and that he carried around carefully, for fear of losing them. He lined them up on his lap – an audience forming for Jim's tale.

'Well, Bennadonner was a fierce giant, one of the bravest in all of Scotland.'

'How tall was he?'

'Oh, at least ten feet high and as wide as Man March's barn.'

'Was he a kind giant?'

'Well, no. He was fierce, and he was having trouble with a giant across the way in Ireland who went by the name of Fionn mac Cumhaill.'

'What happened?'

'Now, Fionn and Bennadonner took to shouting at each other across the sea, hurling insults for all to hear. But Bennadonner, he didn't know how to swim so they couldn't get a hold of each other and fight it out properly. Well, Fionn mac Cumhaill got so fed up shouting at the other giant that one day he pulled up a lump of land from the ground and hurled it into the sea, and then he threw stone after stone after stone to build a bridge so Bennadonner could climb across.'

'And did he?'

'Well, by now Fionn mac Cumhaill was so exhausted he lay down for a nap and fell to snoring soundly, and as he slept Bennadonner came marching across, ready to fight with his enemy. Fionn's wife, Oonagh – she sees this hulk of a giant coming crashing across the waves on the rocks to Ireland and she looks at her husband and sees he'll be no match for the Scotsman who's the width of Man March's barn and over ten feet tall, and so quick as a flash she grabs a baby's bonnet and a blanket and she covers over Fionn and sits the bonnet on his head.'

Lenny leaned into Jim's wide shoulders, smiling up at him, laughing, letting the fire warm up his frozen toes.

'So, when Bennadonner sees this enormous sleeping baby, he shouts, "Where's mac Cumhaill?" and Oonagh chides him and says, "Shush now, can't you see Fionn mac Cumhaill's baby is lying here fast asleep?" And on seeing the monstrous size of the baby, Bennadonner thinks to himself, *The father must be a mountain of a man.* And he turned on his heel and fled, racing so fast that he broke up the bridge that Fionn had thrown across from one country to the other, and that's how it stays to this very day.'

Lenny laughed and let his head drop on his father's shoulder as Jim sipped on the soupy mixture, stirring it round in his mug, watching his young son sleep. Then he lifted him up and wrapped Lenny in the blanket, pulled it close round his face, and placed him in the hammock nearest the fire. There the boy slept, the fire glowing against his cheeks, him far away dreaming of giants and battles in far-off countries.

Only then, when Lenny was settled and protected by sleep, did Jim bend over and sob, his hands shaking, the empty mug fallen in the leaves.

He had told Lenny it would be an adventure. No need to go far from home, in case Mari-Rose came back.

'We should wait for your mama,' he said.

'What if she never comes back? She's been gone nearly a year.' Lenny said it quiet and low, not looking at Jim. 'What if she meant it this time?'

'That woman loves you Lenny, don't you ever forget that – even if it looks like it is not the case, you're her sunshine. Mine too. She's just struggling, is all. What kind of mother just up and leaves? She'll be back, she'll be back for her sunshine.'

He had ruffled the boy's curls, choking back the anger in his throat, not knowing what else to tell the boy, not knowing how to explain what he couldn't rightly understand himself, the way she'd shut in on herself, locking them out.

'She tell you that, that she'll be back?' Lenny asked him, suspicious.

Jim nodded, but he couldn't look him straight in the eye, and Lenny knew it was a lie.

'You're her little prince, that's what she used to call you – on account of your curls, and that story she liked.'

Well, that was true at least. Lenny knew that was a thing she used to say to him when he was little. He remembered her rubbing his head, telling him about a little prince and the stars and a wise old fox and a pilot far from home. She had smelt like roses leaning over him, stroking his hair, singing to him to get him to fall asleep when he was missing his daddy who was never there. That was when she was kind, and still in love, and hopeful.

Then, when Jim stopped calling, she had stopped with the stories and the singing, saying Lenny was old enough to settle himself to sleep. She grew cold and faraway. He would hear her out on the porch at night, drinking alone, or in her room, crying.

She'd been gone so long now he'd almost forgotten what her voice had sounded like, but he remembered what she said, how she had said it, and the ways she had changed.

Jim gathered up more firewood. The night sounds rustled around him. He took the gun from the bag, rubbing it, checking the barrel. Never knew when something might just jump out of the woods – man or beast. Best to be ready for it.

The man at the lumberyard had shaken his head, sorrowful, when Jim had gone to see him that morning.

'I'll take whatever you've got.'

'Got nothin'. We got nothin'.'

The man had looked apologetic and held his palms up to the sky as if waiting for rain.

Jim nodded. 'Well, if you get something, I'm willing to take it, anything at all.'

He looked the man straight in the eye, but the old-timer waved Jim on, not wanting to foster false hopes.

'*Désolé*. Sorry.'

Everyone was sorry. Ever since he'd got back, once the shakes had quietened down and he wasn't talking quite so much to himself, and had started putting himself back together, ever since then he'd been looking for a job. Anything to be useful. At first, Mari-Rose was supportive, though she'd looked so surprised when he had walked back up to the house, dragging his bad leg a little behind him, like an unwanted Christmas gift. When he first disappeared, they'd called to tell her they thought he had been lost in combat, and that they were sorry. There'd be some money, though, once they knew for sure. Then there'd been a phone call, saying maybe they'd made a mistake after all, and there'd be no money. Looked like he wasn't dead after all. Left her so she didn't know what to imagine.

Only Lenny had been excited to see him, swinging off his waist, hugging him tight.

Mari-Rose had looked unhappy but resigned.

'Best get a job,' she'd told him after a week of hanging about the house, upsetting her routine.

'I am trying, Mari-Rose.'

She had snorted at him.

At night, they lay back to back in the bedroom upstairs, the voile curtains she had hung flapping in the breeze for she liked to sleep with the window open on the nights when the air didn't blow the stench from the sinkhole over to Roseville.

Jim wasn't used to the wide bed with its soft mattress and the scent of Mari-Rose lying next to him, and he curled in on himself trying to take up as little space as possible. Mari-Rose twisted and turned, then made for the guest room, pulling the blankets with her and leaving him lying there cold.

Jim wondered why he'd ever come back, what he was doing here with these people he didn't know anymore, had never really got to know, and who didn't know him. And what could he do, when all he knew was elsewhere, when he felt the only place he truly belonged was hurtling through the sky, far away from all of life below.

But when Mari-Rose left – broken by the way her life was shaping up, unable to keep up loan repayments, her mind unravelling, sinking under the weight of it all – Lenny had pulled him through then.

'Well, I hope you're happy,' she had said to Jim the morning she left.

'Look, I've been trying to sell up for the last year. No one is buying. Anyone with sense is leaving, packing up. Roseville's a ghost town. There's nothing here no more. Nothing to hold on to. We're all just sinking into nothing.'

Mari-Rose had cried, wiping her face quickly to stop the mascara running everywhere, but she was angry, Jim could tell.

'What you going to do?' he asked her.

She looked at him, defiant. 'I'm going to make a life for myself. Reckon I've time to start over. Somewhere new.'

He didn't try to stop her. Not even for the boy.

Jim couldn't explain to her, how it was he felt, for he didn't really understand it all himself – the nightmares, the way he'd waken at night, listening, fearful – feeling something terrible was going to happen, and he had to be ready. They had to be ready.

Everything looked and felt to Jim as if he were staring through misty glass. Even the sounds of things pared away from him. Mari-Rose had stood there, pretty and ugly, but he couldn't hear what she was saying to him and so Jim just smiled, gentle, and she kept throwing insults across to him to grab a hold of but he didn't know how to anymore – the fight had gone from him.

He and Lenny had held on as long as they could.

'Roseville's a long way out,' he reassured the boy.

'Those bank folk, most likely, have better things to do with their time. Roseville's closing up, Lenny. Maybe they'll never come. Just leave her as she is.'

Lenny jutted out his chin and smiled at his father.

'It's okay Pop, it's all okay.'

At first, Lenny kept on going to class, Jim waving him off on the doorstep as he ran down the street to catch the school bus early each morning – at least there the boy got something to eat, the teachers kept an eye on him, he was learning something about the world.

The house grew cold and damp. Mari-Rose took pretty much anything she could sell. She left a little of the money, just enough to get rid of the guilt that clung to her, and pushed the agate stone, the *gris-gris*, into Lenny's hand to ward off evil.

The day she went she'd kissed Jim on the cheek, her lips touching the air, and told him, 'Don't go doing anything stupid – that boy needs you now. You hear? It's your turn.'

She smelt clean and hopeful as she shook Jim off her.

He let her go.

She hadn't even waved goodbye to Lenny, unable to look him in the eye, knowing if she let him hold on to her, she'd snap in two. She had spent the night before standing in the doorway to his room, watching his chest rise up and down as he slept, his curls spilling onto the pillow. Mari-Rose had cried, quiet so as not to waken Jim next door, and then she'd pulled the door shut.

When she left, she jumped into the car quickly with Beatriz, the two of them laughing like schoolgirls.

Lenny had watched her go, like she was taking a vacation, not really understanding she was leaving for good.

He had waved goodbye to Arturo, who didn't wave back, and he rubbed the watch on his wrist. It was a quarter to ten. He always remembered that, what time it was when she went, that and the image of his mama with the secateurs clipping away at the garden, huffing and puffing on her knees, beads of sweat on her brow, and her looking happy and calling him her little prince. Those were the three things from Mari-Rose he held on to.

Jim watched his boy sleeping. He sat the gun down by the log. It was a clear night and overhead in the stars he looked for Pegasus and Cassiopeia. Years ago, Jim had been interested in astronomy and space and things we don't know much about, but that were beautiful to watch. He'd studied the stars, and from there came his desire to fly, to reach the heavens.

He lay in the hammock next to Lenny's, pulling the tent canvas aside so he could look up. For how long could he convince Lenny that their nightly campfires and sleeping out under the stars was just a great adventure, for how long could he hide the truth of it from him?

Jim thought this as he counted the stars overhead, patches of light breaking through the shadows of the tall trees, looking for shapes in the night sky. He lay there a long time, chasing sleep as it ran from him, startled away by the night noises of the woods. He kept on counting stars as Lenny snored lightly beside him, for the boy had caught a cold. Jim, not for the first time, was worried.

'If the boy gets sick, there's nothing I can do for him,' he thought, pulling his knees up to his chest, his boots rubbing against the net of the hammock, the damp clinging to the threads.

Lenny slept on. In his dreams, two giants were throwing stones at each other and Lenny stood in the middle trying to get them to stop. But they were too high up and they couldn't hear him.

In the morning, the fire had burnt right out, and Jim was so stiff from the damp he could hardly move. It had been cold where they'd first sent him too – bitterly cold in the nights, unbearably hot in the days, no relief in either and little shelter there. On the ground, the soldiers below carried heavy packs and guns, moving quickly and carefully, the whole place mined – one wrong step and you'd be maimed for life, or blown up and just gone. Jim knew which of the two options he would prefer – sky over land, always. He'd watched the soldiers struggle as he passed by overhead, their faces turned upwards as his jet streaked past.

When he had first come back to Roseville from overseas, Lenny had been full of questions about the war and the fighting.

'What was it like?' he asked with an innocence that floored Jim, who stood mouth open, unable to speak. It was like Lenny was asking how a holiday had been or a trip to somewhere new. He hadn't the heart to tell him. Worse than that, if he started into telling – actually telling, talking to anyone about it – he wouldn't find his way back to Sunday lunches and homework time and looking for a job. He just wouldn't.

'You know,' he said, smiling at Lenny and Lenny smiled back. But the thing was, Lenny didn't know. Couldn't know. For the first time, Jim had felt more of a bond with the child – no longer a baby, now a little man, and all he wanted to do was protect him.

'You done your schoolwork?' he asked him.

Lenny shook his head.

'Well, then, get on with it. War stories can wait.'

The little boy had squeezed his hand and Jim had opened the front door and walked out, leaving him pulling books out of his school bag, and Jim kept walking for a week. In the end, someone saw him wandering halfway along the road between Red River and Denial, and they picked him up and took him home to Mari-Rose, who decided right there and then she wasn't for staying. It was all too much. He was a shadow-man and she couldn't bring him back to life.

Chapter Five

Ubari Sand Sea, 2011

The boy called him Goose. Soon all the nomads were calling him Goose and the man let them because he could not remember his true name and Goose seemed as good a name as any.

The body heals, given time, and after long weeks of rest he could at last sit up unaided. Then he began to walk a little, leaning on the boy who helped him, his leg still bent where it had broken his fall. He found he had some words of Arabic, enough to make simple conversation, and the boy taught him many others each day, both Arabic and Tamahaq, as if he were a child, new born, discovering everything for the first time.

The boy would point or mime, and say words over and over, until Goose could repeat them, a ripple of laughter or appreciation circling the tent.

'*Goooose, Goose,*' the children called after him when he pulled himself up and dragged his smashed leg along the side of the tents, and away from them, over the ridge to pee, his belly full of mint tea.

One day, the boy's mother Tayri gave Goose a pair of trousers, like those the men wore, with a long-sleeved cotton shirt, and a long indigo cloth. He put the clothes on, the cotton cool against his skin. The boy, Izil, taught him how to wind the *tagelmust* around his head.

'Like this, Goose,' he laughed at the man's efforts, showing him, 'watch.'

These desert people, he realised, had no reason to take him in, to look after him, yet they did, and they asked for nothing in return. He wanted to be able to give them something, but as he did not even know who he was, what could he share with them? Instead, he tried to amuse them with badly mimed jokes, and by trying to sing – these were the only offerings he had. He sat at night now by the fire, listening to the men's talk, trying to follow, catching words where he could, smiling where understanding failed him. It surprised him, the light in the desert at night when the skies were clear and he would lie on his back to stretch out his leg as it ached, and wonder at their kindness, which felt stranger to him than the words he did not understand.

Once he had healed enough to travel, the caravan, a group of some thirty men and women and their children, moved from Ubari and headed south and further east. Goose found himself learning to ride a camel, his charge surly and unwilling. At the end of the first day, he had fallen asleep quickly, his limbs tender and sore. He admired the Imuhar for the way they made the desert home – how they travelled through life taking little with them, how they seemed to navigate their way through the endless sands with such grace and ease.

'What is it like to fly?' Wararni, his dark eyes watchful, asked him one evening, as they all sat around the fire outside eating *taguella*, the bread dipped in a meat sauce, passed around by the boy's mother, washing it down afterwards with sugary mint tea. The flames jumped in front of him, and Goose felt a shiver down his spine.

'I don't remember,' he said, leaving them all disappointed.

Several families travelled together, and he was still working out who belonged with whom, and yet it seemed all belonged together as one.

They could not understand his childlike ways. At first, they felt he was hiding the truth from them, pretending to know nothing, but as time passed, they could see that he was lost to himself.

'One day, he will remember?' Izil asked Tayri that night as the man slept outside, a little apart from the group, on a worn mat close to the camels.

'Perhaps,' she said, thoughtful, 'or perhaps he prefers to forget.'

The fire dropped in the night breeze until only the embers glowed. In the shadows, the camels sat, their legs folded under them, resting in the cool of the night.

Goose, too, slept outside. He loved to lie there, swaddled in blankets, looking up at the sky streaked with stars. He could almost feel the earth tip and spin, *or perhaps*, he thought, *it is me that is spinning*. The sky stretched vast overhead, the stars so clear in the desert night that he felt as if they watched over him and he wanted to stay in the desert forever.

Looking up, he saw a comet shooting across the sky. He saw the constellations, patterns familiar to him.

'Orion,' he said and then, sat upright. Orion. He looked at the other stars more closely now, and they too began to take on names and shapes in the night sky above him.

And he began to shake, feeling something slide loose in his mind, something awakening once more.

Chapter Six

Roseville, 2012

The night had been so cold that the damp – the promise of a bad winter ahead – clung to the blanket that Lenny still clutched around himself. At first light, Jim tried to get the fire started again but it was useless, and besides, he had nothing to offer the boy by way of breakfast.

'Morning, Pop,' Lenny woke up, hearing the rustling around him and feeling the slants of the early sun hitting his face.

'You sleep okay?'

'Good, thanks.'

The boy coughed, his cheeks pinkish red, his eyes shining a bit too much. Jim placed his cold hand on the boy's forehead. It felt hot to the touch, but he couldn't be sure.

'Think you'd best spend the day indoors, Lenny,' he said, thinking it over. 'How about we walk down to the library? Warm enough there. You could stay put while I go see what work there is – got a few people I want to talk to, got some options.'

Jim smiled at the boy, his teeth chipped a little at the front, his chin grizzled from lack of a decent shave. Lenny smiled back at him, with a warmth Jim almost couldn't bear, that he felt he didn't deserve but wished he did. *No map for this*, he thought. Lenny started to cough, his chest rattling under the blankets.

Jim took himself off to the stream to try to wash – splashing the freezing cold water on his face. He hated the way he must smell, walking into stores, people standing back just an inch farther than usual from him, a look of embarrassment from them, like they weren't quite sure what to say. He took a lot of that.

'I promised Miss Julie I'd get her a new cookery book,' Lenny said.

'That's good,' said Jim. He wasn't sure about Miss Julie, why she bothered with Lenny, but right now he couldn't go questioning it.

'She sure likes to cook.'

'She likes to try,' laughed Lenny. 'Doesn't always turn out how she'd hope.'

Jim smiled, a wry smile. Oh, but the boy could lift him up. He hugged Lenny to his chest, and it knocked the wind from him, thinking how his own father had never once hugged him, not so as he could remember, like love was something to be ashamed of. Jim stepped back and started packing up their makeshift camp, the fire turned to ash now. On the walk back along the boardwalk, they listened to the ducks making their way through the water, calling out to each other, and they stopped a while to watch a map turtle trying to navigate the slippery bank until Jim lifted it up, its legs dangling an instant.

'Put it back, Pop.'

He shrugged, reluctant, but did as the boy asked him.

'You be kind now to Miss Julie. She sure is kind to you.'

Lenny nodded.

The library was empty apart from an old man who sat in stained trousers and a threadbare jacket reading the newspapers, glasses perched on the end of his nose. On the reception desk was Lucy Albert – at the tail end of her twenties, maybe into her early thirties – Lenny reckoned, younger than Jim anyhow. Lucy was a regular library volunteer and general busybody. She was also in charge of the community campaign against the sinkhole, and when the weekly meetings were on Lenny would often sit in the nearby seats, listening to the talk about the chemical companies,

and the sinkhole nearby threatening the town, and watch as
Lucy would bring everyone together. She had a quiet kind of
power that emanated from her – the way she'd look at you, like
she was seeing things you didn't want to show her.

Lenny didn't care for her much, didn't like how she poked
about in people's lives as if prospecting for sadness. She had
wild curly hair, and a pale look about her like no one much
loved her. She always had her cat, Hervey, with her, usually
on her lap, sometimes sprawled out over on the *Reading
Recommends* trolley. Lenny got a bit sneezy around cats so he
avoided Hervey too – insofar as he could, for if a cat wants to
come up and moult hair all over you and mark you like it owns
your sorry ankle – then, of course, it will.

'Cats presume,' said Miss Julie, who was more of a dog
person. 'Cats take advantage, Lenny. Dogs never do. A dog got
better sense than most people.'

Lenny sat at the opposite end of the room to Lucy Albert and
her one reader. It wasn't a large library – just a few reading
tables beyond the stacks and shelves, and the big hardwood
desk up front, and its tall grand windows to the side, sliding
sunlight over the dusty books. To the back was a staircase, but
Lenny didn't know what was up there, roped off as it was from
prying eyes. He imagined rooms full of books, great big piles of
them, waiting to find a home downstairs.

The building had once been a nursing home of sorts, a
long time ago, in the war days. Miss Julie had told him that,
and Lenny sometimes imagined he could feel those old souls
still holding on to the place. It didn't feel empty to him, not
like some places – instead it felt full of life, all of it hidden in
amongst the shelves.

Lenny went over to one of the round tables, where he
struggled to reach the floor when he sat right back into the
chair. He had Miss Julie's library card in his hand. Since the
bank had taken the house from them he couldn't use his old
card anymore, but Miss Julie liked him to take out books on

hers, and then he'd read to her or she to him, and he always picked her one or two that he thought she'd really like – so it worked well, especially as she didn't much care to go out walking anymore.

'It's too hard, Lenny, too damn hard,' she told him.

Lenny didn't mind at all. He liked feeling useful.

The Jamaican cookbook was still there on the display shelf nearby. He sighed with relief, and lifting it down, he put it under one arm as he browsed around, looking for a story to catch his eye.

He'd read all the adventure books, the space books and the geography atlases – he liked those, how you could travel all those places, he liked that a lot. When Jim had been away, he had looked at the maps, tracing the line of mountain ranges, imagining he was somehow closer to him.

Lenny liked Walt Whitman too – poetry. His teacher, Miss Avery, had been keen on old Walt. He enjoyed the sound of it, like pebbles dropping into the lake, rippling out wide.

The old guy was looking at him over the top of the *False River Courier*. Just staring. Lenny looked away, uncomfortable.

Some folk are just plain weird, he thought, moving on towards the end of the alphabet, ducking behind the next row of shelves out of sight.

Up at the reception desk, Lucy Albert's knitting needles clicked and clacked, back and forth. She was making a Christmas sweater and it only had one-and-a-half arms so far. But she was proud of the brightly decorated Christmas tree she had managed on the front of it, even if that weasel Willie Jones had said it 'looked kinda lopsided'.

She'd always found him kind of mean, and that remark just confirmed it for her. She fined him for three long-overdue books, and he looked at her mournfully, saying, 'Christ Lucy, I was only kidding.'

But she made him pay, nonetheless.

'We'll see about that, Willie Jones. You owe twelve dollars – you won't get any new books until that's settled.'

He had sighed and paid up, walking away scratching his head, a copy of Jane Fonda's *Original Workout* under one arm ('for Callie', he had said by way of clarification. Callie was Mrs Jones, but Lucy Albert gave him a look as if doubting that Callie was a big Jane Fonda fan). She gave Willie the stink-eye as he went.

Lenny knew better than to mess with her. He sat down on one of the wooden step-seats that blocked the aisle and pulled out books, flicking through them, reading some here and there. It was only 10.30 am. Jim had said he would call back to pick him up around 4 pm. Nothing was said about lunch or breakfast, though he had watched Jim talking a little with Lucy, both of them shy of each other. Jim had asked her to keep an eye on Lenny, hoping probably she'd pity him and share the sandwiches that she brought from home every day. Lenny was none too hopeful, and he didn't want her rotten sandwiches anyway.

The morning passed like that, Lenny avoiding the stares of the newspaper man, who kept getting up and going off to the men's room and coming back looking glassy-eyed.

'You thinkin' of taking out any books?' Lucy shouted this at the man just before lunchtime. He gave her a withering look and walked out, not saying a word. Lenny relaxed. He was good at feeling people's energy and the man had unsettled him, made him unhappy without knowing why. Lucy – it was different – he knew straightaway the things he didn't much care for about Lucy, but also he knew she loved books, that she cared about the sinkhole, cared about Roseville, and she was lonely and maybe she wasn't so mean after all, just a bit unhappy. He felt all her energy and that's what it told him. Lenny decided he would go easy on Lucy Albert.

At lunchtime she took out her sandwiches rolled in greaseproof paper, and a flask of hot tomato soup. She slurped at the hot liquid and left crumbs all over the desk. Lenny smelt the soup filling the library, until the whole room became soupy and full of tomatoes and his stomach ached. When he looked up, he was sitting in Lucy's shadow.

'Why'd your daddy leave you here all day?'

She cut straight into him.

Lenny shrugged.

'He looking for work?'

He nodded, embarrassed.

'No shame in wanting a job, you know. You tell him I said that.'

'Okay.' Lenny blinked up at her.

Lucy held out an uneaten half of her sandwich and passed the flask to him.

'Not got cooties, have you?'

Lenny shook his head, blushing.

'Only kidding. Here, have some of this – it's tasty. I made it.'

That surprised him. Lucy had always struck Lenny as more of a tinned food kind of a person.

He took the soup and half-eaten sandwich from her.

'Your daddy's a veteran. That right?'

Lenny nodded, surprised she knew. But then he'd seen how she would light up when Jim was around, like she was taking a particular interest in him, even though they never much spoke, mostly just smiled at one another.

'We get a lot of veterans in the library. Lot of folk who've served. We surely do. Folk like to read. Takes their minds off things. Me, I love to read. What about you?'

She hunkered down beside him now. Up close her skin was nearly translucent, strangely pretty in an alien-looking kind of way.

'I like adventure stories, and space, and Walt Whitman. I'm pretty into space.'

'That so?'

Lenny nodded.

'I'm training to be an astronaut.'

Lucy laughed, then seeing his face fall, tried not to smile.

'Astronaut? That's a pretty specialist career.'

'I just figured …'

Lenny weighed up his thoughts, whether he wanted to tell her or not.

'I figured it must be awful pretty up there. Like we might find something beautiful.'

Lucy smiled.

'That so?'

She looked thoughtful.

'I've got just the book for you.'

She started running her finger along the bookshelf, checking the titles, until at last she pulled one out, a slim book with a boy on the cover, standing on a planet in space, a fox sitting next to him.

'Ever read *The Little Prince*?' she asked him.

Lenny shook his head, remembering the story Mari-Rose would tell him, wondering if it was the same.

'He looks just like you!'

She smiled.

'I think you'll like this one – it's about a boy from space. You want me to stamp it for you?'

Lenny nodded and she took the Jamaican cookbook and *The Little Prince* up to the desk and stamped them both, running Miss Julie's card through the system.

'How come you never use your own card?'

'I ...'

Lenny blushed, ashamed. 'I lost it, and I help Miss Julie out ...'

Lucy peered at him over the desk, raising one eyebrow.

'You want a new one?'

Lenny stared at her. If she knew, then she'd maybe not let him hang around so much in the library. People were funny like that.

'Oh, it's probably just at home, somewhere. I'll find it. But if it doesn't turn up, I'll let you know, maybe a new card could be good.'

'Okay ... What's your name again?'

'Lenny.'

'Okay Lenny. You can't find it, you can always ask me. Miss Julie's lucky to have you helping her out all the time. Man, she sure likes to read – and cook!'

Lenny smiled.

He gave the flask back to Lucy and thanked her for the lunch.

'Lenny, don't even mention it. Besides, I'm slimming. Always try to before Christmas, then if things get out of hand, it doesn't matter.'

She laughed.

'I like the sweater you're making.'

He meant it. It looked cosy and soft, and made full of love, and he wondered who it was for and would they mind that the arms were kind of different lengths – but he didn't mention that point to Lucy on account of it could be for someone with different-length arms and then he'd feel stupid and mean for asking.

'Why thank you, Lenny.' She smiled, pleased.

'You settle over there by the window – best spot in the house! I'll let you know when your daddy gets here. Okay?'

Lenny took the two books over to the table and slipping off his sneakers, placed his wet socks on the warm window ledge, letting the sun's rays through the glass warm him. The cough was still there, quiet in his throat, drier now he was indoors but he knew later at night he'd feel it again.

Lenny opened the book.

He liked the way the pages felt, running his hands over them, unfolding the edges of corners that had been bent up a little over time. He flicked through, staring at the beautiful pictures. He often liked to do this with a book – just flick through from start to finish, soaking up the pictures, catching the rhythm of the words, the sense of direction for where a story was headed – but he didn't like to look too closely at the words, and he never raced ahead and read the last page. That would be just awful, to cheat himself out of a story. The other thing Lenny loved was the smell of a book. If you held it up to your nose, you could smell it, like it had an energy all of its very own. You didn't get that much with things anymore – most things were fake. Fake chairs, tables, rugs, pictures, fake flowers – Lenny had noticed that, how much wasn't real. That was one of the things he loved about Miss Julie's house – she had it full of old furniture – things someone had made by hand, old things built to last, put together with love. He liked to touch the hall table when he was talking to dead Stanley (for Lenny was convinced Stanley was long gone, though he never let on to Miss Julie, for she was none too ready to turn that page). Lenny liked things that seemed alive.

He felt something warm wrap around his ankle. Lenny jumped up screaming. Lucy looked up at him and put her fingers to her lips, saying 'shush' and looking around, cross even, though apart from him and her, the library was plain empty.

Lenny looked down. Hervey looked up and meowed at him. Hervey was a big, spreading, tough-looking kind of a cat, with a black circle around one eye like a patch, and long moulting hair, black and white and a few orangey patches here and there for good measure. He was a mean-looking old cat, a fighter, a scratcher. Lenny pulled his legs up onto the chair underneath him and stared down at Hervey, trying to shoo him away, quiet so as Lucy wouldn't notice him doing it. Hervey didn't look too concerned. He stayed put.

After a while Lenny could feel his nose running and a sneeze coming, and he knew it was because of Hervey. He sighed and got up off the chair and went to the men's room to blow his nose and wash his face and under his T-shirt, and maybe he would wash his feet too while he was in there – he checked for soap.

He washed his feet in the basin with the soap, letting the water run warm, hopping on one foot, then shaking off all the water as best he could before lifting up the other one, holding first left then right for a spell under the heat of the dryer. Lenny loved standing there, feeling the hot air blast down, warming him up. He went back out to his seat by the window where Hervey had moved looking at him through the slit of a half-open eye. Lenny would have liked to tip that seat right there and then but on account of Lucy he let Hervey have this one.

Instead, he took the damp socks, turned them over on the window ledge, warmer already in the sun, then he took two big heavy atlases and placed them on their edges in front, by way of covering up what he was doing and then he went and sat at the other side of the table, which wasn't as cosy a spot but at least Hervey left him in peace.

He heard Lucy talking to someone and looked around, peering between the bookshelves. It was an old lady – not super old, she looked more like forty-five or fifty maybe, in-betweenish – not Miss Julie-old but older than his dad or Lucy Albert. He wondered if she was somebody's grandmother, or a schoolteacher, or if she worked in one of the stores that they kept closing on Main Street.

'Roseville's just shrinking, the sinkhole is growing and Roseville is shrinking, I tell you.'

She was sure telling Lucy. Lucy nodded, captive.

'Joey's barber's is gone now – you hear that. He closed last Tuesday. Packed up everything and they's headed up to Shreveport. No sense to that.'

'Crying shame,' intoned Lucy.

The woman clucked in agreement.

'We're losing everything now. Since the storm too … fishing camps gone, levees bust, whole place just left to ruin. People getting sick, worrying about their kids, folks got no money. That's the problem. No use in having all these things to buy if you can't afford them. Just makes your heart sore.'

'Ain't that so.'

Lucy kept on knitting, the short sleeve getting longer. Lenny watched how she moved the needles without looking at what she was doing, her hands just tapping them together.

'I hear tell that Pat's grocery store is thinking of shutting up too. Imagine!'

'Oh my,' Lucy tutted.

'I know.'

The two women shared a look.

'This keeps up the whole place will be a ghost town by the summer. And that's no joke. That's exactly what's happened in August, and in Anchor and Denial. You go up there now and you'll find one crazy old guy with a shotgun spitting tobacco on his porch and the rest of the place boarded up.'

'To think we live in these times,' Lucy soothed her companion.

'I know. It's not right. Not right at all. And I heard tell that vagrants were bussed down to the parish border and just dropped off at Red River Crossing, and now they're holed up in folks' empty old houses over Alma ways.'

She exhaled sharply, her large chest rising and falling at the shame and indignation of it all. Lenny watched her as her arms flailed like she was swimming but drowning and no one could save her. The woman's cheeks grew pinker.

'You go there now, you got no idea what you're walking into. None at all. Lawless. The whole damn country goin' to hell and nobody knows how to fix it.' She sighed.

'Though I know you're trying, Lucy – saw your poster about the sinkhole campaign. You've a good heart. If only other folk cared enough too – then we wouldn't be in this mess.' Her arms waved again in the air.

'Maybe you'll join us?' Lucy asked her. The woman shook her head.

'I can't, Lucy. My boy works up at the plant. Can't go causing him trouble. Doesn't mean I don't think you're right, though.'

Lucy pursed her lips but said nothing and a silence fell between the two women. Lenny watched as drips of water plopped from the wrung-out socks onto Hervey's head as he lolled on the chair right up against the window ledge. The cat let out a big meow of indignation and Lenny took to laughing, a belly-aching laughter that filled the room and brought the attention of the women on him.

'What's so funny, Lenny? Hervey okay over there?'

Lucy sat up high behind the desk, making to come over.

'Sorry,' said Lenny, pulling himself together.

Lucy turned again to the other woman who was taking out three books: one was *How to Be Happy: A Beginner's Guide*, the second was titled *Finding Your Inner Animal Spirit* and the third was a racy-looking romance, large print.

She made no commentary on the choices, for she considered the library to bear a resemblance to the sanctity of the confessional.

Books people choose, it's their own business, Lucy thought, though she also thought that she could have also pointed the woman in the direction of *Life After 60*, which she might have liked too – though you could never tell and she hated it when folk came back in and gave her back recommended books and thumped them down on the desk, sighing and saying, 'Well, I don't know what you were thinking, Lucy Albert, I really don't ...'

No, sometimes it paid just to listen.

Over in the corner, a small pool of water from the wet socks had seeped into the grey carpet that was already pulling up and the damp would only worsen the situation.

As the woman left, putting her books into a creased plastic blue-and-white bag, and thanking Lucy as she went, the door swinging shut behind her, Lucy came over.

'Lenny, where's your socks?'

She pointed to his bare ankles as he peeked out from behind his book.

'I splashed them with water – they got wet, so I washed them. Sorry. They're just drying over there. Won't take any hurt.' He gave her his best winsome smile.

'I don't know. We're not a laundromat, you know. Folks generally keep their socks on in here.'

She stood, her hands smoothing down the creases in her skirt from sitting so long. Sometimes Lucy liked to walk around the library and if no one was watching, she'd do a few stretches and bends from the waist, and sometimes even her Wonder Woman dance, '*Baba-ba-ba-babababa ...*'

That made her cheeks sparkle and look less wan, and it made her feel more alive. But she couldn't dance with Lenny there – so instead she sat down beside him for a heart-to-heart.

'Lenny, things okay at home?'

He nodded, his eyes fixed on the carpet.

'Just you're spending a lot of time in the library.'

She waited for him to look up.

'You're here most days in fact. What about school? Aren't you supposed to be in class?'

Lenny buried deeper into the book, sensing her circling him.

She sighed. 'A boy your age ought to be in school.'

He looked at her at last. 'My mama's sick.'

'Oh, I'm sorry to hear that.'

'Yeah, so I don't go to school at the moment, but it's okay – my dad's home-schooling me and he looks after her – all day, he's looking after her, when he's not searching for a job that is, and I just come here to give her a break and because it's safe and warm and *quiet*, you know.'

He placed a lot of emphasis on 'quiet'.

'What's wrong with her?' Lucy wasn't going to let it go – he could tell.

'She has cancer.'

'Well, I am truly sorry to hear that, Lenny. That must be very difficult for her and for you ... and your daddy.'

'It is.' Lenny agreed, almost wishing for a moment it were true and that Mari-Rose was just holed up in bed upstairs, wasting away, waiting on redemption. But it wasn't true, and Lucy knew it.

'And what kind is it?' she asked.

'It's ... I don't know what they call it. It's a bad kind.'

'A bad kind of cancer. Gee, that sucks.'

'Sure does.'

'Well, okay then, I guess you can dry your socks there – just this one time, mind.'

She raised an eyebrow and stroked Hervey's extended belly as he lay there purring at her.

Lenny sighed with relief and then he felt ashamed. It was a stupid lie. He felt bad about trying to trick her into feeling sorry for him, but if he told her the truth, she would have him packed off to school in seconds – and then who would look after Jim? No, *sometimes a stupid lie is necessary*, thought Lenny. He touched the socks. They were almost dry.

He picked up the book again and realised he'd been staring at the first page over and over, listening more to the women and watching Hervey give him the stink-eye, not reading as such. He had too much on his mind, and Lenny felt his cheeks warm, his throat scratchy, and his body sleepy and he just bent over the book, his head on the table and fell asleep in the muggy warmth of the room.

Chapter Seven

Ubari Sand Sea, 2011

The mind when it is in danger protects itself by closing off those parts it considers to be non-essential to functioning, or perhaps it protects the parts most personal to us – Goose wasn't sure which way around it was, but he was beginning to remember.

He took to walking at night far from the tents. The darkness didn't frighten him. It soothed him.

First sensations, then images, came back to him. The sense of freedom, of flying, the jet tipping hard, breaking through the clouds, seeing the land far beneath him. His thumb on the control stick. Goose saw the ocean, blue and gold where it met the sand, villages and towns of stone houses, clinging to the coast and the mountains, fringing the country, seen from far above. He felt the jet turn in the sky, the pressure against his brain, the blood dropping towards his feet, the G-suit squeezing him, the exhilaration and a sense of free-falling through the blue.

There was a man talking to him, talking to a room full of men, all dressed the same. 'Fire-and-forget!'

The voice boomed at him. Laughter ricocheted around the room, the men smiling at one another, some shifting uncomfortably, others at ease.

'Do it right,' the man told them with a solemn look. Goose remembered. His thumb on the control stick, the crackle of the transmission, the breathing of the men on the ground, the fear in their voices, hearing them running, screaming at him in panic.

Flashes coming back to him.

But still he did not know who he was.

Goose started to run.

He ran up the dunes, sliding down the far side, breathless, then clambering, running up again. His leg was still stiff and sore. It did not bend as before, but he was stronger now. He pulled his damaged leg with the rest of him. He ran at the desert. He flung himself at the dunes over and over.

From the ridge above, the boy watched the sky devil, fighting the sand seas in the dark.

Chapter Eight

Roseville, 2012

Lucy didn't have the heart to waken Lenny, but the sky had turned to inky blue and it was time to go home. No sign of the father, though. She'd gone outside to check he wasn't just standing out there, waiting, but there was no one on the empty street. She felt an ache in her gut, seeing no sign of the man.

I don't know, she thought to herself. *I just don't know.*

It was plain as day to her that things were not going well for Lenny, and that story about his sick mama, not a word of it true, the way he'd looked away from her. Lucy knew about such things. She'd buried her own mother, two aunts and her older sister – all thanks to cancer – and she knew that the boy had no idea, not about that. Still, if he thought it was worse than cancer, worse than lying about that – well, then it had to be pretty bad.

She would speak to the father. It wasn't right, him just leaving the boy here on his own. Lucy felt nervous. There was something about the man that unsettled her – the way he looked at her with his sad, pale eyes, like an injured wolf. He was in need of fixing and Lucy was a fixer-upper. She liked nothing more. Some folk called her a meddler, but she didn't see it like that.

'Sometimes, folk need a little push, that's all,' she would say.

She thought about taking the boy home with her. She lived above what had once been Eddie's Fish & Bait on Main Street – in a small apartment, just one room with the bed as a couch during the daytime and opened out at night. There was a small kitchen corner with a couple of rings for cooking and little fridge that made a loud whirring noise at night and kept her awake, and a window that looked out over the street so she could watch comings and goings from the comfort of an old moth-eaten armchair, its springs half-gone, but cosy nonetheless. She'd knitted a crochet throw for it and it made the place look homely. Lucy didn't have a job – not a proper paying one (for who had one of those these days?) but she'd held on to her inheritance money and the money from selling her mother's house when it fell to her (back when folks were still foolish enough to buy) and she lived off of that and if she was careful each month, the money would last a long time, for she didn't need much. But children needed a lot of looking after and spending money on – feeding them, dressing them, sending them to school, medicine and doctors when they took ill. Lucy looked at Lenny, exhausted, his chest rising and falling with a slight rattling sound as he breathed out. No, she couldn't just take him home with her.

She watched the hands on the clock on the wall until it was long gone 7 pm. Usually, she closed up at 6 pm sharp. There was no sign of the man. It surprised Lucy how much she had been looking forward to seeing him again, how she had wanted that. She had finished knitting the sweater. She packed away her needles and the ball of wool, folding over the sweater and putting it in a plastic bag under the desk. Later on, she would wrap it in shiny paper and hide it away in the wardrobe in her room, until Christmas Eve, when she would take it out and sit it on top of the busted armchair and when she would wake in the morning it would be there, and she would look at it, all surprised, and say, 'My, oh my,' and take it out and hold it up and put it on. It would be a perfect fit and she would be happy. If she could just keep Willie Jones's words out of her head, she would be happy.

Hervey knew it was home time. He could see Lucy standing there waiting. Going over to Lenny, he used the boy's leg like a scratching post. Lenny woke up, startled, and kicked him gently away.

'Time to go home, Lenny. Didn't your daddy say he'd come by to pick you up?'

Lenny nodded, half-asleep.

'Well, I'm sorry, but he's not here, and I need to take Hervey home.'

'Oh.'

'You understand?'

Lenny took his socks, dry now, off the ledge and put them back on before bending over and tying the laces on his sneakers.

'It's okay, I remember now, I was gonna walk home actually. It's fine.'

'You sure? Someone at home to let you in? What about Miss Julie?'

'Yeah, I need to bring her her book anyhow, it's okay.'

Lenny pulled on Stanley's old sweater again, putting it over his denim jacket. It was so big on the boy, swamping him. Under one arm he held on to the two books.

'You sure you're okay to get home? It's getting dark soon.' She asked him, once more, locking up as they stood together outside, her switching off all the lights and setting the alarm – though in truth no one cared to steal books.

'Thank you for the book.' He smiled at her, waving goodbye before he ran off downhill into the falling dusk, back towards Miss Julie's and the swampland on the edge of town.

It was kind of late to call with Miss Julie. She never usually opened her front door after sunset. Just locked everything up and went to sleep, waiting for the morning light.

'Night can let in the devil,' she would say.

He hugged the heavy cookery book to his chest, and it helped cut out the chill of the wind. Could be a storm was coming, wind was up, leaves swirling on the path down to the edge of town. Looking back over his shoulder he watched Lucy pushing against the wind, struggling with it. Hervey hung draped over her shoulder, his claws catching in her hair, and a plastic bag full of knitting spinning from one wrist as she walked home alone. He could tell she'd been disappointed his father hadn't shown up. He sensed something between them – like electricity fizzing – the way they didn't really look at each other much when they would talk, the way she would ask after him, say something nice each day for Lenny to report back. She hadn't believed Lenny's lies earlier either, so it had been a day of disappointments for her. He knew she hadn't believed him from the way she'd looked at him and he knew he regretted saying it and was angry at Mari-Rose, blaming her for a moment just because she wasn't there.

Lenny pulled the sweater up around his cheeks. The wind was bitter, blowing up the late autumn leaves off the ground, swirling them in a blizzard of faded reds and golds around him.

Back by the river, he looked for Jim, but there was no sign of his daddy. Lenny even went into the swamp a little, calling out for him, but no answer came. Back on the street, the only houses with lights on were Miss Julie's and further down, Mr Gomez's. Lenny went and leant on the fence of the old house. Sometimes he would climb in and sit on the steps to the back yard from the kitchen, just like he used to. Jim had been angry when the man from the bank came and had waited until they packed up what was left, and then waited until they'd taken everything out on the lawn in front, and the bank man waited until it was all sold or given away, and he waited until they had left, carrying two bags between them, and then he'd gone to the back of his pick-up truck and lifted out a heavy sign on a stake, and he'd hammered it into the lawn out front, locked up the house and left.

The house was as they had left it a few months before. The man never came back. No one bought it – even though it was an okay kind of a house with Mari-Rose's beautiful roses all the way along the fence at the front and back, even with that no one wanted it. The sinkhole saw to that.

'Why can't we just move back in?' Lenny asked Jim one evening, just as the days were getting cooler and he had grown tired of their nightly camping adventures.

'Because ... it's not ours anymore.'

'It's not anyone's, Pop. No one wants to live there. It's just empty. Can't we move back in? Please?'

Jim had gone very quiet. His face went sheet white and he looked like he might just keel over. His eyes got watery and he walked off leaving Lenny sitting there in the dying sunshine thinking about it all.

When he had returned that night, hours later, Lenny had been curled up, his knees up by his chest, hunkered down into the old orange box as it leant against the back fence of the house. He had seen his daddy coming down the road, swaying and muttering and Lenny had known he'd get no sense from him then.

He wondered if that was where his Pop was now, holed up in a bar off of Main Street somewhere, running up a drinks bill he couldn't pay for, getting drunk so if they beat him up afterwards for not paying, then he wouldn't feel it too much.

Times where Jim would be fine, kind even, like he wanted to be around Lenny. Then times when a sort of darkness would descend upon him, like he was far away in his mind and Lenny couldn't reach him none, and that's when his daddy would just take off, like he couldn't bear to be around him anymore, and the only thing he'd pay heed to was the drinking. Somehow it steadied him, numbed him from the fear he felt. Least that's what Jim thought, how he'd tried to explain it, make sense of it to the boy as he'd sat in the grass crying at having left Lenny alone on his own in the dark. Lenny didn't understand adults much at all.

Now he looked at the empty house, its shutters pulled closed and he wondered, *Who's going to care? Who would notice?*

Almost the entire street was empty. The house on the far side had a cracked window that the curtains flapped through and the lawn had grown tall and untidy. Lenny had kept the old lawn neat – running Miss Julie's mower over it after he finished doing hers.

'I appreciate that, Lenny,' she said, as if he did it for her so that she didn't have to look out on a garden gone to ruin.

He looked up at the window of his old bedroom. If he climbed up the side, he could probably reach the window ledge and the window never really locked there on the inside – if he pulled at it, he reckoned he could get it to open.

Lenny dropped down onto the lawn, the books still wedged under his arm. His stomach rumbled again, hours since lunch. Next door, he could hear Miss Julie's TV on loud. He went to the back of the house and climbed up, scrabbling, holding the branches of a vine that clung to the side of the building, and once up on the window ledge he prised it open slowly and carefully, so as to not damage the frame, and he slipped it open and clambered into his old room.

It looked kind of sad now. He went to switch on the lights, then hesitated, wondering if they'd even work anymore, wondering if they'd call attention.

Best not, he thought. The room was empty, even the bed was gone, sold in the yard sale to a Chinese family who bought most of the old furniture and loaded it up into a van, taking it with them. Lenny placed the two library books by the wall and had a look around the rest of the house.

It was completely empty, like the heart had been ripped clean out of it. He touched the walls, trying to remember happy moments. Instead, he saw Mari-Rose, her mouth twisted in unhappiness, and his father looking sad and standing by the door, shifting from foot to foot, always looking for the way out of enemy fire.

Lenny tiptoed downstairs and knelt in the middle of the living-room carpet where the couch used to be, and put his hands on the floor, his fingertips burrowing down, drawing circles, one inside the other, until his heart slowed down and the fear and hurt numbed within his chest, and he could almost make out the shape of Mari-Rose's footprints, barefoot on the carpet long ago. He lay down, sideways, looking at the room from down there, curled up in a ball.

Mari-Rose. Barefoot. Probably somewhere far away, dancing. Free. Lenny could not understand how she could leave him as she had. If he could only go back in time, talk to her, let her know that he loved her – that even when she was mean or upset, he loved her. How he wished for that, holding tight to the agate stone buried deep in his pocket. Had she been there, he would have asked her why, but only the memory of her lingered in the space. He squeezed the stone, the *gris-gris*, in his pocket, and tried to hug the damp carpet to him.

Lenny closed his eyes and slept.

Chapter Nine

Roseville, 2012

As she walked home, Lucy nodded in passing to Appleby Bertrand, the accountant who never seemed to have any clients but who kept an office up from the library on Main Street, its door wedged open most days, just in case. She had heard Appleby call out to her, Hervey clinging on to her shoulders, obscuring her view of the sidewalk, hiding the man from view, Hervey a giant ball of fur trembling around her neck.

'Evening, Lucy.' There was a nervous, pleading tone to it.

She couldn't see the man, could only smell the pools of dark sweat under his arms, could picture the anxious look he carried with him, could hear his plaintive tone chasing after her, and she was glad of Hervey's backside up against her cheek as she passed by. Something about Bertrand was awful sad, like he was missing some part of himself with no hopes of ever finding it. Needy. He was plain needy. She nodded in recognition in his direction and hurried on, thoughts of Jim filling her mind.

'Don't take up with a needy man.' Her mother, Delfy, had warned her of the pitfalls of modern romance before she died.

'If you feel the need to tether yourself to another human being, make it someone practical and level-headed. Watch out for the dreamers and the broken ones. No use to themselves, let alone anyone else. You have to be practical, Lucy-Lu.'

That was what she called her, even when Lucy was a grown woman.

Her mother's words were steeped in her own sorrows and experience, and she'd given Lucy such a fierce look that the girl almost swore to everlasting celibacy there and then.

As a young woman, Lucy had brought home a few beaus – no one special, other than that they liked Lucy enough to call over, or perhaps they came because her elder sister Marcie was real pretty, or because they'd heard how her daddy had put his shotgun in his mouth one Thanksgiving in the living room before pulling the trigger, and they were curious to visit and stand in the same space – to feel close to death. People are ghoulish that way sometimes.

Lucy would have liked to think it was because they liked her and found her interesting – if not as pretty as Marcie. But her mother sized these suitors up so quickly it got so some of the young men didn't even make it across the front porch, seeing this wild-haired woman waving a shotgun at them, firing it at the steps as they followed along behind Lucy, taking cover, panic clouding their features before they'd run off, stammering excuses.

Later her mother would say, 'What, Lucy-Lu? You embarrassed I chased him off? If he'd been any good, he would have stayed. I was only foolin' with him. A man has to have a sense of humour. Little bit of crazy in all of us. Nothing wrong in that.'

Then she'd polish the shotgun and put it back in the case that hung over the long dining table. She had refused to have it moved out of the house after her husband shot himself with it.

'Constancy. Staying the course. That's better than any fancy notion of love. Some folk think they need to be hurting to call it love. That, right there, that's a lie.'

When the pain got to be unbearable for Delfy, and the drugs no longer worked, she would have Lucy help her out to the steps of the porch and she would sit there, slumped against the wooden railings and scatter bird seed near her so that the pigeons would come close to her, and then she'd ask Lucy to fetch her the shotgun, and she'd shoot at them, horrifying

Lucy who just stood there wondering how it was she had been born into such madness.

Her sister had high-tailed it to California, leaving Lucy and Delfy alone at the house. Then Delfy died, and the old house passed to Marcie, who never wanted it anyway and had no intention of coming back. In the end, caught up with sickness of her own, losing her looks and her health, her beautiful face and figure bloated with medication and anger, Marcie gave the house to Lucy.

'I want nothing to do with it,' Marcie had snapped down the phone at her, as if somehow everything was Lucy's fault. Even though Marcie had been sharp with her, Lucy went to her sister's funeral all the same, and grieved over her too, and then, as soon as she could she sold the old house.

'That's a fine-looking shotgun,' said the man from Mississippi who drove over to buy the place, standing by the dining table, looking around at the walls with hungry eyes.

'I'll throw it in for free.'

Lucy handed the man the keys, sold up, and left without looking back.

She took a motor coach up towards Pointe Coupee and the False River in search of solitude and lakeside living. She got as far as Roseville, and realising the need for long-term economies – for she could not bank on her own life being cut short like Delfy or Marcie – she gave up the reckless dream of a cabin on the lake and settled instead for the apartment above Eddie's Fish & Bait – less romantic, more level-headed. She imagined her mother looking down on her, approving.

It was around then that Lucy took on the voluntary role of librarian in Roseville. At first, just for a few hours a week then later as the main librarian, learning from old Betty who was ready for retirement and mint juleps in the garden, and was selling up to move to Houma, moving out, following her family. Lucy would bury herself in a stack of books and the challenges of numeric coding and reshelving, and try to forget what she'd seen: the muffled cries of her mother at night-time, or the wild deranged look that had filled the woman's eyes towards the end, Delfy's hands reaching for morphine, just to numb the pain of it all. Cancer. It ate away at anything good.

She read all the medical books and journals she could find. Trying to find ways to make it less painful. To make sense of it all. Was it God's will or just plain bad luck? Why then Marcie and not her? Why'd her daddy have to get so crazy? She had answers for none of it.

Lucy resolved to live in as simple and careful a way as possible. Maybe then the ill fortune would pass her by unscathed. She didn't need much, she reasoned.

Besides, if she squinted when she looked out from the apartment window at the back, she could make out the line of trees edging the waterline, so she knew the lake was just there, even if she couldn't see it. Wasn't that enough? She tried as best she could to settle down into quietude and routine.

Lucy had holed up above Eddie's Fish & Bait, with only Hervey and the regulars at the library for companionship. Though even that grew burdensome to her now that her campaign to stop the sinkhole was gathering enthusiasm – all these lonely folk, with a surfeit of time to give, all eager to attend the weekly meetings, all ready for action, wanting her to lead them into battle.

Needy folk, always in need of attention, she thought as she fumbled with the lock on the door, shrugging Hervey down off her neck, letting her bag of knitting drop on the ground.

She was annoyed that Jim hadn't come to claim the boy, to take him home again. All day she had sat there waiting for the moment when he would swing open the door and give her that mournful look that he had about him, like he was taking up too much space, just by being there. Lucy knew that feeling.

She had thought herself happy. Protected by the quiet routines she had chosen, the limited circle of interaction, the containment of emotions, the status she gleaned as custodian of the library, the warmth of Hervey next to her, his disdain for expressions of affection – it had all shielded her. Except now the boy and his father had become preoccupations for her. She found herself unable simply to observe them, as she tended to do with others. When Jim stood next to her, she felt herself reaching out to him, her spirit and heart seeking to tug free. With the boy, she felt the need to protect him, stronger even than the need to protect herself, stronger than the desire to hide away from the sharper edges of everyday living. And yet, she had let him go home alone.

'I couldn't take him home with me, Hervey, don't look at me like that. I just couldn't.' She put the kettle on and set to making an evening meal of *grillades*. Nothing fancy. Just what she always had on a Thursday. She switched on the radio – KPCP 88.3, for she liked to listen to the old-time tunes.

Perhaps it was better Jim hadn't come to collect the boy. She could feel herself unravelling a little around the man, her heart lurching, a feeling she hadn't had before. He made her nervous of what she might do.

'Year of Decision' by The Three Degrees played out, the sound of the vinyl scratchy over the airwaves, Hervey mewing along with it, clawing at Lucy's boots in search of supper.

Chapter Ten

Ubari Sand Sea, Libya, 2011

When the men came in the convoy of jeeps with their dark-tinted windows, the nomads had already long left, the caravan snaking further south. All that remained behind were the dead embers of the night fire, the dips in the dunes where the tents had been and a camel trail that petered out quickly.

'Must have known we were coming!' one man joked, wiping the sweat from his forehead, cursing the desert heat. Although used to harsh weather conditions, he still cursed the sands and the wind that when it came could turn a man crazy.

They had been searching for the pilot since the crash. This motley group of strangers, all battle-scarred, all off the books. No one (except those who needed to) knew they were there, deep in the Ubari. They represented no government, no nation. For hire to the highest bidder – that was the drill. Dropping down to earth silent in the dead hours, silently spinning in the night sky – this was what they did. This job, however, was a little different – a man lost in the desert, the NATO command reluctant to send in search parties, no one wanting to draw attention to the fighter jet that should never have been there, so far off course, and should never have crashed.

'Find him first.' That had been the order.

They had found the lone parachute not long after the crash, the smoking wreckage guiding them, the parachute peeking up from underneath the sand where it had been buried. Why had he buried it?

There had been a local outcry, the plane's falling wing demolishing a shepherd's stone home when it dropped from the sky. *Someone could have been killed.*

Now the pilot was gone, no one knew where, or if they did know, they weren't saying. These men had to bring him back.

They didn't want him falling into the wrong hands.

'Bloody expensive mess,' the commander had boomed at him. Elliot shrugged. His men were expensive for a reason – they could do things that other men couldn't. They kept the secrets, erased evidence, resolved the unresolvable. And that came at a high price. Elliot smiled at the older man who sweated in his jacket in the midday heat.

'Clean it up before the press get wind of it.'

This was what Elliot and his men did. They cleaned up.

He had looked at the airman's record briefly – training in Texas and California, time in Yemen, Iraq, now Libya. Irish roots. His father and mother dead years before. What happened there? And the man seemed fearless. Always keen to be sent out into the thick of things, like he had a death wish. Not much of a family man perhaps. A loner by inclination, it seemed, happiest in the skies. Only basic Arabic skills.

Elliot doubted they'd find him alive. Probably killed in the crash. Looked like the parachute might have jammed, but he'd managed to release it, hadn't he? So, where was the body? And if he didn't hide the parachute, who did?

A man doesn't just disappear. Not even in the desert.

Chapter Eleven

Roseville, 2012

Jim was sorry to leave the boy with Lucy Albert. He truly was. But he didn't know what else he could do.

He had gone up Main Street, planning on asking around in case anyone needed a worker, he was a strong man (once anyway) – surely someone would need a man like that? But when he got there and found Vincent opening up his bar, Jim had stepped inside out of the sunlight and pulled up a barstool, and began the day early, knocking back whiskey, alternating with beers, sipped slowly throughout the day. By evening-time he was telling Vincent the same story for a fifth time and the man was looking at him with a mixture of compassion and hate.

''Bout time you went home, Jim,' he said, refusing to pour another glass, shaking his head.

'Home?' said Jim, laughing. 'That's a good one, Vincent. That's real funny.'

'Not being funny, Jim. Closin' time.'

Jim made a show of feeling about his pockets for his wallet, padding down his shirt and trouser pockets.

'Oh damn, Vincent, sorry. I've come out without my ...'

The man waved him away.

'It's alright Jim. This time it's on the house. Just bring it by next time.'

Jim bent his head and nodded, trying to steady himself as his feet made contact with the floor of the bar and he stood swaying back and forth.

'Door's that way, Jim.'

The bar owner pointed him in the right direction and followed him to lock up. It had been a slow night. Only Jim and a couple of fellas down from Shreveport who had sat in the corner minding their own business, crouched over two beers and a plate of potato chips.

Vincent's son had been in Iraq. The boy was nineteen and cocky as hell. Nothing Vincent or his wife Stacey had said could change the boy's mind. Vincent had listened to Jim and wished the man could have talked to his son before he signed up – maybe then the boy would have understood, what it does, what war does to a man.

Things kept up the way they were headed, he'd be closing up soon too – just like everyone else. The bars were always the last to go.

Their girl, Evelyn, she was over in Florida – near Fort Lauderdale – maybe they'd go live with her, look after their grandchildren, get soaked in the Florida sunshine. Maybe it was time.

Vincent locked up and switched off the lights.

Jim had stumbled out into the cold night air, his breath frosting a little in front of his face. He looked up – it was a clear night and the stars were clustered overhead. Jim needed to relieve himself – all that whiskey and beer sloshing about inside him. He looked around, and not seeing anyone, went over to the side of the street. There, at the side, was a doorway. Jim pulled down the zipper on his jeans, his hands frozen with cold now, pulling at the zipper, and sweet release ... *Ahhhhhh*. He watched as the liquid spurted forth, spraying up against the woodwork of the door.

Above his head he heard a window pull open.

'Get away from there!'

A woman's voice called out. He looked up, startled.

'Oh, sorry,' his words slurred. Her face came into focus, surprising him.

'Didn't realise it was you lived here.'

Lucy Albert looked down at him angry as all hell.

'What do you think you're doing?'

'I ... I needed to go.' He looked sheepish and sorry.

'Folks live here. Ain't no way to conduct yourself. You should be ashamed.'

'I am truly sorry.'

He looked up at her thinking how much prettier she was when she was riled, and how she had the stars twinkling all around her and that was pretty too, and how he really liked her. Yes, he did. And here she was. Like it was a sign or fate or something, except now she was mad at him.

'You left that poor boy alone all day, never came to pick him up, didn't leave him nothing to eat, deserted him. I should call the police – in fact, I'm half-minded to do just that.'

'Damn,' said Jim, remembering Lenny now and looking about him, trying to figure out what to do.

'Where's Lenny?' he asked her.

'What? You're asking me? That's just incredible. Really. Like – Father of the Year right there.' She looked at him, waiting.

'You gonna invite me up?' he asked, hopeful.

'You're drunk.'

'It's real cold.'

'You're drunk and you're a bad father to that boy.'

'I'm truly sorry. I didn't know.'

She looked at him for a heartbeat. Lucy Albert believed in fate too.

'Well, maybe you better come up. I'll fix you a coffee then you go find that boy – I sent him to Miss Julie's house. Pained my heart to watch him go.'

Jim nodded.

'Hope you don't mind cats none?' She was already downstairs, opening the door, standing in her slippers, a robe wrapped around her and her hair up in bunches. She'd just been about to paste on a cucumber mask for tightening pores when she heard him vandalising her door.

'Well, come on up.' He followed her, putting one hand to the cheap plywood partition wall on the stairway to steady himself. She opened the door to her room, in one corner the bed was already out, next to it an armchair all bust at the seams, that fat old cat of hers sitting on it, and next to the kitchen corner she'd a small radio on the counter playing Philly soul, sounds of the sixties floating out into the night air around her.

She looked at him.

'I don't usually have late-night callers. Here ...' Lucy turned down the radio some and pushed the cat off the seat, gesturing at Jim to sit down. Standing up, he took up most of the room. Sitting down, he was manageable. She set the kettle to boil and brought out the coffee (she'd go without in the morning, she reasoned, on account of this being a special occasion).

'Thank you.' He fell into the seat. Hervey jumped away from him.

'Hervey doesn't like strangers.'

He looked around, terrified for a second, thinking *Who the hell's Hervey?* Then, on seeing her stroke the cat, he realised and felt his heartbeat slow a little.

'I like cats,' he said, blushing at the untruth of it.

'That so?'

'Sure is.' He kept going.

'You're about as bad a liar as your boy.'

Lucy looked over at him as she measured out the coffee grinds – just enough to make it taste like a proper cup of coffee.

'Lenny told me his mama has cancer. That's why he can't go home, doesn't go to school, spends all day in the library, washing out his clothes and waiting for them to dry.'

'That so?' he asked.

'Sure is,' she replied.

They eyed one another, her breath catching a little. *She was like a truth-seeking missile*, he thought, and could feel her locked on him, unswerving.

He closed his eyes and leant against the back of the seat.

'She left us.'

Lucy inhaled, and held it there.

'She wanted more than I could give her, so she left us.' Without meaning for it to happen, Jim felt the tears coming and he bent over, forward in the chair, his head to his knees so she wouldn't see him cry.

She brought over the coffee in a chipped white cup and set it down on the floor beside him.

'Coffee's goin' cold,' she said when five minutes later he was still doubled over, wiping away the tears.

He sat up.

'Sorry, I ...'

'It's okay. Really.'

He nearly knocked over the cup. She inhaled again. This time he noticed, and seeing the cup at his feet, he lifted it, grateful now, and sipped it down, letting it burn the insides of his mouth a little.

'That's fine coffee,' he said at last, noticing she wasn't having any.

'You not having one?'

'I don't usually drink coffee after midnight.' She looked at the clock on the radio, its numbers glowing in the low-lit room.

'Oh, sorry. I best not keep you.'

Jim looked ashamed of himself now – he liked her, felt his spirit lighten around her, and what had he done? Defiled her front door, cried like a baby in front of her, drunk her last dregs of coffee, kept her up late.

'Shall we start over?'

She smiled at him.

'I'm Lucy,' she said, holding out her hand. He took it, surprised she wanted to let him touch her. Her skin felt soft and warm, even though she looked like it might be cold. She surprised him alright.

'Jim,' he offered in exchange, even though he felt like she knew that already, like she could see into the heart of him, the way she looked at him.

'Jim.'

They sat in silence a while, their hands still touching, both recognising in the other the same feeling, both surprised by the force of it, but knowing it was there all the same.

'Oh ... Lenny,' he said, life slowly coming back into focus. 'I've got to find Lenny.'

'I sent him to Miss Julie's house.'

Jim looked up worried.

'I thought someone would be at home for him. I ... I should have let him stay with me, but I ... I'm so sorry.'

Lucy looked guilty now, her forehead all puckered up, realising that the boy was perhaps out there on his own, and here she was only thinking of how long she could keep Jim with her, kept him in the spell of inebriation and the drowsy heat of the room, before he would leave again and she would be alone.

'Thanks for the coffee,' he placed the cup back down on the floor by the armchair, 'but I've got to go find Lenny.'

He wavered, unsteady on his feet, seeing two Lucy Alberts blurring in front of him. He looked from one to the other, unsure which one was actually there, the drink befuddling his mind.

She nodded, reluctant, holding out her hand to steady him, knowing he was right and it was the right thing to do, and how she liked him better for knowing that, that he had that instinct and yet ... she would have liked him to stay and she could have given him a bath in the small tub off of the room, and cut his hair, and helped him shave, and fixed him up. Instead, she hugged him.

Her warmth surprised Jim, who found himself hugging her back – though he was not one of life's huggers in general. That too, caught him off guard – that she did not recoil from him, or pity him, or find him strange.

She wanted to ask him to come back – once he'd found the boy – but she couldn't. Too much pride, Lucy Albert, too much damn pride.

He leant forward, almost kissing her forehead, then pulled back, not wanting to startle her or presume. Instead, he stumbled back out into the night, Lucy watching him go, until he was a shadow in the distance.

Alone, Lucy lay down on the pull-out bed, and looked out at the stars. The heavens had sent this man and his child to her. The heavens would tell her how to proceed. She felt her heart lift in a way she hadn't known before. Lucy closed her eyes and went to sleep, and she dreamed of giants and battlefields and a boy with straw-coloured curls, and when she awoke, she felt like she had slipped into someone else's dream, and she felt alive.

Chapter Twelve

Ubari Sand Sea, 2011

'Where are we going?' Goose asked Izil, more confident now in his words. The boy, who clung to him as if Goose belonged to him and he, and he alone, was responsible for this broken sky king who the heavens had sent to them, said, 'To a special place. Where we go every year. We take the herds to feed and rest.'

Goose watched as the women packed away mats and pans and tied them with rough rope to the backs of the camels, and the men took down the tents and rolled the goatskins as dusk fell. Little by little their camp disappeared.

'And what is it, this place?' he asked Izil.

'You'll see ...'

Izil looked at him. The boy looked worried, and Goose realised he had begun to talk in his sleep, sounds spilling out of him, parts of his life he could no longer contain, but that his mind still would not show him. He noticed the tension in the way Izil's father Wararni watched him. He felt the interest of Tayri, the boy's mother, her eyes following him around, Izil chiding her, quietly, pulling her away. There was talk amongst the men, some of whom would turn away as he approached, a sense of unease growing. Were they happy to have him there amongst them? He was no longer sure.

The caravan travelled on for hours that night, having left in the darkness when it was cool enough to journey. Wararni had decided that they should leave. He had a sense, he said.

'They will come for him.'

Goose heard this, the whispering in the tent between the men, something being planned. Part-way on the journey, some of the men had split off from the main group, had left the camp in the sand, and kicked over the tracks of the main caravan as it continued south. Goose had watched the men go and knew they were doing this because of him. He felt Tayri's watchful eyes on him, but he asked nothing, affected not to notice as the men split off, shadows receding in the darkness.

As daybreak came, the caravan dipped down over the peaks of dunes, the camels sliding in the sand.

'There!' cried Tayri, who rode a little ahead of Izil. She turned to smile at him, her eyes catching Goose's, who smiled too on seeing the sudden green spreading before them – a large oasis of thick green palms circling a glistening lake, ringed with black sand, in the middle of nothing but rolling sky and desert.

Seeing the green against the dunes made something twist in his stomach – the unexpected beauty of it.

Izil jumped down and, in a race with the other children, ran towards the shade of the trees. Soon everyone was splashing in the water, sliding down the steep sides of the lake, holding tight to the reeds that clung to the sandy bank. All around him, Goose could hear everyone laughing, a few of the men began to sing, soft gentle songs offered up. The water was cool against his skin and as Izil splashed next to him, Goose watched the trees' reflections on the surface bend, the world turned upside down in the water, sky now below and above, and he shivered, a memory tugging at his mind, the sensation dizzying him. The water tasted salty on his tongue. Then he clambered out and sat in the sun to dry, running his fingers in the sand over the animal trails that surrounded the water's edge, and he watched beetles rise and fall between the indents of the tracks – whether digging down for shelter or up to escape the pull of the sands, he was not sure.

Tayri, who had moved further up the lake with the women, turned and kept a watchful eye on the stranger, sitting on the bank, lost in his own world apart from them all, even here.

Later Goose helped set up the tents once more. Now they were masked by the dense tree cover, shaded from the day's heat. Then, as the smell of supper cooking filled the evening air, he took himself back over to the lake and leant awhile against the trunk of a tall palm in the shade by the water's edge, looking out at the oasis ringed in fading desert heat. At night, it would be bitterly cold once more and he would wrap himself in blankets and watch the lake fill with stars and the moon. From the camp, he listened to the singing, and the sound of the women playing drums and the mournful song of the *anzad*, and the children danced, kicking up small clouds of dust by the fire in the distance. Goose pressed the back of his head to the tree trunk and closed his eyes, for once not fearful of the dark. He felt the life of the desert pulse through him.

In that one moment, how perfect it all seemed.

Chapter Thirteen

Roseville, 2012

When the sun came up it broke into the living room through the open window, and warmed Lenny awake – first his toes and the stripy socks, then his frayed jeans, then the navy sweater he had put underneath and around him like a sleeping bag, then his cheeks and his forehead and his curls. In the sunshine, lying on the carpet of his old home, Lenny felt safe and loved and warm, so that when he woke up it took him a minute to understand why it was he was on the floor downstairs and not up in his own bed. Then he remembered.

He went into the bathroom and peed into the bowl, watching a dead dragonfly all curled up on the rim of the basin next to him. The water from the taps still worked and he drank from it, the water icy cold, running down into the pipes from the back of False River and the reservoir. It tasted of coming winter. Lenny washed himself carefully, peeling off each item of clothing only long enough to get washed and dry, drying himself in the warmth of the sun – *air drying*, he thought, thinking of Miss Julie's plates.

Then he rinsed out his T-shirt and underwear too, and let them dry in the sunshine while he wrapped himself up in the huge sweater, pulling it down over his knees as he sat cross-legged on the floor, his back to the bedroom wall, reading *The Little Prince*, the story like the old one his mama used to tell him. It was a pretty book – and he liked the pictures, and the opening part, and that Lucy Albert had picked it out for him, like a gift. So, he read with an open heart and soon he was sitting laughing out loud on the floor of the empty room in the empty house at the man who couldn't draw a sheep but could only draw a box in which to hide a sheep – and Lenny thought that was pretty good alright.

In the sunlight, he could almost imagine his mama there with him, happy as she had been once. What if his daddy had never learnt to fly? Had stayed put in Roseville instead. And if the chemical companies hadn't come, if there was no sinkhole? What if he could change it all, wind time back, let it roll out differently? Would it have been enough for her to stay?

Lenny, half reading, half daydreaming, blinked into the dust imagining other planets, similar to his own, yet different all the same.

Meanwhile, Jim woke in the clearing, tangled up in his hammock. For a split second he forgot he had failed to find Lenny and that things were pretty bad, no doubt about it.

He couldn't remember much of the night before. He recalled sitting in the bar telling Vincent a story about fighting and the two of them talking about war and how it turns you inside out and how you can't get back to living afterwards, not like before, and how Vincent wished Jim could have talked to his boy – what was he called? – Jim couldn't remember. He remembered the row of shot glasses next to the empty beer glasses stacking up beside him – Vincent leaving them there just to make a point. *None too hospitable for a bar owner*, Jim thought, though he'd let him leave without paying ... probably. He wasn't sure. Maybe he'd just walked out. Damn. He'd have to go apologise – when he could go back and pay him. That could be a while. Jim sighed.

Then he'd come back for Lenny.

Wait – and then Jim remembered. Lucy's face shouting at him out the window, her bringing him upstairs, her sad little one-room home looking out over Main Street, that fat old cat scowling at him. Jim bit his bottom lip. Had he made a fool of himself with the girl? What had he said to her? He remembered talking about Mari-Rose. Oh, Christ. And crying. That too.

What would she think of him now? He had liked her – that sad, lonely look she tried to hide, there was something to her, and something between them. He had felt it too, and now he'd probably gone and wrecked it all.

A crow cawed on a stump of a fallen bald cypress next to him. The ground was cracking underfoot, sun slicing through the tall empty trees. A few birds called out back and forth in the early morning light, but it felt quiet, like the place was emptying out.

A storm was on its way, and he had lost Lenny.

Jim, now sobered up, was hopeful the boy would be with Miss Julie. Where else would he have gone?

You should have been there for him.

He berated himself, angry now at his own selfish stupidity. The boy needed him and all he'd done was let him down. Time and time again, like he didn't know any better. It all just weighed down on him.

And Miss Julie, she'd be worried sick and angry as all hell.

Jim howled into the trees, like a wolf. He didn't know what else to do.

At home, Miss Julie was for getting up and about her day. It took her a goodly long time to get organised in the mornings on account of the stiffness she felt in her bones. Just getting levered out of bed took her maybe ten minutes on a good day, her back having pretty much given up on her long ago. Then she liked to take her time in the bathroom – *No point in rushing*, she'd think. *What's to hurry for?* She liked to approach the day steady and calm. On the days when her hands shook badly, it took even longer to do up the buttons on her dress – so sometimes she would just pull on a cardigan over the top, leaving it open at the back where she struggled to reach and where she was worried that if she managed to do the buttons up, she might not be able to undo them and then she'd be well and truly stuck and it would be an embarrassment to go in search of help. That was an admittance that she couldn't manage, and Miss Julie wasn't there yet.

She took her time cleaning her face each day, counting the wrinkles, sometimes gurning into the mirror to scare herself and make herself laugh – because you've got to keep a sense of humour, she reminded herself on the days when she really had no idea who it was stared back at her in the mirror, but it sure as hell wasn't her.

'Boo!' she'd say, then fall about the place chuckling, a smile on her face for the rest of the morning.

That particular morning, she was feeling extra tired on waking up, the sun glancing off her bedcovers, stealing in through a chink in the curtains where she left them open at night so she could see the moon a little. She let the sunlight warm her hand and yawned. She had a sense that someone else was nearby. This was confirmed now as she heard the water pipes from next door gurgling, water running. And listening real hard, she thought she could hear someone moving about.

Burglars.

Miss Julie had pulled up the blankets a little higher.

Perhaps she was imagining things. It can get like that sometimes when you're older. Your mind wanders, you see things, hear things that other people can't. You become more sensitive to the universe and young people mock you for it, so you stop mentioning these things in case they get you shipped off to a 'care home' somewhere. When you're old, you're not allowed to feel things. You're just supposed to sit there, nodding. *Well – to hell with that*, thought Miss Julie, who had never been, nor was about to begin to be, a bystander. Oh no.

She needed to look in the top drawer of her bedside cabinet – there was a number somewhere she'd been given by Sheriff Lentement to call in case of emergency. What if this was an emergency? This was an emergency. She had heard the water pipes. What more evidence was needed?

She levered herself out of bed, put on her robe, pulled the drawer clean out and tipped the contents onto her bed covers. In addition to a collection of lint, there were a couple of Christmas cards, one from 1951, another from last year. The first was from Stanley – it had been their first Christmas together there, when she was only twenty-two and he had bought her the card and a huge bouquet of roses, and brought her to the house – for then Roseville was brand new and everyone wanted to live there, and he'd bought her the house before he had to go overseas, so that he knew she'd be happy when he was gone. They'd arrived with three suitcases, a crate of furniture, two large wooden boxes full of Stanley's belongings, and a brand-new golf bag for he planned, when he got back, on joining the new golf club they were advertising on all the billboards nearby. It was a fine beginning. Miss Julie touched the card.

'Oh Stanley,' she sighed.

'You never said you'd be gone such a long while.'

She kissed the card, just where he'd written inside – *To my darling Julie.*

She set it down.

The other card, a picture of a robin on the front, came from the real-estate company that had wanted to buy up the whole street and knock down the houses and build new ones. Every year for five years they had sent her a Christmas card – each time promising a cheque if she would sell up, but she just tore up the letters inside and put them in the waste-paper basket. *What would Stanley think?* she thought, tutting to herself, angry for several days afterwards each time the cards came.

'Determined to ruin Christmas, those people,' she had said to Lenny who asked her, 'Why didn't you sell?'

'Some things are not for sale, Léonard,' she'd said, giving him a stern look. But Lenny wasn't one to let go of a question once he had it in his mind and he came back to her about this, asking, 'But if they give you more money, and you could buy a bigger house, somewhere better than Roseville?'

'Better than Roseville?' She had looked at him, disappointed.

'Nowhere's better than home, Léonard, nowhere. Why – anywhere else you're just a stranger. Besides, how would my Stanley find me?'

The boy nodded, satisfied.

On the last year that they sent a card, though, she had been tempted.

'You have to watch out for the devil,' she told Lenny one afternoon, when she was sitting there thinking about it. This was back when Lenny was seven and Roseville, then, was a place people were still coming to, rather than leaving.

'What's the devil look like?' Lenny had asked, genuinely concerned.

'That's the clever thing of him,' said Miss Julie, 'he hides in weakness, buries deep in people's hearts so that they can't see him there, and that's how he gets into things – he looks just like you and me, Léonard, isn't that something?'

Lenny's eyes had bulged.

'But don't worry Léonard, we'll not let him in.'

'Mari-Rose says the devil is in the detail,' said Lenny, looking around as if being watched from the shadows.

'Well, that's true too.'

'And my pop says there's no such thing as the devil, or God.'

'That so,' murmured Miss Julie, looking at the boy who sat on the carpet of the front room, his legs crossed, a beaker of milk in one hand.

'Well, some folks are very certain about everything.' She left it, diplomatic like that.

Lenny wasn't sure what he believed. Believing was for adults.

Apart from the cards, there wasn't much else in the drawer: a half-eaten packet of mints, some coins for the jar downstairs and there at the back, rolled up, the envelope with a number scribbled on the back of it, to call in case of any trouble.

She stared at the numbers, the ink faint in the creases.

But who would be fooling around next door? Probably local children, or maybe one of those homeless people from up in Denial. Miss Julie had heard all about what was happening on one of her rare trips up to the post office off Main Street, when Betsy, Lionel's wife, had told her how her boy James had been up in Denial, doing some clearing work for one of the construction companies that wanted to tear down the old houses – 'no use anymore to no one and just going to wrack and ruin, anyhows'.

'Aren't we all,' Miss Julie had said, and Betsy had belly-laughed at that.

'And you won't believe what my boy found ...'

Betsy paused for effect.

Miss Julie sat down on the chair next to the counter, for she was tired standing and her shoes rubbed the inside of her soles.

'Well?'

'Only that they checked all those old houses, shouting and hollering and making sure they was empty.'

'But?'

'When they came to bulldoze them down, suddenly all these people starting climbing out of the basements, James said, all dirty and dusty, filthy they were ...'

'Hush now, what way's that to talk, Betsy? People better than that.'

'I's just sayin' what James told me. It was the shock of it, y'know. Here they all were, just hidin' away.'

'Hoping to be left in peace, no doubt.' Miss Julie had pursed her lips and was tapping the counter with the ridges of her fingernails. She'd always had strong nails. They didn't split or tear easy.

She looked at her hands.

'Anyone give them any help?'

'Hell no. James said the driver of the bulldozer started chasing after them, foolin' with them. They took off out into the fields. I don't know where they went – maybe up to August. Hear they got problems too.'

'We all got problems.'

'Well, that's true, Miss Julie, but wasn't it the darndest thing. James says they pulled down all those houses, just tore them down. He was working at it for ten days, clearing the place.'

'What they want with the land if no one wants to live there anymore, no one that can pay?'

'They're gonna harvest. It's one of those California companies, some newfangled kind of seed they planting. Has to be far from everything else. And the land was cheap. Experimenting. That's what they're at. We're just all one great big petri dish.'

Miss Julie shuddered. She was glad she hadn't sold up – even when it got tempting, because they couldn't do anything to the house if she wouldn't budge, and she liked that, sticking it to them that way. Besides, if she moved, where would Stanley come home to? No. She was staying put.

Miss Julie went downstairs now, remembering all this. Some days she found it easier to remember things that were past, long past, than to recall what she had only just done or said. The nearer a thing was to her, the better it hid from her in plain sight.

Someone was ringing the bell. She pulled her robe, padded with pink and gold flamingos on it, tight round her. She had not yet gotten quite ready for the day. She held the phone number, the envelope creased up in her hand as she answered the door.

There on the steps stood Jim Lockhart looking sorry for himself.

'Good morning, Miss Julie.'

'Morning, Jim.' She peered around behind him.

'If it's about the sweater, you don't need to come complaining or thanking me or bringing it back – it was a gift for Léonard.'

Jim stared, surprised, then his face kind of crumpled up and caved in a little.

'So, Léonard's not here?' he asked, his eye twitching a bit on the right, jumpy.

'No, not so I know. I haven't seen him … *pas çe matin*.' She looked at Jim, smelling him on the breeze and hesitating. 'You want to come in a moment?' She was big on manners, and not one for long conversations on the doorstep. Besides, he was letting all the warmth out of the house – that cold winter air seeping in behind her.

'No, no, thanks, won't bother you if he's not here. If you see him, could you hold on to him for me? I'll call again later to check if that's alright?'

He looked down at the flamingos on her robe, standing on one leg like that, wonder they didn't topple over.

'Okay, but shouldn't that boy be at school? Where's he sleeping at night? You've not moved back in, have you?' she asked him, wondering if that's what she'd heard.

Jim blushed.

'It's not our home anymore.'

She knew not to press him.

'Well, I see the boy I'll tell him you're looking for him, okay. He can stay here. Léonard's always welcome here. I like the company. He's a good boy, helpful. He's welcome, anytime. You might want to think about that.'

Jim nodded and turned to leave.

'Hold up, Jim. You had breakfast?'

He shook his head.

'I've got some pancakes left over from yesterday that I can't finish up. Was going to bring them down to old Gomez, see if he'd care for them, but it's a cold day for walking and slippery out. Could you do a kindness and deliver them? Take some for yourself – for the trouble. I'd be most obliged.'

Jim shuffled on the steps, nodding, his cheeks burning under the stubbly beard.

Miss Julie went back into her kitchen, and soon came back with a dish stacked with cold pancakes.

'You tell him, I need that dish back.'

'Sure, will do.' He took the dish from her and thanking her went off out the gate, closing it on the latch carefully behind him as he went. Jim waited until he was around the corner before opening it up and eating the top two, wolfing them down, then ashamed, wrapping up what was left and bringing the stack down to the Gomez house at the far end of the street, ringing the bell and hollering through the screen door – 'gift from Miss Julie, she wants her dish back'.

As he passed back once more by the front of the old house, he thought he could hear Lenny laughing, and he almost stepped up and rang the bell to check, but what man rings the bell to his own house like that, so he kept on going, up the street and back out into the swamp in search of the boy.

Chapter Fourteen

Ubari Sand Sea, 2011

It hadn't taken the pilot long to get used to life in the desert. The Imuhar had made him welcome, had worried over his recovery – taking pride in the fact he had survived the sky fall. Whatever they felt about the fighter planes, about the work he had been sent there to do, however it sat with their own loyalties, they said nothing, asked nothing. Instead they were curious about his family but here he could not yet answer and they came to realise that he had lost a part of himself in the fall, and so they were gentle with him, pitying him even.

'You have no family?'

Goose shook his head, uncertain.

'But everyone has family,' Tayri said, incredulous.

'I can't ... remember.' He fought for the right word, so they would understand.

'The fall ...'

She looked at him with pity, and a quiet kind of hopefulness too.

Goose nodded, accepting it now. At first, he had been terrified. To not know who he was, what sort of a person, to have lost even his name – it could cause a mind to unravel. Instead Goose sought to take refuge in his anonymity and wore it about him, fending off questions. All he wished was to be able to forget – yet he saw splinters, glimpses of things, and he could not know if they were things he had done or witnessed. It was that which would make him cry out at night, frightened of his own possible selves.

Tayri looked after him most. She would bring him food or sugary tea, and although she sat far away from him, throughout the day he could often feel her eyes on him.

Seeing her with Izil brought to his mind another child, a boy. Himself perhaps? Was that what he remembered? It frightened him, how his mind had let go of everything that had gone before, as if it were of no future use to him. A whole lifetime erased in one moment.

Time worked differently in the desert. The day reversed, as the dry searing heat shaped the patterns of their travels.

As the days passed, time surfaced slowly once more for him. He found, amongst the nightmares, odd partial memories like the voice of a man he took to be his own father, a sensation of being trapped somewhere, perhaps as a child, a sense of fear that cut right through him. He couldn't be sure whether it was himself he was seeing or a memory of someone else.

'I can't see them,' he told her one day, his hands shaking, a wildness about him.

'Who?'

'My family, I … don't know if they exist.'

She had stopped braiding the hair of the child who sat on her lap, a little girl belonging to one of the other women but who clung to Tayri as if she were her own mother. Tayri put her hand on his, her eyes not leaving his. Then she moved away, the little girl turning around, looking startled to see them so close.

'You are amongst family here,' Tayri smiled at him, her words meant to reassure, but he pulled away, uncomfortable and uncertain.

Chapter Fifteen

Roseville, 2012

Inside the old house, Lenny's T-shirt and pants had dried in the sunshine and he put them back on, stretching his legs after sitting cross-legged for so long. He was halfway through the book and had spent the morning caught up in the adventures of the strange little prince, and had nearly forgotten all about Miss Julie and bringing her the Jamaican cookery book, that when he realised the sun was high in the sky and it must be nearly lunchtime, he reluctantly left the book, face down on the carpet, open on the page he was reading, and went next door to see Miss Julie.

He opened the back door quietly and slid out that way, pulling it shut behind him, having left the bedroom window upstairs slightly ajar. He took the cookery book with him, and jumped over the fence, vaulting over the rose-beds – all looking spare and thorny and sharp in the coming winter air – hoping she wouldn't notice that he'd come in from next door.

He knocked on the screen door at the back and called out for her, 'Miss Julie …' She opened it eventually, a wide smile on her face, her dress flapping open at the back, a creased envelope held absent-mindedly in her fist.

'Well, if it isn't the little explorer. Your daddy was here a while back. You talked to him yet?' She looked at Lenny, her head tilted to the side in the way she had to hold it these days, bird-like.

Lenny's cheeks reddened. He was still angry with Jim for not showing up, for leaving him alone all night. Even when his father had gotten really drunk before, he'd always come back, always come looking for Lenny ... So now, didn't he care at all anymore?

'I haven't seen him. No.'

'Well, you can stay and keep me company. How's that sound?' She tried to sound cheerful – like it would be fun. And it was fun because Lenny enjoyed Miss Julie's stories and the way her eyes twinkled when she told them, or when he told her jokes and her belly would shudder with laughter and ache so hard she'd have to say, 'Oh Léonard, stop kidding now, you're making me weep.'

But it was a good kind of weeping. With Miss Julie, he could laugh and cry about life. He could breathe. She didn't make him feel guilty the way Mari-Rose always had, or awkward like he felt around his daddy, who looked at him sometimes like a stranger, like a boy he didn't rightly remember. With Lucy Albert, Lenny had to be on his best behaviour, always alert to which way her questions might suddenly swing like the boom of a boat, caught in high winds. And Arturo wasn't around anymore. No, it was only Miss Julie he could belly-laugh with, so hard that sometimes he'd need to go stand out on the porch and just catch the air in his lungs. Just breathe.

'Léonard, can you help me?'

He looked inside and there was Miss Julie pressing her bony hip to the heavy console table in the hall, trying to push it away from the wall.

'What are you doing?'

He rushed over before she would topple the table over and send Stanley smashing all along the hallway.

'I want to move Stanley.'

'Okay, why don't we ... um ... just lift the picture?'

Lenny's fingers brushed the silver frame a second as her eyes lit on him. Miss Julie nodded, blinking into the sunlight, looking down at the narrow table and the line where the paint was brighter from behind it.

'You lift Stanley, come on. I want to show you something. Put him over there a second.'

Lenny set the photograph in its frame down gently by the television, so that Stanley could watch the news if so minded.

'Stanley okay?' she hollered to him from the hall.

'He's fine.'

'Good boy. Help me then – let's move this.'

She was still pushing at the table, scraping the floorboards.

'I've got this Miss Julie, stand back.'

Lenny lifted the table in the middle and half-pulled, half-dragged it – scraping the woodwork further as he pulled it off the rug and over by the screen door.

'Sometimes, Léonard, you forget to change things. You live with them in a certain way ... you get used to things being a particular way, you know what I mean?'

Lenny nodded, not really understanding why the old lady had gone a little crazy and taken to rearranging the whole house.

'Here, roll up that rug.'

He bent over and let the rug fall in heavy thuds as he turned it over upon itself. Underneath was a trap door. Lenny felt a slightly sick taste in the back of his throat.

'Um ... Miss Julie ... I'm not sure this is such a great idea.'

'Nonsense, Léonard. I just remembered something I had been meaning to show you. I think you'll appreciate it.'

'Well, I ...'

She motioned at him to pull open the trap door, which he did, standing back away from it, fearful of what lay beneath.

'Stanley used to keep all his ...'

She coughed as a cloud of dust came up with the opening of the door and a stale, slightly damp smell emerged.

'I've not opened this place up in a long, long time.'

She tutted, staring down into the gloom.

'Here, pull on that string, that's the lights ... well done!'

The strip lighting flickered on and Lenny could see down beyond the short set of steps into a basement – the walls lined with certificates and shelves full of books and sports trophies, and at one end an old record player and a stack of records, and in the other corner a telescope standing proud.

'That's what I wanted you to see!' She smiled triumphant, the bend in her back helping her for once, to look down into the room below.

'I was just sitting thinking about Stanley earlier and I thought about what you were saying yesterday, about going into space. Go on – fetch it!'

Lenny looked at her, uneasy for a split second, imagining her dropping down the door and leaving him in the dusty room where no one would ever find him again, but the prize was too great and besides he'd be ashamed if she knew what he was thinking, so he swung himself down and began to drag the telescope across the ground. He had to put it down a couple of times on the steps, before hauling it up into the daylight.

'Wow!'

'Wow indeed.' She smiled, delighted at the look of joy on the boy's face.

'You ever used one of these?'

'No ma'am.'

'Well, there's nothing complicated to it. Let's bring it out to the garden and when it's night-time you can look through it – and Léonard, you'll see all the stars. All the stars.'

'Pop ...' Lenny blushed, 'he likes the stars. He knows all their names and stuff like that. Sometimes he'll tell me ...' he puffed as he pulled it down the steps to the back yard, Miss Julie watching his progress.

'Well maybe he can show you them better through this.'

Lenny shrugged, unsure he was ready to share his find with his father, angry still at being abandoned alone all night.

'Maybe.'

'My Stanley used to love looking at the stars. I would bring him out a flask of coffee and he'd stand out here for hours on end on a clear night, just wondering about it all. He could have been a fine scientist, you know, if they hadn't sent him to war. Stanley was never a fighter. Not like your daddy, not looking for a fight in life. Someone did wrong by Stanley and he would be the one apologising all the same. He had a kindness to him, a gentle soul. He never went looking for trouble. Like you Léonard – you've got kindness at the heart of you.'

Lenny looked away, embarrassed by the old woman's words and the tears that had gathered in the corners of her eyes, talking about Stanley like he was already gone. They moved indoors once more, leaving the telescope out on the grass.

'Let's put Stanley to rights,' said Miss Julie, switching off the light in the basement and gesturing at Lenny to pull back the rug and the table while she fetched the photograph and sat it back on top, tilting it just so.

'There, all looks just the same as before now, doesn't it just.'

She shuffled off to the kitchen in search of tea and a sandwich for the boy, along with a plate of buttermilk biscuits for them to share. Afterwards, she went to sit a while in the last of the late autumn sun on the porch while Lenny took a duster cloth out to clean the telescope up and to hold on to it gently, daydreaming of travelling up into space and floating weightless and free – looking down at the earth, trying to make out Roseville and there, by the edge of the swamp, to make out his old house and the telescope on Miss Julie's lawn, its lens winking at him up in space.

'All time is elastic – like a rubber band – watch!'

His father had told him this once, slapping a band back on his cheek, gently so as not to startle Lenny. It was just before Jim went to the war.

'We think of it as one day added on to the next,' Jim had smiled at Mari-Rose as he spoke over Lenny's blonde curls, 'but that's not so. You can shrink it right down or draw it out long.'

He concertinaed the band back and forth in front of Lenny.

'So, I'll be gone a while, but you and your mama can fill that time right up full of good stuff, make it real short, and I'll be back again before you even get used to me being gone.'

Jim had smiled at Mari-Rose who looked sorrowful and mad because this was back when they were still interested in each other, each still seeking answers in the other's warmth at night. While she found no answers, Mari-Rose found a comfort of sorts in Jim back then. She loved his handsome dark curls and his pale Irish pallor and the way he walked around with a shadow of sadness.

But for Mari-Rose, time did not shrink – it stretched endless once he left and as long months passed and Lenny grew taller and missed his father more and more, and the seasons came and went, all the while she wore that elastic band on her wrist and she would fiddle with it when the sadness would wash over her.

Then she would take herself out to the garden and kneel in the dirt and tend to her roses, whispering to them, singing to them – anything to get away a stretch from her son who reminded her too much of his daddy, who she'd let walk out the door and go off to fight other folks' wars because of the itch at the heart of him, and the sadness that followed him, and with which she could not help him.

The band had rubbed the skin on her wrist raw – a thin tight groove against the skin – she let it chafe, until one day the band snapped as she was standing in the kitchen looking out at Lenny and Arturo kicking a ball into her rose-beds. The band snapped and fell from her wrist as she hammered on the glass window, chasing the boys off the lawn. Mari-Rose picked up the two pieces of elastic and dropped them in the garbage pail and after a few weeks the marks on her wrist faded and she began to think differently on Jim's absence until it was like he had never been there at all, and time began again for her. More urgent this time.

None of this Lenny knew as he polished and cleaned up Stanley's telescope, but he thought about his father and how Jim's hands now shook in the mornings more and more, and how he hardly ever told him stories these days or talked about the stars. And a sadness tightened around Lenny's heart, squeezing the boy hard.

Chapter Sixteen

Ubari Sand Sea, 2011

Goose didn't want to ever go back. His hands shook and he would take to holding his head and weeping.

'He needs to go home,' said Izil's father to Tayri one day.

'And where would you send him? He doesn't know who he is.'

'But they do.'

'Who?'

She looked up. Her husband had heard it first, the whirr of the helicopter overhead.

'They can't see us ... the trees.'

'If they want to take him back, they will. Sooner or later.'

'He was sent to us ...'

'And we have helped him as best we can.'

Wararni was ready for Goose to leave. The men talked of what to do with him. Some wished to protect him, others planned and schemed in conversations whispered, looks exchanged. It was not right, he felt. They had welcomed him in, waited for him to recover, waited for him to leave. But the man did not leave, and if he did not leave soon, it would bring problems. Wararni knew this, knew too that the man had a value, a high value perhaps. But then, how to value a life? For as long as Wararni held control of the caravan, they would respect him, though, wouldn't they?

Then there was the way his wife looked at the pilot, watchful over him, attentive. He didn't like that either. They had all looked after him, helped him recover, had treated him as an honoured guest. The rest … the rest he would have to work out for himself.

The helicopter circled above them.

Wararni made to get up.

'Don't!'

Izil darted to him and held on to his sleeve, pulling him back into the shade of the trees. From above it would be difficult to see them there, hidden as they were by the dense leaves.

'You see anything?' Elliot asked the helicopter pilot.

The helicopter circled once more.

Goose heard it too and looked up. But he didn't stand up. He didn't run out into the sand. He just sat there, shaking, and on hearing Izil cry out to his father quietly not to break cover, one word – a boy's name – seeped into his mind, bleeding over and over.

Goose felt at last like he had found a missing part of himself, something he didn't need to be ashamed of – something precious he had left behind – and he wondered what it meant.

'Anything?' Elliot asked, peering down.

'They have to be here somewhere. We found five men heading east. Swore they were travelling alone. Take us for fools. You see anything?'

'Nothing, sorry. Let's look north again … there's nothing here.'

Elliot sighed, frustrated. The man had been missing now almost ninety days and no one had claimed him. There had been no ransom request, no torture video, no demands. He really had just disappeared.

He looked down on the sands that spread for miles … the borders of one country blurring into another, Africa stretching before them. The helicopter turned, heading back.

Things were difficult now in the country. Too many soldiers, pilots, warships – everyone waiting for something to happen. Everyone saying time was up, for how long could one man strangle a country? Things had to change.

Something was coming. But it was something ugly. Elliot could feel it, and here he was sent out on a wild-goose chase in the desert.

Chapter Seventeen

Roseville, 2012

Lucy Albert woke up with a strange fluttering feeling in the pit of her stomach. Today would be a big day. She could tell these things. Intuition. Some folk have it, some don't. Lucy was full of it.

Hervey squinted at her. He sat curled up in the busted chair in the slant of sunlight, watching her get herself ready for the day.

Lucy almost tripped over the chipped cup, still on the floor by the armchair, where Jim had placed it the night before. She had left it there after he had gone. Leaving it, it was as if he had only just left, rather than the hours that had passed, hours in which she had slept and dreamt and seen a snake slithering between the bald cypress and she had heard the steps of a child thudding along the slats of the boardwalk, running, running towards Lucy Albert until she had jolted awake – sitting upright in the folded-down bed, listening to the thud of her own heart in the quiet night hours, the dead time between the day just gone and the new day to arrive. A shiver passed through Lucy and she had reached out her hand to touch Hervey's fur and stroke the cat – just to feel its heartbeat slow and steady and certain – unlike her own.

When the day finally put in an appearance, Lucy sat wide-eyed waiting for it, unable to think of anything other than the man's sad eyes and the way he had looked at her.

The fluttering in her belly rose once more as she bent over and picked up the cup, setting it in the bowl of the sink, still not ready to clean it and set it up on the shelf out of sight.

'You were here,' she whispered, her fingers tracing the ring of the china, her nail scratching the chip on the rim.

Hervey stretched out long and looked at her as she got washed and dressed, brushed her hair and put on her happiest dress, even though the feeling rising in her gut was not an altogether happy one.

Out on Main Street she let the sun wash over her, a bright empty sun and a chill in the air. She took what warmth she could from the day.

A short queue of early morning readers, her growing band of sinkhole warriors, had formed outside the library doors, ready to have their meeting, looks of disgruntlement and relief as she arrived to let them in.

Lucy glanced at her watch – gone eleven. She had come late to the day after all.

Chapter Eighteen

Ubari Sand Sea, 2011

'Where are you going?' Goose pushed his way up the sand dunes, following Izil who had run off, upset.

The whirr of the helicopter overhead had long passed, the danger gone for now.

'You don't care,' Izil shouted back to him. 'Stay and talk with my mother – that's what you really want!'

'Izil, wait!'

Goose dragged his leg, which still did not bend as before, up the dunes and down, and then up again, grains of sand caught on the breeze, hitting his cheeks, him pulling the blue cloth tighter around his face, the dye staining his cheeks a dark inky shade as he sweated in the heat. The boy was faster than him, and anger had a hold of him, tossing Goose's shouts behind him.

'Izil, whatever you are worried about … you're mistaken. Look, come back.'

The boy's figure grew smaller as he put distance between himself and the crippled pilot, smaller until the boy was just a dot of blue and white moving against a sea of waves of sand. Goose stood on the top of a ridge, watching him go. He should let him work it out for himself – blow off steam, take it out on the desert.

Meanwhile, Goose could go back and sit with Tayri and drink tea and try to forget about the voices that were beginning to crowd into his head. She would soothe him … Her husband had left too, taking the herd and the men with him on a trip to the border, so Wararni was not there to be disgruntled, nor Izil now. He could perhaps, even … Goose thought about Tayri, her eyes, her hands, her beauty, the way she smiled at him. He felt himself grow weak.

Yet he had promised the boy that there was nothing, that there would be nothing. No challenge to honour, no breach of the complicated web of hospitality rules of which he was only faintly aware, no misstep. But the boy had been so angry. Goose wondered – had she said something?

Perhaps it's just the damn heat.

He looked again at the horizon. The boy was still there, a faint dot in the distance. Goose sighed. No, he would have to go to him, bring him back, make peace. He edged forward over the steep ridge, sliding sideways down the dune, trying to angle his descent to use the minimum resistance. It would take him a long time to catch up with the boy. Only if Izil stopped, stayed in one place long enough, would Goose catch up to him. He hoped for that. His leg ached, a dull heavy ache below the knee. It did not wish to hold up his weight for long, so he pushed on, wiping the sweat from his forehead, wrapping the scarf around his head more tightly. No matter how hard he tried, he could never have the easy grace of the Imuhar, as at ease here in the sands as he was in the skies.

He no longer called out to the boy, saving his energy instead for the walk, the sun still too high overhead. Twice he lost sight of him, climbing a dune just for the blue dot to disappear. But he waited and squinted and eventually he could make out the boy once more.

It had been several months he had lived with them in the desert now. Would they let him stay? There were days he felt it possible, in fact believed it the only possibility, for how would they explain him away if he were discovered amongst them now? What problems would it cause them? He was a burden, of that he was sure, but he was beginning to feel that in the life he had left behind perhaps he had been a burden too – and he wondered as they travelled from oasis to oasis, setting up camp, sleeping under the night sky, taking little with them – if perhaps this is what love is, what life is.

A hawk circled overhead. The boy was closer now, sitting with his back to him. Goose tried to approach him as quietly as possible, frightened he would run off once more and he would have to start again to catch him up, but the boy did not move.

When he was a few steps behind him, and sure Izil could hear him, he called out his name, gently. The boy did not turn his head.

'Izil, I'm sorry. Let's be friends. Whatever you think, honestly, there is nothing to be angry about. Let's talk ...'

Goose stopped.

He saw the snake dart up from the sand and slither over the boy's arm. He threw himself forward. There was nothing to take a hold of. Instead he hit at the snake with his headscarf, pulling it off his head, the fabric unrolling, the snake sliding away.

'Oh God, Izil.' He picked up the boy who was pale, glassy-eyed, his skin punctured.

'No.'

Goose panicked. He tried to think of all he knew but had tried to forget. Why had he hit the snake, hit the boy? Had it bitten him before or after? He could see redness on the boy's arm and in the distance, the tents of the caravan. By the time he carried him back the boy would be dead, surely? Perhaps. He flung the boy over his shoulder and started, dragging his leg as fast as he could, desperate to bring the boy back alive. The hawk followed him as they went.

He could hear Izil's breathing, rasping. Could feel the boy's heartbeat against him. *He's alive, he's still alive.* This is all Goose thought, all he needed to make it back to Tayri, where he dropped the boy at her feet.

'A snake.'

He described the snake, how it had bitten the boy. Tayri, looking at him horrified, knew what to do. Immediately, the women gathered around the boy. Goose was pushed out of the way, unable to see and frightened to watch. He took himself outside of the tent and waited. Much later she came to him and hunkered down beside him on the sand. She was crying.

Goose put his hands over his eyes and bent his head. He had failed her.

She put her hand on her heart.

'*Shukran*,' she said, resting her head on his shoulder.

'He's okay?'

'He's okay. If you hadn't found him …'

She shuddered and put her hand over her mouth, the pain of the thought of it too much for her.

Goose rocked on the sand beside her. One word came ringing back to him. The same word as before. Lenny.

This time he knew what it meant.

Chapter Nineteen

False River, 2012

Jim sat on the edge of the boardwalk by the banks of False River. This was a quiet, peaceful spot he loved to come to when Lenny had only been a baby and Jim would sometimes sneak away on his own, exhausted from the child's cries and the broken nights when Mari-Rose would stumble from the bedroom out into the hall and then to the child, leaving Jim alone in the bed wondering what had become of his life all of a sudden, how it was he had ended up in Roseville.

He had sworn not to repeat the mistakes his own parents had made, and yet somehow everything was broken before it had begun. And it was like Mari-Rose kept the boy from him, fearful he would never return.

'If you don't come back, you're leaving me a widow. What do I tell him then? I can't. I just can't.'

'I won't get killed. I'm coming back.'

He looked at her, seeing the fury in her eyes, knowing it was all a disappointment to her too, and now there was Lenny, caught between them, and Jim had not counted on any of that, had been caught clean off guard by it all.

He dragged his fingers through the frogspawn on the surface of the water, making it ripple a little out from the bank. He watched a dragonfly hover over the rushes, darting between them, its wings emitting a low, persistent buzz. Jim shivered even as the sun caught his cheeks. He closed his eyes and leant back against the moss on the bald cypress behind him, its roots breaking up through the planks of the boardwalk, forcing it to bend and arch.

In a war zone you have to be ready to bend, let the day mould itself to you. Some men took pills, others drank a lot, some just had a kind of steel in them that carried them through the days. There were things he loved about it, things he hated. Mostly, he hated what it had done to him, how far it had taken him from who he wanted to be. *Some things you can't undo.*

He remembered his mother shouting that once at his father, the man looking at her with a fury about him. But she had been right. In the end, she'd dulled her days with sleep pills, anxiety pills, pills to make you happy. Jim wasn't sure she'd ever been happy. He only knew he'd never made her happy either and when he'd signed up for training and aced all the examinations, the only thing she'd said was, 'You were always more like your daddy.' Six months later, she was dead, and Jim was alone in the world. Free.

The dragonfly's buzzing came closer, louder now. Jim felt a twitch to the side of his left eye. He raised his hand, his fingers wet from the river. A heaviness sank over him and he let it take him as he fell asleep, shutting out the morning light and the thudding in his head, his fear over Lenny's disappearance and his guilt mixed in with empty relief, that perhaps he was free of the boy. The terrible responsibility that he felt towards him, and the panic knowing he was broken, not capable perhaps of being a father to the boy, then shame and unease as he thought of Lucy Albert, how pretty she had looked, and the fear that threatened to sink him when he thought about how he would care for the boy, how he would feed him, protect him.

Yet for all that, it was only Lenny who kept him afloat in the world around him, who tethered him to Roseville. He could not abandon the boy. What little love he held on to in life, he saved for him. Only it had taken him so long to realise and what if he was too late, what if he couldn't undo the mess he'd made of his life? He wanted something different, better, for Lenny.

Sleep took over. The dragonfly buzzed louder still in his mind, the whirr, the whirr like the blades of a helicopter overhead and the flash of something on the water's surface. Jim's mind drifted, unconscious, far from shore now.

Chapter Twenty

Ubari Sand Sea, 2011

Goose had noticed Tayri watching him all the time now ever since he had saved Izil, the way she would smile with her eyes, little creases at the sides of them. Dark soulful eyes, that watched him all day long. He tried not to look at her. He didn't want to cause any problems. He just wanted to stay but he sensed Izil's father, Wararni, watching him closely, asking him more questions now.

Izil, recovered, had helped him learn so much that Goose could follow their conversations without much difficulty, if he put his mind to it. He would lie on the mats at night, pretending to sleep, but instead listening, trying to make out what they were saying.

'It is dangerous for us ...'

'When have you ever been afraid? When?'

'I am afraid for you, for Izil, for the others – not for myself.'

Wararni sounded affronted.

'They will come looking for him.'

'Let them look. Izil wants him to stay.'

'The man has a life somewhere else.'

Tayri moved away from her husband.

Goose had opened his eyes and saw the hurt in her face. He turned over to face the canvas, feeling like he had intruded, without meaning to, that here was something he could never truly be part of and that they had been stupid to imagine it possible. He was not Imuhar. The desert was not his home. The man's words echoed in his mind – *a life somewhere else.*

What of that life now?

When he slept, the nightmares came. Burning villages, children running screaming, blood on clothes, missiles exploding – but he could not hear them, and it was as if he were watching it all from far above. Different countries, different missions. The same fear, and for what? What had he done?

When he woke the heat of the day was already up, his cheeks were wet, and Tayri was wrapping a damp cloth across his forehead, her hand stroking his hair. He was frightened for her, but Wararni had left again.

'Shush … The men have gone to the markets, beyond the border.' She pushed him down as he made to sit up.

'Just sleep, you have fever. Otherwise they would have taken you with them.'

She poured a warm salty drink down his throat. He coughed at the bitter taste. Izil came in, and she moved away, her eyes blank now.

'Why didn't you go?' he asked Izil.

'I am to watch over you.'

He said this, his tone matter of fact, his hand on a small silver knife tied to his waist.

'What? I'm your prisoner now? Is that it?'

Goose laughed, but the boy did not laugh back.

Goose, his mind spinning, drifted back to sleep until the fever left him.

When he woke, Tayri had placed stew by him so he could eat, then she went to sit with the other women in the far corner of the main tent. They had grown used to him now, ignoring his presence amongst them, this ghost of a man fallen from the sky. He wanted to talk to her, but he knew whatever he would say, it would not be enough.

The day passed in feverish fits of sleep until the cool night air came.

In the dark, his mind stilled. He took his mat outside and just lay looking at the stars.

In the morning, he let Izil teach him more new words – making him practise over and over, so that the Imuhar would no longer laugh at his accent and his fumbling for the right words. But now, he was not sure why he learnt, why he stayed.

Then, the helicopters were back. One night, three flew overhead in formation – he heard them, and he knew that he would have to leave, sooner or later. He was starting to remember everything.

Chapter Twenty-One

Roseville, 2012

Lucy couldn't remember rightly how it was she had come to be the leader of the RSCAG – the Roseville Sinkhole Community Action Group – but perhaps due to her trusted role as librarian, or perhaps because she had given over the library space for the weekly meetings, or perhaps because it was her who had brought everyone together in their discontent, whether she wished it or not, the others felt her the rightful group leader. Therefore, it fell to her to organise the meetings, to corral the morning stragglers into one unified voice resolute against the chemical companies and the damage they had brought to the waterways and the air and the townships along the bayou.

Willie used to work for one of them, in a place that made all sorts of plastic coatings, but he'd left when his skin had broken out in a rash and hives that no cream from the doctors could heal, and his breathing had grown heavy, catching on his words when he spoke. He'd begun passing out sometimes, could be driving the station wagon or walking down Main Street or even sitting in the yard listening to Callie, a beer in one hand – and thud, there he'd go, falling again. It had got so Callie was terrified and plain refused to let him continue at the works, even though it meant they had to rely on the children – all grown now and living in Mississippi – to send them money each month, just to get by.

'Morning, Willie,' Lucy said, pushing past him, opening up the library. Hervey was winding around everyone's ankles, marking them with invisible scent and wafting ginger and white and black cat hairs.

'Morning? Why, it's practically lunchtime time, Lucy,' said Willie, indignant. 'What has you so late?'

She looked up at him, saying nothing, swinging open the door, letting them crowd in behind her, her small anti-sinkhole army, all chattering amongst themselves, muted conversations about the week gone, the days ahead. Small gentle courtesies exchanged between them before the anger would be summoned forth, around the meeting table, electric in the air between them, crackling through the silence of the library.

'Lucy, you hear about Denial?' Betsy asked her, the woman pulling her fine-knit cardigan around her shoulders, shivering with something somewhere between pleasure and fear as she relayed news out of Denial, where the local remaining townsfolk – having heard of the RSCAG's formation – had taken it upon themselves to do the same, only to be shut down by Sheriff Lentement, law enforcement in action.

'A night in the cells they spent, for trespassing, like common criminals!'

Betsy sighed, part-envious, part-fearful.

Lionel, her husband, laughed.

'Can you imagine Sheriff Lentement doing that here? I used to teach that boy. So did old Julie Betterdine Valéry. That boy knows to respect his elders. No, there'll be no nonsense like that in Roseville. Folks have a right to protest.'

Willie Jones nodded his head, stealing a quick glance at Lucy, anxious for her approval. From across the table Appleby Bertrand, beads of sweat dotting his high forehead where his hairline had receded back, watched Willie watching Lucy. Under the table his knuckles clenched white, but he put on his best smile and tried to ignore the provocation. What did Willie want chasing after Lucy's attention – hadn't he a wife at home already? Some folk just plain greedy. That's what Appleby, who had never had anyone love him, felt.

Lucy felt the eyes of the group on her. She cleared her throat and tried to empty her mind of Jim with his tears and Lenny with his wet socks, and focus her mind on the task in hand.

'Lucy, you darn well made us wait long enough already,' Willie called out.

She gave him one of her sternest looks then, her eyes sweeping around the table, dropped her voice to an almost whisper.

'Is anyone familiar with the Almata Park Campaign?' she asked. '1956, a whole community devastated by poisoned water, locals banded together to take action. Stood up directly to the company involved. Snuck in at night and took apart all the equipment, so they'd no choice but to stop. Now I'm not saying what we have here in Roseville is the same situation, nor even directly comparable, but ...'

'You think we should ...?'

Lucy looked at them all.

'I do.' She sighed.

'Letter-writing only takes you so far. Folk here have been complaining for years. Waiting on survey results, following all the official channels, writing, documenting their concerns. These companies are wise to all that. Someone complains, they put someone kind and concerned on it, with a gentle face and a soft voice, send a pretty response, promise action and whatnot. And what happens?'

'Nothing,' said Appleby, whistling through his teeth.

'Exactly. A whole lot of sweet nothing.'

'Isn't ... well, isn't it illegal? Like couldn't we get into a whole heap of trouble?' Alma-Mae asked, timid now and uncertain. The girl, a new recruit, a student of Lionel's before he took early retirement, and who cared deeply about nature and the living world and the air she breathed, and for those reasons and out of loneliness too (like the others, truth be told) she had gravitated towards the group one week. She liked the *idea* of doing something. But actually, going ahead, and doing something, something that could land them all in a heap of trouble, she wasn't sure about that.

'Anyone else feel the way Alma-Mae does?' Lucy levelled a glance at them all. 'No one has to get more involved in this than they're comfortable with – but we have to find a way to stop them. Before it's too late. Before there's no Roseville left.'

There was a quiet murmuring amongst the group. Hervey leapt up onto the table and wound his way through the cups that shook, half-full of water, his tail tickling the polystyrene. He stopped in front of Appleby, giving him the stink-eye.

'Hello there, kitty,' said Appleby, reaching out to stroke Hervey, forcing himself to extend out his arm. Hervey hissed at him and jumped down onto the floor.

Willie sniggered from across the table. Lucy pretended not to notice.

'Well,' she said, 'unless someone has a better idea, I think we need a show of hands. Who is with me on this?'

For a moment, the group fell silent, each examining their own conscience and motives, each wondering at the inexorability of it all, how they were being sucked into a course of action, once undertaken, from which they would be unable to return.

Lucy's eyes shone clear, evangelical almost. One by one their arms raised until all six, Alma-Mae reluctantly raising hers in the end too, were in concordance and there could be no going back.

'That's decided then. We'll work out a timetable and a plan of action – unless anyone comes up with a better idea before next week's meeting – and then we'll put it in motion. All in favour?'

The same show of hands again, some wavering a little now, but all choosing to stay the course.

'Constancy,' said Lucy, smiling at them all, her sinkhole warriors.

Lucy looked over at the tables by the window. There was no sign of Lenny. Usually, when the RSCAG would meet, he would be sitting nearby, eavesdropping, his eyes lit up, his body tense on the edge of the seat, for Lenny – Lucy Albert knew this for certain – had that warrior spirit to him, and he was just looking for a way to set it free.

In that moment, as the small group of activists broke apart, each going out blinking into the daylight, Lucy thought about the man and his son – how they had been sent to her. The universe had plans for Lucy and Lenny and Jim. She could feel that. She was drawn to it, magnetically pulled into a swirl of emotion and uncertainty and need.

'Don't go getting needy, Lucy Albert,' she muttered to herself under her breath. Hervey looked up at her, disapproving.

Chapter Twenty-Two

Roseville, 2012

Miss Julie had decided to tackle jerk chicken from the cookery book and sent Lenny off in search of coconut cream, chilli and limes, or as close as he could find in the few remaining stores of Roseville.

'Says here we need the paste, and thyme and garlic, ginger, spring onions. Well, I doubt you'll find everything at the grocery store, but ask all the same. We can make it up, our own version, as we go. Just do the best you can.'

Lenny had taken the list and the money from the jar in the kitchen as instructed, and he had set off, trailing the empty orange box behind him.

'Good for carrying provisions,' Miss Julie had winked at him. 'And buy some marshmallows for toasting, that's if you want to stay over …'

She hesitated.

'You can camp out here in the living room, do some star-gazing with the telescope on the lawn if you like. Keep me company.'

Lenny hadn't answered though his heart had lifted at the thought of him and his father sleeping indoors, curled up on the couch in Miss Julie's living room rather than swinging out in the damp hammock in the woods, sheltered only by the canvas of the tent strung up in the branches and hoisted over them for cover, the night's dampness cutting into his chest and chilling him to the bone. Then his spirits sank once more as he remembered that Jim had not come to find him the night before, and that perhaps he was never coming back. Gone, just like Mari-Rose, without even saying goodbye.

Lenny coughed a little as he walked, his eyes shining, the box swinging off his arm. Miss Julie had noticed the cough when he'd turned up that morning but said nothing, giving him a hot lemony drink instead with honey dripping off a spoon stirred into it. She figured a well-cooked spicy chicken dish and a warm night's rest would set the boy to rights once more. For a while, at least. Lord knows what they would do in the winter.

As he walked up Main Street, Lenny hovered by the door of the library. He peered in through the frosted glass to the side. There at the front desk sat Lucy Albert, stroking Hervey. Lenny wondered about whether to go in or not. He wanted to thank her on account of letting him wash his socks and dry them out and not making a big deal out of it, and for the book she'd chosen for him with its strange story that had filled his dreams that night, and for the way she'd shared her lunch without worrying about cooties. For all those reasons and because she'd only raised an eyebrow when he'd told those lies about Mari-Rose having cancer, and for the fact that she didn't seem to notice that his daddy smelt of drink and sadness and dirt if you stood too close to him – for these reasons too he wanted to do something kind for Lucy Albert, who had her own sadness about her too.

What Lenny really wanted to do was invite her to supper at Miss Julie's but that would be to presume and so instead he peeled himself away from the glass pane and continued on up the street, his sneakers kicking in the dust.

When Lenny left the house, trailing the box with him, Miss Julie went and stood by Stanley. Just leant on the back of her armchair to steady herself, then touched the wall, its flock wallpaper bumpy against her hand, as she wept. She sobbed in a way she hadn't done before. It was the tears of over sixty years – tears she had been saving up for a special occasion, one she had now found, for Miss Julie in opening up the trap door to the basement, in sharing Stanley's special place with young Léonard, had opened up the trap door to her own heart and out flew the dust and hope of a lifetime of wishing and hoping and not wanting to know the truth of the matter, wondering all that time what had become of Stanley. And she knew why she had decided to move the table and let the boy have the telescope – and if Stanley had been there, he would have wanted it too – she knew the reason why because she held it in her hand, crumpled up in her pocket and pulled from the back of the drawer in her bedroom that morning. It had a phone number scribbled in pencil on it, the envelope yellowed and unopened, the letter inside – she held it tight in her fist, kept it in her pocket and the past and all her memories of Stanley had rushed to the surface when she found it there. Sooner or later, she knew, she would open that letter – though for now it stayed deep in her pocket.

'Stanley, what shall we do?' she asked him, wiping her cheeks. 'How can we save him?' Stanley didn't answer. But then, he never did. She looked at the front door, remembered the way he'd looked at her before he left, so hopeful. They had both been so hopeful. Then the door had closed, and he was gone.

Chapter Twenty-Three

Ubari Sand Sea, 2011

'The stars are the secret to the human soul.'

Goose held a faint memory of these words, of someone telling him this as a boy. He remembered standing in a wide, open space, looking up at the night sky, a sense of adventure to it all.

This too, the desert, had been his adventure, his solace. He watched Tayri over by the fire. Even with her back to him, he could still picture her smile, the way her eyes held his, and there was an ache in him now.

Here in the desert the stars were different. He spent long evenings talking to Izil and even Wararni, when he was there, about them. It was something that marked him apart, as a stranger of some substance, that he should know such things too. For with the stars go grace.

'Goose, what is that one?'

'Where?'

'That group, all stuck together.'

Izil had pointed at a cluster of stars.

'That is Hercules, and above it, Lyra ...'

'Oh.' The boy sounded disappointed, like he had expected a more poetic name or explanation.

'I call it the fox, that little one – see how it has ears that point upwards,' Izil said pointing at Lyra, happier now, retrieving control of the situation. Goose smiled at him, at his childlike way of making the world fit to him, not the other way around.

'The fox is a fine name. I'll call it that too from now on.'

The young boy yawned and rubbed his eyes, his head dropping as they sat apart from the warmth of the fire.

'Time for sleep, Izil,' Tayri called out, watching the two of them lying there looking up at the night sky.

'Night, Goose,' he said, getting up, going over to his mother, kissing her goodnight, then going into the tent to sleep.

'He is a fine boy,' Goose said to Tayri as she passed by. He told her this at least once a day but it always made her proud and happy, and she always felt he meant it, for why would a man say something he did not mean?

'Like his father,' she said, surprising herself at the mention of Wararni, whose presence normally surrounded their conversations but did not intrude, instead hanging silent and heavy in the air between them.

'No, like you,' Goose said, making space for her to lie down on the mat beside him, the other women having gone ahead of her into the tents to settle the younger children.

She looked at him askance, wary and keeping her distance.

'I want to show you the stars,' he said.

'I know the stars.'

Looking around to make sure no one could see, she lay down near to him then edged away a little, leaving a gap between them, stretching out her arms on the damp sand to the side.

'I live with them, every day of my life. They guide us when we travel at night. You think you are the only one to read the sky?'

He laughed, surprised.

'I just wanted to impress you.'

She smiled at him and held his gaze.

It was then that he heard it: the sound in the sky – unmistakable.

'Quick, waken everyone, get them out of the tents. Hurry!' he shouted at her, pulling her up.

He was up and shaking off the sand, running to the tents, shouting, forcing the women and children out and away from the tents.

'Stay away from the animals. Stay low. Scatter,' he shouted, his voice hoarse, no longer his own anymore. Tayri looked at him, fearful. A young woman was crying, dazed and half-asleep, the baby in her arms awake and howling, not understanding, no one understanding what had happened to turn the sky devil crazy. They all ran.

As they ran, a first, then a second fighter jet shot by overhead. They passed high. High enough.

The nomads hunched down in the dips of the sand. The children whimpered. Goose cursed under his breath. They stayed like that a long while, the children growing cold and crying in the night air. Eventually, when there was no sign of a return, only then did he wave them back.

'I told Wararni I would look after you all,' he said to Tayri, who stared at him now as if a stranger.

'I'm sorry. I thought …'

'You thought what? That they would bomb us, shoot at us?'

'I couldn't be sure. The tents … at night, they could be mistaken for something else.'

'We are not a mistake.'

She looked at him, her eyes searching his, but it had broken, the spell of the stars. The sky devil was after all – just that.

Yet to the pilots above, who had seen nothing, they had only been shadows in the sand.

Chapter Twenty-Four

Roseville, 2012

Lucy saw the small boy's shadow crouching by the library door, just before he moved off. She had counted: one ... two ... three ... slowly to herself, each beat a stroke of Hervey's patchy fur, each count expecting Lenny to swing open the door. Lucy's heart had tightened in her chest as she wondered if the father would be with his son, and she felt herself not quite ready to see him again in the daylight. She waited but the door remained shut, the shadow moved away, and Lenny was gone. Lucy felt a strange ache, like it was the last time she would see the child perhaps, like she had missed something important, something meant for her and sent by the universe, a pulse or quickening that she could feel echoing in the space of the library and then it ebbed away, gone with the boy.

Then a moment later, the door swung open.

Lucy's heart leapt again, letting happiness in. Willie smiled back at her – surprised by the uncommonly warm welcome.

He had the Jane Fonda video cassette tucked under one arm. Folks didn't much bother with cassettes anymore but he had a player that worked just fine, and never saw the need to change to something new. *If it works, leave well alone,* he thought, approving of the long shelf of dusty videos just waiting to be discovered in the library.

'Afternoon, Lucy.'

She tilted her head in his direction.

'Afternoon, Willie. Surprised to see you in here, so soon again.'

'Callie asked if I could bring this back in, says it's too fast for her, all that bending and twisting.'

He laughed, cautious quick laughter, nervous still after her sharpness the last time he'd been in.

'She wondered if you mightn't recommend something else instead. Something … um … less ambitious.'

Lucy raised her eyebrows, unwilling to be so easily drawn in.

'Go and look over in that rack over there – that's what we have.'

Then relenting, she offered, 'The yoga one at the end is quite good, bit slower paced if that's what she's after. More focused on the breath, meditation, being mindful.'

Willie came closer to the desk, dropping his voice.

'She's trying to lose weight – doctor says she has to lose it, or she's headed for a stroke. Callie's always been proud of her looks, but since the change, well, the weight just sticks to her. She's got so she's crying about it all the time, she won't hardly leave the house. Hardly ever. And we used to go dancing or take the bicycles out around the lake for a picnic, even liked to go birdwatching together. Now she's just sad all the time.'

He looked at Lucy – a broken man.

'This here is all I can think of to help her.' He hung his head.

'I see,' said Lucy, softening, seeing that perhaps there was more to the man than she'd given him credit for. She went over to the shelves and pulled down two tapes, then from another shelf a couple of books.

'These should help. Did you know Betsy has a ladies' walking and singing group? They step out most days – idea is you sing as you walk. Callie might not feel up to it, but the ladies swear by it.'

Lucy leant over to Willie and whispered, 'Annabel says she lost fifty-six pounds just from walking and singing every day. Did her the power of good. Cleared her depression right up … not that I'm saying Callie is depressed, but sometimes these things get on top of a body …'

'Annabel Robins? I'll be sure and tell Callie that.'

'You do that. And if she likes, ask her to join the group against the sinkhole too. You could both do that together. Might not be as romantic as birdwatching, but we could do with more strong souls. Happen she'd want to join us?'

'Well, I don't rightly know. Callie doesn't socialise much these days.'

'Ain't socialising, Willie, it's social action. Just ask her.'

Lucy stamped the books and videos and passed them to Willie who winked at her, his heart and spirits lifted somewhat.

'You're looking mighty pretty today, Lucy, if you don't mind me saying so.'

She blinked at him, sensing it as just what it was – a compliment, a way of saying thank you. Instead, she thought of Jim, the way his eyes had held hers before he took to sobbing over Mari-Rose. She smiled, without meaning to.

'Right, well, thank you kindly, Lucy,' Willie stammered, seeing this look of pure happiness on her face, not knowing how to read it. He left with the books and tapes under his arm.

Lucy kept an eye to the door for the rest of the afternoon, but Lenny and Jim never came.

Chapter Twenty-Five

Ubari Sand Sea, 2011

Goose grew terrified of sleep, preferring to sit outside, wrapped in the blankets. Tayri would slip out of the tent at night and sit beside him. Wararni and the other men were still gone. The journey to the border was long, the crossing dangerous, people sometimes taken as slaves, disappearing if they weren't careful. Wararni had wanted to bring Goose with them this time, but the man still struggled to walk and would only slow them down. Besides if it was discovered he was with them, it would bring trouble. Better he stay hidden, for now.

The border zone was a lawless kind of no-man's land, but the prices they would fetch for their goods would be high, and the smuggled goods they would bring back to deliver to Ghat and other towns along the rim of the desert paid handsomely too.

'They go to sell the things we make ...' she told him. 'At least, that is what he tells me.'

She had looked at Goose, a searching look as if there was something else that she wanted him to understand but that she could not say out of loyalty to her husband.

'You know, it is easy to fall into a well, but not so easy to climb out.'

She looked at him again, 'You will be in danger if you stay. Wararni has protected you, first as our guest, then because you saved Izil, but the others ... It's war and fighting, it makes men crazy.'

She stroked his cheek. Goose had felt a jolt shoot through him with the warmth of her skin against his.

He had a life somewhere else and it was beginning to call him back.

'Are you crazy too?' she asked him, laughing.

'I must be,' he smiled back, struck by how beautiful she was and how much she seemed to know of him when he did not even know himself.

'All men are crazy.'

They heard something rustling at the back of the tents.

'Wait there, I'll look.'

Goose lifted a heavy pan from beside the fire and went to investigate, nervous, realising that it was up to him to defend the women, with Wararni and the other men gone. Had he ever killed someone? Is it murder if you can't see the person's face, if you're hundreds of feet above in the sky? He wasn't sure. It was something he had thought about, over and over. When Izil had found him, rescued him, he had been flying somewhere. To do what? What was his mission?

He gripped the handle of the pan tight, hearing a rustling to the right, behind the flaps of the main tent.

He felt a chill pass down his spine as he inched forward. Pulling back the flaps, he found a fox eating a dead hawk. This was their fearsome night-time intruder. Goose sighed with relief. He let the pan drop. Behind him, Tayri laughed.

He turned.

'My hero!' She laughed at him, her eyes dancing. Had someone been there, she would have dealt with them. Just as she had refused to run and hide when the planes had passed at night. Goose could see that now. Tayri was not given to fear. Only when Izil had been ill, only then he had seen her frightened, uncertain and grateful. Now her eyes mocked him, and he wanted to kiss her.

'What's going on?' Izil, sleepy-headed, peered out of the tent.

'It's okay, go back to sleep. We heard something. He was protecting us. It's okay …'

'It was just a fox,' said Goose, feeling foolish.

The boy looked at him, uncertain.

'Go to bed,' he ordered his mother, acting like a little man already. She looked at him, then at Goose. Izil refused to budge.

'Ah, may Allah protect me from the protection of men.'

She spat on the sand, and went back inside, leaving Goose staring after her.

'I couldn't sleep.'

He said this to Izil, as if it were an explanation.

'You shouldn't talk to her, alone like that,' the boy warned him. 'My father wouldn't like it. And besides, you promised.'

He looked at Goose, disappointed and worried.

For a moment, Goose wanted to go after her, to shake Izil off, but the boy stood there like a sentry waiting for him to come back into the tent.

Chapter Twenty-Six

Roseville, 2012

Lenny was easily distracted. As he walked up Main Street, he took to counting all the *For Sale* signs that swung from the old storefronts. Place was half-deserted, folk not even waiting for sales anymore – just gone. The stench from the sinkhole when it blew over Roseville was practically pushing folk out of town.

Lenny leant against the front of Eddie's Fish & Bait, opposite Vincent's bar, and waited. He was sure Jim would be in there, sitting quiet and sorrowful in a corner or up at the bar, on one of the high stools, full of fighting talk and jokes to share with the barman. He had watched his father before through one of the small windows to the back. Jim never noticed him and eventually Lenny would tire and wander back down to the river to wait.

His throat felt scratchy and his forehead clammy, and so he rested against the peeling green paintwork and kept watching the comings and goings from the bar, wondering if he shouldn't go straight in and pull his father out if he was in there. But the shame of it would be too great. He let go of the thought. Was it Jim or Mari-Rose he was maddest at? Lenny wasn't sure. There was an ache at the heart of him where they had both just left him empty and wanting.

Coconut milk, thyme, chilli – Lenny began to doubt that the man who ran the grocery store would even know what half of these things were, let alone have them.

He pushed the door open, and found the owner behind the counter, sitting reading a newspaper that he put away on seeing the boy come in. The air was stale and cloying, as if the door was rarely left open to let in the day.

'You for buying something?' The man gave Lenny a hard stare. Usually kids came in and tried to lift a packet of gum or a chocolate bar, just to get a rise out of him.

Lenny showed him the shopping list.

'I have to pick these up for Miss Julie.'

The man looked interested now. An actual paying customer.

'Let's have a look then ... my, oh my ... what's she cooking?'

Lenny just shrugged. It wasn't that he didn't like the man, except he sort of didn't, if he was honest with himself about it. He didn't care for the man's attitude, the angry look he had about him ...

Lenny walked around, looking at the shelves, not feeling hopeful.

'You got any ginger?' he asked, unsure what that even looked like.

The man watched Lenny as he walked around the shelves, all crowded with packets and boxes.

'You sure you're not plannin' on stealin' now?' the man asked him, crossing his flabby arms, staring down at Lenny, like he was king of his castle.

'I'm watchin' you.'

His eyes, mean-looking and squinted narrow, locked on to Lenny, like he meant to make trouble for the boy. Lenny sensed the man's temper rising, ready to swing towards him.

'Sorry, but I've got to go. Miss Julie's waiting.'

'What about your ginger?' the man called after him.

Lenny shot out the door, his heart racing now, leaving the man standing there alone, sweating and angry.

He ran down Main Street shaking off his discomfort. *Adults were so messed up sometimes*, he thought. That man reminded him of a big old black bear – little sad eyes, but ready to swipe at you all the same.

He squeezed the agate stone in his pocket and for an instant he missed his mother so much. She would have shut the man right up. Mari-Rose was used to unwanted advances and downright crazy behaviour. Lenny had watched how she'd handled the men of Roseville who had gathered around her when Jim went to war.

'You'll be wanting company,' he remembered one, Willie Jones maybe, saying to her, one day in broad sunlight while she was taking Lenny to the school bus.

'If I wanted a pet snake Willie, I'd buy me one. Run back home to Callie now, before I tell her you losing your way.'

It didn't take much. Sometimes she'd just look at them and sigh in disgust, and that was enough too.

'Don't ever let anyone take advantage of you Lenny, you hear me?'

She had shaken him hard one day after an old tramp had followed him back from the bus stop to the house asking for food and a place to sleep, and the boy had felt sorry for him.

'People's all kind of messed up. Doesn't mean you should indulge it.'

He had nodded, shocked, but sensing her fear too as she pressed him to her, having called the cops on the old guy who was refusing to leave now he'd been invited in.

'I can't always be there, Lenny. You got to do this stuff for yourself.' It was like she was mad at him for making her care, making her weak.

He had never thought she'd really go, make good on her threats, nor stay away so long. Sure, he'd heard her and Jim fighting over and over, sometimes shouting, sometimes it was just the way they moved around each other, saying nothing, their silence doing all the talking. A dance between them, their love – or care, or whatever it had been that had once been good between them – long gone now. And he couldn't help them fix it. That was the thing Lenny found hardest.

He remembered the day Miss Julie had found him sitting on the back steps crying like a baby. She hadn't mentioned it, hadn't asked what the matter was. Just called him and hugged him over the fence, burying his face in the roses.

It was funny how she just kind of knew when his heart hurt. Miss Julie, he reckoned, could see sadness in other people before they even really saw it for themselves.

'We all got gifts, we all got sorrows to bear,' she told him one day when she was stiffer than usual and struggling to walk. 'Sometimes Lenny, sometimes you just have to let things be what they will, even if it's not to your liking.'

So, he let go of Mari-Rose, when he couldn't make her stay, couldn't make her happy, couldn't fix her. Didn't make his heart any happier, though. And he noticed Miss Julie never let go of Stanley, though he didn't bring that up.

Lenny felt exhausted. He was a good distance from the grocery store though he could still see the shape of the man, standing on the street, watching him go. He shivered, the empty orange box somehow heavier now in his hand.

All he wanted was to sleep, to curl up in a bed – an actual bed with a coil spring mattress, and cool clean sheets and a soft feathered pillow for his head – to sleep and close out everything. Main Street began to spin. He was near the library now. If he could just get to the library. Lucy would look after him. Lenny felt his skin go cold, with goose bumps running up his arms. Everything started to go hollow and he felt himself falling, his knees buckling as he tipped sideways, his head hitting the sidewalk.

Chapter Twenty-Seven

Ubari Sand Sea, 2011

Ever since the snake had bitten Izil, the boy changed. He no longer laughed as much, nor sat as long with Goose. He seemed to grow tired of helping the man, as if Goose had become a shadow that he wished to shake off.

Instead Izil spent more time with the other children, and then when the men returned, bringing with them Wararni's younger brother, Hamou, who had been gone a long while having been involved in the fighting in the north, then Izil preferred to sit with the men and listen to Hamou tell tales of great cities swallowed up by the sand on the coast, of rivers running under the desert and of the great garden cities that would rise when their enemies were defeated and the country was free again.

Izil's dark eyes would still follow Goose, who tried to help the women, or who would sit close by to Tayri, not speaking to her, nor looking at her, yet Izil felt he was watching her all the same.

'Ask him where he is from, this fallen sky devil of yours,' Hamou told Izil one evening, gesturing at Goose.

'He doesn't know.'

'Perhaps. Or perhaps he is just pretending. Ask him what he has done. Why would he be here? Why would he stay, if not a spy?'

Wararni waved away his younger brother's harsh words, warning Izil with his eyes to say nothing, Goose only catching parts of the conversation between them all.

'Have you forgotten, brother, that here a stranger is welcome?' Wararni laughed a little, uneasy, a look of anger passing between the two men.

Goose sought out Izil's reassurance, smiling at the boy, but Izil did not smile back. Instead, he moved towards his uncle, leading him away from the camp, walking off towards the camels, the boy and man talking together, their words lost on the wind. Izil turned only once, shrugging his shoulders as his father raised a hand as if to beckon him back, then they disappeared over the ridge, leaving an uneasy silence in their wake.

Goose watched the fire embers burn low, lost in his thoughts, wondering about the questions the man had asked, not quite knowing all the answers yet.

Chapter Twenty-Eight

Roseville, 2012

Lenny woke to a splash of cold water. He spluttered, and feeling disoriented for a second, pulled himself up off the ground.

'You okay, son?'

Appleby Bertrand, stepping out of his empty office next to the library, looked at him with concern. Wasn't every day he saw a child faint on the sidewalk. Most days in fact he had no contact with anyone on account of most people having no money, and therefore no call on his accountancy services. Things kept up this way, he'd have to leave soon and go back to Baton Rouge, which was a crying shame for he loved the fishing at the levee – at least, he had done when there were fish. These days they were coming belly-up downstream, killed no doubt by chemicals in the water or salt seeping up from the Gulf – *folk needed to speak up some*, he thought. Months before, he had seen Lucy's flyer in the library window, some sort of community meeting to address the issues. He had marked it in his calendar and now he went every week – as regular as churchgoing. With this week's meeting just gone, he was waiting, waiting for the week after, and the week after that – all precious moments with Lucy that he gathered up, storing them away. He wasn't brave enough to talk to her outside of the formality of the meetings. That would feel too raw, too personal. The mere thought of it made him perspire. Until the next week, he was always just sitting in his storefront office passing time.

The boy keeling over like that, just in front of his window, did him a favour, took him out of himself.

'You okay there, son?' He called out to Lenny once more, leaning over him. Slowly the boy came around and looked up at him, sitting up, unsteady, his hands pressed to the ground.

'I'm fine.' Lenny wasn't sure but he said it anyway, just to check he could still speak. His head hurt where he had smacked it on the concrete. Appleby went back inside and brought him a cool soda from the ice-box and a cloth wrapped with some ice cubes for his head.

'Here you go.' He passed them to Lenny, sitting beside him on the curb. The boy nodded slowly in thanks and took the offering, pressing the cloth to his forehead until the skin felt numb and cold to the touch, then still shaking, he got up to leave. He didn't want Lucy to see him all in pieces, covered in dust. He didn't want that sad-eyed look from her.

Something glinted on the sidewalk.

'You dropped this?' Appleby called after him, sad to see the boy go already. *Never good with kids*, he thought, they always unsettled him, like they saw through life and were judging him somehow for the dullness of his own. But this kid didn't look at him like that, didn't hardly look at him at all. Bertrand felt invisible.

Lenny held out his hand, the palm scraped from the ground, and clasped the agate stone, taking it from Appleby. It was supposed to protect him – wasn't that what Mari-Rose had promised? Just a dumb, fake promise, was all. Lenny's hand smarted from the fall.

'Thank you,' he called out to the sad-eyed man who stood there, the ice cubes melting through the cloth, watching him go, Appleby wondering why he couldn't just be more natural around other folk. Surely then the boy would have stayed a little longer, they could have talked about fishing maybe. Don't all kids love fishing? Appleby wasn't sure.

He walked down after the boy and then tried to peek into the library through the frosted glass to spot Lucy Albert. He truly had a soft spot for Lucy. Couldn't tell her that, though. But he'd go to her meetings. He'd do that alright. He watched the boy double back up on the opposite sidewalk, heading now towards the end of Main Street, and he had a moment of panic. *Should I have let him go? What if he hit his head hard? What if there's blood on his brain? Or concussion?*

But Lenny was too far away to notice the accountant worrying about him.

Criss-crossing the road back up past Eddie's Fish & Bait, trailing the orange box with him, steering clear of the grocery store, Lenny peered in through the grime of the windows to the side of the bar, but Jim was not there, only Vincent standing behind the bar polishing glasses and singing, low and quiet, to himself.

By now feeling somewhat recovered and refreshed by the soda, Lenny had forgotten about the shopping for Miss Julie, clean forgot all about their grand plans to make jerk chicken, as the indignity of having been abandoned by Jim hit home to him and he felt himself deeply alone and unwanted in this world.

It shamed him to feel this way, this sinking way, everything falling away from him – first Arturo leaving, then Mari-Rose, now Jim. What was it about Lenny that made everyone just take off like that?

His heart and head sore, he set off down in the direction of the river and the woods to the back of the bend of the river, kicking up scuds of dust as he went, his eyes low, looking for wild roses in the grass verges along the way.

He thought about how Mari-Rose used to call him her little prince. That felt so far away. Lenny pulled Stanley's sweater, the sleeves trailing long around him. The damp in the air cut through the holes. He couldn't go back to the clearing – not without Jim. Couldn't be out on his own again another night.

The leaves of the sugar maple trees were starting to drop, making a carpet to stamp through as he made his way down to the boardwalk by the river. There was a place in the bayou, round on the far side of the river, along the walkways where Jim would go to sit and think sometimes – Lenny had seen him before, leaning back against a bald cypress by the water's edge, his eyes closed, like no one was watching.

Was it the path on the left or right? Lenny hesitated, trying to remember.

Lenny had followed him there one day and waited. He'd seen his daddy cry. Jim hadn't meant for him to see that and Lenny had never mentioned it, but he'd held on to it all the same. If he could pick the right path, he'd find the spot. Maybe Jim would be there. Maybe he'd be sorry for having left Lenny alone. Maybe there was a way of fixing things, if only Lenny could find out what that was.

Lenny squeezed the agate stone in his fist and walked on out into the bayou.

Chapter Twenty-Nine

Ubari Sand Sea, 2011

In the desert, the lorry bumped along the track left by countless other journeys, sand sticking to the wheels as they sank down further with each rotation. The driver, from Ghat, cursed under his breath as the wheels stuck, the engine revving and pulling helplessly against the dunes.

'Get down,' he shouted to all the men and the lone pregnant woman who travelled with them, bringing her two children with her. For a moment, no one stirred, as if believing if they said nothing, did nothing, perhaps the lorry would decide to move again. After all, they had spent all morning in this stop-start pattern, each time with the driver growing more morose and emphatic in his muttering.

'Push! Or would you rather we bake in the heat here?' he berated them, signalling at the high sun, pushing his passengers out of the overheated lorry, far too many bodies all squeezed into one space, some faint with exhaustion, others sick with fear.

'You said we would be there by now,' one young man called out, pushing his shoulder to the back of the lorry along with three others, the wheels loosening a little, only to drop down even further.

'We are lost,' said another, a young man too – for they preferred the young to fight, finding them easier to mould, less attached to life, understanding less what they were surrendering, so letting them pass at the border with the guards paid to turn a blind eye to the shadows at night.

'He does not know where he is going,' said the woman, tutting under her breath, pulling the children close to her.

'We are lost. We will die here.'

A silence fell over the group. They had already travelled thousands of miles north, crossed borders, evaded capture, and this, the final stretch should have been easy. After all, the driver had taken their money and told them it was a route he covered every week. The men looked about them. The track was faint ahead, sand blowing over the tracks of the vehicles that had gone before them, for as far as they could see – only sand.

But a madness took hold, a collective fever, and once it became clear that the lorry would not move without chains, and that they had almost run out of water, the men began to walk, covering their heads with shirts and scarves, following the track as best they could.

'Come back, fools,' shouted the driver, shaking his head in disbelief.

The woman stayed in the sliver of shade cast by the side of the lorry and let her children sleep on her chest.

The driver, believing she slept too, lifted his seat and took out a large container of water, sipping it carefully before hiding it once more. Then he radioed for help.

Izil, standing on the top of the ridge of dunes, saw the line of men moving like ants away from the lorry. Sometimes he would see these overloaded vehicles pass by in the distance, men hanging from the sides and back, as they crossed to the north. The men came from far away. They came in search of work – some finding it as soldiers, others as labourers on the great engineering project that sought to siphon the desert seas buried deep below the surface, tunnel the water out to the north to create a new green kingdom, a land of miracles, they said. Others returned to the south, disillusioned, broken by work or war, realising they had simply swapped one set of despairs for another.

This time, though, something had happened. Why were the men walking in the desert? With little shelter for days, they would soon die in the heat. He wondered at the strangeness of it, then he rode his camel down the bank towards the lorry, looking over his shoulder, conscious that his mother would not approve, having warned him many times before not to get close.

'Why?' he had asked her.

'Because I say so,' she replied, making him more curious about these people crossing the desert sands.

'Where are they going?' he persisted.

'Somewhere else,' was all she would say.

Izil marvelled at this: the idea that there was somewhere else that was not the desert or the edges of the desert. It was this in part which had drawn him to the fallen sky king, but Goose could tell him little of the world beyond. He began to yearn to see it for himself, to know what was beyond the edge of the sand seas, to discover worlds different to his own.

Approaching the carcass of the lorry, its tarpaulin flapping in the breeze, black smoke pouring from the front as the engine complained fiercely at its punishing treatment, he saw the woman standing at the side. She put one hand up to cover her eyes as he came near. He called out in greeting.

'*Salaam.*'

'*Salaam alaikum.*'

She gestured at him for his water bottle, and he passed it to her, watching her force open the mouths of her children, making them waken in the heat to drink before taking a drink herself, and passing it back to him, having made sure not to drink it all, even though she was faint with thirst.

'Thank you.'

In the front the driver was snoring, his belly rising and falling in the heat.

Izil lifted the woman up onto the camel, bending down so she could step up on his back, and then he helped up the two children, handing them to her, a boy and girl both mute with exhaustion. He walked alongside them, taking them back to the caravan, east of the direction from which the men had set out. The woman said nothing, only held tighter to her children, leaning against them to shade them from the sun as best she could.

Tayri and Goose, seeing Izil return, bringing these strangers with him, went out to help, lifting down the children and their mother, bringing them into the cool of the tent, Tayri giving them milk to drink. The children stared at her, at the light quick way she moved as if the heat were nothing. They stared too at Goose with his damaged leg, seeing him a stranger also.

Tayri passed a goatskin flask to the woman who drank, grateful.

'What about the men? The driver?'

Izil, having run off to explain all he had seen to his father, asked him, wondering what it was they should do.

'We must help them,' said Wararni, reluctant, sensing trouble. But later when the heat dropped from the day and when the men from the caravan travelled back to where Izil said the lorry had been, they found it had disappeared and the men were gone. There was little they could do, only wait for their return.

Chapter Thirty

Roseville, 2012

Waiting was something Miss Julie was an expert at. She had waited so many years for Stanley to come back – this, she reckoned, made her an Olympian of the waiting world, and therefore short waits – waits on letter responses, on coupons off, on Lenny coming back with library books and shopping, waits on relatives ringing or writing, or rarely visiting, all those things she bore with grace and equanimity.

But the chemical companies, not responding to the legal letters she had sent about the sinkhole and the toxic fumes and the statistics that showed – CATEGORICALLY (she had written in capital letters) – the illnesses affecting the good folk of Roseville, that kind of waiting her nerves were growing thin for, because she *knew* they did not care.

No shame in them, she sighed, listening to the radio presenter complaining again about the plants dying, and interviewing local folk who told sad stories about how everything was perfect before, and now, well now they were ashamed ...

Everybody is ashamed of something, she thought. If she could just find that weakness in the chemical company. *Find that*, she thought, *shine a light on it and they'll do something. There's nothing so bad, it can't be put right.*

That morning she'd received a flyer through her screen door, just dropped onto the mat. She almost threw it out without reading it, but then she had seen:

Community meeting of the RSCAG – SINKHOLE Action Group – Roseville Library

Miss Julie had pinned it to the wall above her vanity table in her bedroom. Now here were some folk actually doing something. For the first time in a long while she thought about leaving the house, taking herself up to the library to see who these people were, what they were planning on doing because clearly letters alone weren't going to fix the problem.

She did not leave the house much these days, on account of her pain and the length of time it took her to get anywhere. She had one of those mobile scooter things, sitting underneath the porch at the front, that she had used only once. Arturo had laughed at her and she had been ashamed – not because she was old and arthritic and embarrassed by her own mortality, but because she had attempted to run him over, just to teach him a lesson, and Mari-Rose had caught her in the act and told her off for 'reckless endangerment'. An irony not lost on Miss Julie when she thought how that girl ignored her own son and broke his heart with her drinking and mood swings, so frequent the child didn't know what normal looked like anymore.

'You aren't fit to be a parent! *Pas du tout!*'

She had shouted that at Mari-Rose, reversing the scooter just to show the woman that she was unrepentant.

'And Arturo should respect his elders!'

After that she had parked up the mobility aid and left it alone – afraid of what she might do, given half the chance. But she kept the battery charged, just in case.

Life is oftentimes a matter of just holding it together, she thought. But sometimes she remembered how it had felt, the breeze in her hair, the speed of the thing whizzing up Main Street, how it had lifted her spirits. Sometimes life is a matter of tearing things apart too.

Where was that boy? She looked out her window up at the lights coming on now. He had been gone a long time. It would be dark soon enough and her belly was rumbling. She had been imagining the jerk chicken so much all afternoon she could almost taste it. Miss Julie tapped the window frame.

'Stanley, I've said it once, I'll say it again. Folks got no wit.'

Stanley said nothing.

Being a world champion of waiting, though, she would sit a while longer before drawing the curtains and wait for Lenny. She would wait even as the darkness fell.

Maybe too she would go to that meeting next week, see what this Lucy Albert was like, and maybe it was time to take the mobility scooter out of retirement. Just this once.

Sometimes you have to try a thing: even if it seems impossible, you have to try.

Chapter Thirty-One

Ubari Sand Sea, 2011

For a long time, they knew nothing of the fate of the disappeared lorry. It was only much later that they would hear, from family in Ghat, how the lorry, fixed once more, had travelled on, picking up the men as they walked, only for it to be turned back on reaching the outskirts of the town, and that the driver became lost as they journeyed back through the desert at night. The radio battery had died, and they were alone, trapped in a sandstorm. Many of the men who had travelled with the lorry were found weeks later, their bones picked over in the sand.

'The desert is no place for those who do not understand,' said Wararni, shrugging his shoulders on hearing the news. 'For those who cannot respect it.'

The woman, Malia, and her children decided to stay on with them, terrified of what had happened and unwilling to travel further alone. She told them of life in her country to the south, of the fighting and why she had chosen to risk her life, her children's lives, in this journey across the desert.

'One day, I would like my son to have a future,' she confided to Tayri. 'At home, he would have been forced to become a boy-soldier, to fight. What could I have done, only leave?'

'Here, well in the north, they would have him fight too,' Tayri warned her, shaking her head, placing her hand on Malia's arm.

Izil sat listening to the women talk, wondering, not understanding – after all, why would she not wish her son to be a warrior? He had heard his father and uncle talk of the fighting in the north of the country, arguing over whether to travel there or not.

'If a man holds up the moon and stars, do you believe you can take them from him?'

Tayri had asked the men this, on hearing Hamou talk of how well they would be treated, what riches would be paid, how life would improve for them all if they gave up this rootless wandering and the men decided to join the fight.

'I will go back,' Hamou said, after a long silence.

'You will go alone,' said Wararni. A divide had opened up between the brothers. Wararni's cheeks were wet as he held his brother close and they embraced for a long time. Izil was left wondering why his father chose to remain behind if it made him so sad. Not for the first time, he thought perhaps his father was wrong and his uncle right, and that he too was like those men from the lorry, or like Goose, trapped in the desert, never free, never knowing what lay beyond the edges of the sand.

'Take me with you, Uncle.' Izil had waited until everyone slept before waking Hamou, pushing him on the shoulder until the man's eyes opened.

'Shush Izil, go back to sleep.'

'I'm serious. I want to fight too. Take me with you.'

'I can't. Your parents would never forgive me.'

Izil sat there, unblinking, until at last the man, seeing the boy had set his heart on going, agreed to take him – only on condition that when Wararni discovered him gone, should they chase after him and find him with Hamou, he must say he had stowed away and it was not his uncle's fault.

The boy, his eyes shining in the dark, nodded in eager agreement.

Goose, lying nearby, heard the boy's plans and felt a shiver pass through him as he drifted back to sleep. He dreamt he was flying above a twisting silver river, but that the water was turning red, and the plane was falling to earth, Goose parachuting out only to see too late that Izil was there, trapped inside, Goose unable to save him.

Chapter Thirty-Two

Roseville, 2012

It was getting dark and still no sign of Lenny. Miss Julie had switched on the lamps in the front and sat in her chair waiting for him. Outside looked like it was going to be a gusty night, a wind coming up. He should have been back by now. She folded over the corner of her blanket in her lap. Miss Julie had spent a lifetime waiting so she knew, she knew when someone wasn't coming back – and that was what she felt about Lenny. *It's my fault*, she thought, looking at Stanley.

'What will I tell his father?'

For a moment, she stopped and turned her head. She was sure Stanley said something – *something* about the sinkhole.

'What's that, Stanley?'

Her voice trembled. She got up and ran her hand over the picture frame. *Old age playing tricks on me*, she thought. She sat back down as the light of the day died away and she waited.

Up at the library, Lucy had held on half an hour later than usual, partly on account of opening up late, partly because the group against the sinkhole had run on long that morning, but also because she had been hoping Lenny or Jim would stop by. There was an ache in her belly thinking of her quiet little rooms, the loneliness of it all, and how the man and boy, with the need they had of her, how that had made her feel important somehow.

Locking up, she cast around. Appleby Bertrand next door was locking up too and nodded 'evening' to her. Lucy had

Hervey in a rucksack on her shoulder. The cat mewled, indignant and hungry, his head poking out into the wind. Really, she ought to take Hervey home. But something stopped her.

As the cool night air and little gusts of wind hit her, Lucy felt with the utmost certainty that Lenny and Jim were in grave trouble. Danger even. Her gut told her this, so she unlocked the library doors again and went in, over to the card index in the green plastic box she kept on the counter and flicked through until she found Miss Julie's address.

If Lenny wouldn't come to her, she would find him. She owed the boy that, she reckoned. Hadn't she abandoned him the evening before, perhaps even kept his daddy from finding him? In fact, the more Lucy thought about it all, the more she blamed herself, and it became clear to her that she would have to put things right.

She found the card and address. Hervey's supper would have to wait. She set off down Main Street, waving to Appleby who was always late locking up, always there as she passed by, she thought. He waved back at her, as he always did, a sad little smile on his face. She felt sorry for him.

But tonight, she hadn't time to worry about that. She had a mission – to find Lenny, to find Jim, to fix everything. *There's nothing can't be fixed*, she thought. In fact, she didn't believe that to be quite true, but it had been a favourite saying of her late mother – whose death which took her by cancer just went to prove, in fact, that some things cannot be fixed – but nonetheless, it was a comforting thought, and so Lucy held to it in times of need.

She would find Lenny. She would find Jim. She would fix what was broken. Somehow. 'Just you watch, Hervey', she said as she powerwalked down the street, 'just you watch.'

Chapter Thirty-Three

Ubari Sand Sea, 2011

The days before leaving passed quickly, Izil spending more time than usual with his mother, hugging her, then pulling away, afraid that her presence would weaken his resolve. With his father, he was solemn and quiet, and he no longer played with the other children, seeing their games as babyish.

'Is Izil strange to you?' Goose asked Tayri one evening, wondering whether he should tell her of the boy's plans, or try to reason with Izil in private. But Izil seemed to no longer listen to him and Goose feared he was already too late.

'He is busy becoming a man,' she sighed, seeing how tall Izil was growing, his arms too long now for the worn red top he liked to wear, and spying him wrap the *cheche* around his head, practising when he thought no one was looking.

'You should tell your brother not to go north,' she said to Wararni that evening, watching him, too, grow anxious as the days passed.

'Perhaps he is right to go …'

Her husband became sullen, and Tayri, seeing him struggle with his thoughts, left him alone.

'Izil?'

She called for her son, discovering him at last standing away from the caravan on the ridge looking out to the north. At first, he did not seem to see or hear her, standing as he was on the edge, looking out across the sand, and when he turned, hearing the faint call of her voice, his face darkened a moment, unhappy that she was there, watching him.

'What?' he called back, not moving towards her. For a moment, Tayri said nothing – but she knew in that instant that he meant to leave.

'Izil, come here.'

Reluctant, he walked over, kicking the sand with his heels.

'What would I do without you?' She looked at him, his eyes downcast.

'Tell me that.'

She held out her arms and pulled the young boy to her.

'You know what happened to the men who were lost in the desert?' she asked him. Izil nodded, thinking of the vultures picking over the corpses, the bodies rotting in the heat.

'It is easy to get lost, Izil. Much harder to find your way back. Things look the same, but they are different. A man can be lost forever in an instant like that.'

From below the ridge, Izil heard the camels, all settling to rest for the night as the sun dropped low. As night fell, he came to the fire and sat with his father, away from the other children, feeling himself older now.

The boy watched a shower of shooting stars fall across the night sky, or perhaps it was the light from a far-off plane dropping explosives across the sands. From so far away, it was hard to tell the difference with the naked eye.

That night, his father sang a desert poem, *tahengemmit*, a song of love and belonging and loss, and when he finished, he embraced his brother, who saw how the boy had had a change of heart, and he was glad of it. The boy, despite his warrior heart, was too young for war.

And for Goose, who sat listening to the singing and seeing all this, and who also feared the loss of the boy, his mind flooded with images – a red barn, a twisting silver river, a name echoing over and over, and the night filled with the scent of wild roses filling the desert air.

Much later still, when all the singing and music had ended, Izil stood with the rest of the caravan, his mother's hand on his shoulder, as he watched Hamou go, taking a few of the men with him, their silhouettes on the camels growing smaller in the darkness, until they were only one more shadow flitting across the desert, swallowed up by the night.

Chapter Thirty-Four

Roseville, 2012

The swampland was alive, full of noises and sounds – some familiar, others unknown to the boy – as Lenny made his way along the rickety boardwalk. The slats were draped in Spanish moss, and on either side of the path ducks and turtles swam by, cutting a path through the duckweed that floated on the water's surface. From the distance came the smell of sugar cane burning, carried down the river, a sweet, cloying, smoky smell filling the evening air.

Lenny started to tell himself the story of *The Little Prince* once more, as a way of calming his mind and nerves. He was not afraid. He told himself this. No, he was brave. He would find Jim, find the sinkhole. Somehow, he would fix everything that was broken before it was too late.

Life didn't always offer up all its answers to you all at once. Lenny knew this. Sometimes it was a matter of waiting and figuring things out.

Lenny sat by the water's edge, watching the ants make their way down along the fallen leaves towards the bank, like they had a plan. In the undergrowth up ahead, something flickered by, a flash of colour. Lenny glanced up, seeing what looked like a fox's tail disappearing into the dark green foliage ahead. He shivered.

'It's the things we don't know, don't rightly understand, that frighten us most.'

He recalled Lucy saying this at one of her meetings, telling everyone not to give up – not to let fear win. Lenny shook himself gently and picked up his orange box. He kept on walking, hurrying now, as the day's light began to fall.

Chapter Thirty-Five

Ubari Sand Sea, 2011

In the weeks since his uncle had left, life had returned to normal in the desert. Izil played once more with the other children. He no longer put distance between himself and his parents. He befriended Goose once more – and they would talk of desert life. On the days when Goose's leg or head ached and he would rest, Izil would help with the herd, sometimes stealing an hour or two to himself to sit in the shade, for they had moved to a different *wadi* blessed with water and trees, date palms embracing a dip in the dunes, protecting the water from sucking back into the sand.

'They are stealing the water.'

Izil overheard his father say this one night to the other men, all nodding, one spitting into the sand.

'What man steals a hidden ocean?'

There was silence.

'It is true, the water is low this year. Next year there will be less again.'

'Until?'

No one had an answer. These things happened far away, carried out as if by some invisible force.

'Soon there will be nothing left.'

Wararni's face darkened.

'Have we not always survived? You think they would help us? The same men who take from us?' He laughed. 'Only when the wells run dry will they understand what they have done.'

Overhead, Izil and Goose heard the planes pass by, high up against the stars, the sound drowning out the voices of the men for a moment. Each night now they would count the fighter planes as they flew over the desert. Where had they come from? Where were they going? The men too paused from their conversation to look up at them, Goose flinching as the sound reverberated in the night air.

'Sky devils!' Wararni said, angered then quieted, turning back to the fire, remembering Goose was amongst them.

Izil thought of his uncle far away and the planes, and he was glad now he had stayed in the desert. Did that make him a coward then? He thought about this, and he thought of the movie he'd watched long ago in Ghat, the pilots spiralling in the sky, one called Maverick, one Goose. Which one would he be?

Time in the desert moved slowly. The fighter jets seemed out of place, out of time. Lost in the night sky.

Izil slept, and as he slept he dreamed of giants, thundering through the dunes, swatting away the planes like flies, their feet sending tremors along the sand sea, the desert cracking open all the way to the ocean, revealing an underground river running through the heart of it all. One of the giants stopped and looked down, seeing the ruins of a city rising up from the sand. Below him, people ran in all directions as the earth split and the waters rose up. The giant caught one of the planes in his fist, and shook it upside down, watching a man fall to the ground, a tiny figure swallowed up by the sea.

Goose too dreamed of giants, of planes and a silver gleaming river, and of a boy and his mother calling out to him across the desert sands.

At dawn when Izil awoke, rolled up tight, close against the side of the tent, he felt as if he were on the edge of something, as if something ugly was about to happen or had happened and now its echoes shook the sands, the giants a warning for them all.

Chapter Thirty-Six

Roseville, 2012

The chemical companies had come to the state a few years back. Word was that there was natural gas to be found underneath the swamp – if a man had the inclination and the expertise, that was – and that there would be profit to be made in such an undertaking. For years, many companies had operated all along the river, drilling, setting up factories, making everything from plastics, electronics, parts, chemical products – prospecting, turning a profit, all the while employing the good folk of Louisiana. Now it was the turn of Roseville.

At first the idea was sold to the local people as job creation – opportunity. That was the word they always used.

'Isn't that how evil strides out in broad daylight?' Miss Julie had said. 'Opportunity.'

To begin with, the companies did everything by the book – community meetings, the sharing of plans, sketches, maps. There was plenty of discussion, plenty of what they called 'stakeholder engagement'. And then they got to work.

But no one had banked on the sinkhole.

And then opportunity quickly morphed into something else, something sinister sucking huge swathes of tupelo and bald cypress trees and swirling, bubbling away, eating up the very land itself, and no one – not even the companies, it seemed – were able or willing to stop it.

All this Lenny had listened to in the library week after week, as Lucy and her group of eco-angels, as she called them, took to figuring out a way to get these chemical-industry folk to fix the problems they had brought to Roseville.

'People are dying!' Lucy had said, standing there by the desk, Hervey sat on the table next to her scratching his back against the large-print romances. 'Dying!'

The small assembled group – consisting of Willie Jones, Appleby Bertrand, Betsy, Lionel and that young girl whose name everyone kept forgetting, basically library regulars with nothing else to do with their time – had stood looking at her with compassion and not a little fear. They all knew Lucy had had a rough time of it, more so than most, that she had lost loved ones to illness too, so they understood for her it was personal. Lenny though, not knowing this, could only see the way Lucy was preaching her gospel, and how he thought she was right, and the sinkhole sounded like it was the cause of all of Roseville's problems, including his own.

If it weren't for the sinkhole, he thought, *Mari-Rose would still be here.* She would have never left. The bank wouldn't have taken the house when it couldn't be sold nor paid for when she couldn't keep up repayments. His daddy wouldn't have had to go to war – here Lenny was hazy on the detail, and had you asked him how a chemical company and a war could be connected he might have struggled to explain it other than to say he felt it in his gut – that one thing was connected to another, for good or for bad – just as the stars were connected, the constellations connected, all of it pulsing and creating energy and putting it out into the universe. That much he knew from Jim. But he knew it too from sleeping out in the woods, or from climbing the willow and oak trees by the water's edge and looking out over Roseville and False River from up high, he knew it in his bones – this connection between all things; good and bad. He remembered the last meeting in the library.

'We have to stop them!'

A cheer had gone up from Willie, who found himself admiring Lucy Albert, so fervent and determined.

'Shush!'

A disapproving tut came across from the history section where Waverlee Herbert was browsing for battles. She hated noise at the best of times, but the library, like the church, was meant for sanctity and peace, not this political agitating. She would have to have a word with the mayor. Lucy was a fine librarian, she really was – Waverlee acknowledged that in the girl – but this was going too far, and besides what use did it do, any of it? If it wasn't the sinkhole, it would be something else and that was just life.

'No point trying to roll a boulder uphill,' she had muttered to the group, placing her finger over her lips to make the point about silence being golden. Lucy frowned at the old woman, her cheeks reddening. She had not intended to get carried away. It just got to her, that was all. Anyway, what could they do – only rage.

'Sorry,' Lucy whispered back, blushing, meeting adjourned.

'Thanks for coming, Willie,' she had said to him as he went, warming to him more now. 'Next time bring Callie.' Willie had ducked out the door quickly, wanting to avoid a long conversation with Waverlee, who was apt to hold on to perceived slights and grievances and air them extensively (this he knew for her yard neighboured his own and he could feel her watchful of him – ready to report back to Callie or anyone else who would listen). The group followed after him, only Appleby lingering, aching, unnoticed.

'Library's not meant for that kind of thing, Lucy,' said Waverlee, giving the girl a fierce look, thumping down a weighty tome titled *The Story of American Freedom* on to the countertop.

'Willie, hold up, I need a ride, you mind waiting?'

Waverlee called after him, but he was already gone.

'I just ... I think we have to do something and besides, the library's a public space, space for folk to come together.'

'To read, not to riot.'

Lucy didn't say anything at the time, but she felt admonished and perhaps the old woman was right, perhaps it was a lot of noise and fuss for nothing. Because how could they change anything? She wished Waverlee Herbert a good evening and took out her knitting.

Lenny remembered all that, but Waverlee had been wrong. Some things you could change. You just had to believe in it. And Lenny believed.

Chapter Thirty-Seven

Ubari Sand Sea, 2011

The caravan was heading for the east now. Only the stars lit their way for it was still night – everyone having risen at midnight to avoid the heat of the day.

The men had returned from another trip to the border. It was clear they had not gone just to sell the jewellery the women made. Goose knew this. He listened to the conversations that were whispered in and around the tents, and he knew that even here – in the heart of the desert – the war had seeped into everyday life. He realised, that to some of these men, he was the enemy. He saw Wararni too, watching him, a dark look about his face.

Their hospitality began to seem forced, the warmth gone, the men less inclined to joke or talk with him. Even Tayri was cooler towards him. Something was happening in the country, more talk of fighting in the north, something changing and Goose didn't know what it was, but he knew he was on the wrong side of it, and the desert plains that had felt like freedom to him, began to feel like bonds, tightening around him.

There were thirty of them travelling together, thirty-one including Goose, then a string of camels, with the children all riding up front. Goose was at the back, keeping a little distance from the caravan, thinking about how to leave them. Now that he was beginning to remember who he was, was he able to leave? Was he free to go? He wasn't sure. Perhaps he was a hostage. He watched Wararni up ahead, Izil riding next to him. Hadn't they been kind to him, though? Hadn't they saved him, nursed him, fed him, looked after him as if he was ... what, family, friend? Other people's kindness had always unsettled him. He had grown up never expecting to find kindness in others, so when it happened, he didn't know how to recognise it.

And Tayri? His heart tightened when he thought of her – her touch, the scent of her skin. He blushed, thinking about it, though he had done nothing, never crossed the unspoken line between them. Yet he had wanted this life, this desert life.

Overhead the helicopter found the caravan as they made their way east. It had been a piece of good fortune, Elliot thought, that someone had heard someone in Ghat talking about this pilot fallen from the sky, and how he had become one of the Imuhar, that they'd taken him in down near the border.

'And you said we'd never find him!' Elliot laughed at the pilot.

'A nomad, no less.'

'No wonder you couldn't find him.'

'A nomad in the desert.'

The helicopter crossed overhead, and the Imuhar looked up watching it curving past, trained on them.

'Sky devils!' Wararni cried out.

Goose, looking skywards, was caught up in tracing the path of the helicopter, its shadow above, with its night vision trained on them, and he knew it was not by chance that they were there, that someone had sent them to find him. There would be no escape. He stopped a moment, staring up as the helicopter turned and came back towards them, so he did not notice what Wararni was doing until it was too late.

From under the mat draped over the back of his camel Wararni had pulled out something long, dark, metallic, that glinted in the moonlight. The caravan had stopped.

'Sky devils!' Wararni shouted again, with a ferocity that Goose had only ever guessed at, never witnessed.

'They will pass us by!' Goose shouted back at the man, who held the weapon on his shoulder pointed at the sky, thinking he could stop them, bring them down.

'Stop! Don't fire ...'

But it was too late.

Above in the sky, the pilot saw the caravan, and the missile, veering sideways away from them.

'What the hell was that?'

'Not very welcoming.'

'Can you see him?'

'They all look the same,' said the pilot, circling back.

'But did you see our man?'

'No. It's impossible.'

The missile burst into flames, landing in the sands, missing the helicopter completely. Elliot put his hand on the pilot's shoulder.

'Take us down.'

'It won't be friendly.'

'No.'

The man stared at him, a second.

'Do it, now. Before they hit us.'

The nomads watched as the helicopter whirred overhead, coming closer. Wararni was trying to ready another shot, seeing the sky devil coming straight for them now. Some of the women were screaming, children whimpering, panic setting in.

The helicopter was making to land.

As it descended, the helicopter let free a sudden volley of gunfire ... aimed at the shadows in the sand.

All Goose could hear were the screams. He turned his camel, hitting her with his heels, forcing her away from the caravan. The sound came again, the shells piercing the night air.

Men were jumping from the gunship, two figures coming across the sand towards him.

'Izil!' He heard Tayri cry out up ahead. Izil had fallen to the ground. Goose circled around. He could make out her outline, standing over the crumpled body on the sand, holding her son in her arms. The men, machine guns on their shoulders, sent rounds of gunfire into the caravan, and were blocking his path, cutting him off from the others.

'You!' shouted Wararni to Goose, a fury upon him now.

'You did this. You brought this to us.'

Goose didn't move. The helicopter whirred, the noise louder, filling his ears.

Wararni walked towards Goose, his hands raised in anger. Goose still did not move.

The sand shook – something exploding in the sand around them and Wararni was flying into the air, his head twisted to one side, his body limp as he fell to the ground.

Goose climbed down from his camel, staring for a second at Wararni, then he ran, away from the men towards Tayri and Izil. The boy had blood bubbling from the corner of his mouth and his nose. He had been shot. He would die, there was no way to save him out here, not from this, and Wararni was right – it was because of Goose. He was to blame. It was his fault.

The men from the helicopter grabbed a hold of his arms, dragging him over the sand, Goose twisting around to see Izil.

'Take the boy, *please*, he needs a medic. Take him!'

The men ignored him, as if they heard nothing, saw nothing.

Tayri watched Goose leave, her screams cutting the night air. Around her lay the bodies of children, women, men. Animals were screaming in pain. Only a few of the caravan had survived, a handful of women and men staring wild-eyed, a few children stumbling on the sand, disbelieving.

Goose was lifted up into the helicopter, the blades spinning, sand fanning out away in circles from the base, rising up into the sky, the caravan growing smaller and smaller in the distance, until, at last, it was gone.

Far away, Tayri's cries rang out and echoed across the sand sea.

Chapter Thirty-Eight

Roseville, 2012

When Miss Julie was a young girl, she had wondered about how her life would turn out. She had been bright at school, often top of the class, and was interested in everything. She had a facility for learning that made it hard for her to understand why sometimes other folk could be slow, or could struggle with things, when to her they came easily.

Her mother Myra was a great beauty and she was clever too, though she had cut short her own schooling when she married a white Creole man, and it had been a terrible scandal at the time, causing a break with her family for years. But whatever bitterness Myra felt about being cast out, whatever resistance she may have faced from her family back then, she never passed any of that burden on to Julie, instead reminding the girl that beauty wasn't what others saw on the outside but how you treated people. That was what you would be measured by in the end, and if folk judged Julie on account of her being different, being part one thing, part another, then they were fools, not worth worrying over, for they understood nothing of what mattered in life, nothing.

Perhaps it was this, this feeling of going between two worlds all her life that made Miss Julie feel a particular sympathy for Lenny, for she saw something of herself in the child, and wanted to protect him as best she could.

She had always imagined she would have a family of her own – a house full of boys and girls, a home full of love, and laughter and noise – and Stanley wanted that too, and he didn't care in the least that Julie stepped between two worlds, he just thought her the most beautiful woman ever, that he was a man who could not believe his luck, that she would love him too. But then when Stanley went to Korea, none of what Miss Julie had planned for her future happened.

Of course, other men came calling after a decent time had passed, some encouraged by Julie's mother, for she did not want to see her girl waste away. But Julie's heart lay with Stanley and she would wait – if it took a lifetime, she would wait.

She had gone back to her studies, and became a teacher, and had taught in the towns round about, travelling from Roseville each morning. For nearly forty years she taught, took the local kids and showed them that the world was far bigger than that which they knew. She had students she was proud of, some she worried over, some she despised (though she knew that wrong, she couldn't help it, for some were impossible, even for her). Many stayed in touch and wrote to her, and that was how the letter-writing had started in a way, and then as the students' letters tailed off and they became busy with families and lives and worries of their own, then she began writing to companies instead for by then she was in the habit of it, sitting each day, putting pen to paper, closing the envelopes, and sending them off into the world.

And each letter was a challenge, a challenge to the one she kept in her pocket now, the one she had held on to for such a long time.

Chapter Thirty-Nine

Libya, 2011

Goose was exhausted. He had split himself in two – two lives, two languages, two possible futures. The effort of it left him dazed. What if he never went back? Just asked them to leave him here? He thought about this. It was as if he could just switch off his heart, cut ties to the half-life he had lived before, a desert storm dropping down over him, masking any love he might feel, any guilt, any doubt.

By the time they got him to the base medics, he was hallucinating, his lips parched, his eyes bloodshot and dry. He was a strange half-dead man, covered in dust, speaking Tamahaq with a strange accent, dressed as if of the Imuhar, a cripple, his leg, dragging along behind him, unwilling. He no longer looked like a combat pilot, nor a man with a mission. He appeared broken, a shadow man. Elliot looked at him, bemused, how one man could cause so much trouble.

They took him back to the north, to the ship where the doctors shook their heads and stuck needles in his veins, and told Elliot he would have to wait, if he wanted the man to be of any use to him, he would just have to wait.

Chapter Forty

Roseville, 2012

It was getting darker now and Lenny had lost sight of where the turning might be that he needed to take to find Jim. He rubbed the agate stone in his pocket and hurried along the boardwalk watching the twisted lianas and branches turn into strange eerie creatures, the path darkening before him.

He found himself thinking of Mari-Rose, and of the nights she left him alone in the dark while she sat outside crying. Where was she now? She'd been gone a long time. Long enough to make it so he didn't want to miss her anymore – it hurt too much. It was easier to accept she was gone for good.

And with Jim there, he could have just about borne it, but Jim too had failed him. Lenny felt the night pushing in on him. He tried squinting at the display on his watch, covered as it was with tape, and he began to cry, the path blurring before him. Then he was running, running like he was training to be an astronaut or a fighter pilot. Running hard until he could feel his heart pounding in his chest and a stitch aching in his side.

Lenny ran into the night.

Chapter Forty-One

Texas, 2011

It had begun as small shakes of his hands. Jim would rest them on the edge of a table or on his lap, and they would begin to jig and tremor and he would pull them back down into his pockets to hide it from himself as much as anyone else. He had not much cared for the interrogation when it came, though he had expected it – but what could he tell them? *Was I a hostage? I don't know*, he said. *I don't think so … Was I mistreated?* He thought of the nomads, and the feeling he had of belonging (a feeling he had felt nowhere else in his life). *No, I was not mistreated*, he said. But they held you against your will, surely, why else would you stay so long? He did not know how to explain it – *I felt safe. I felt loved, accepted, wanted.* None of that made sense to these men. *I couldn't remember anything for a long time*, Jim said. And that was true. But you remember now? They asked him. *I do*, Jim said.

In the end, he told them about Wararni and Hamou, and the lorries full of people, and the journey beyond the border and the weapons, and how that was something – though he did not know what. They left him in peace after that. The man had been gentle with him, the few bruises he had would heal quickly. He would soon be ready to rejoin the real world, they said, once the doctor gave the all-clear. But he would never fly again.

Goose. They took to calling him Goose on the base. Someone had overheard him mention it to the doctor and now it was a joke of sorts, except that it made him picture Izil – but the image he had of the boy now was of him lying on the sand, blood seeping into the dunes, his mother bent over him. Goose was a name he no longer wanted, but the flying – that Jim fought for. It had been the only place where Jim had felt like it all made sense. It was what he had spent so long training for, preparing for. But now when they would send him up, just to see, he would come back shaking and crying, test flights cut short.

'PTSD,' diagnosed the base doctor. 'You're still living it – in your mind, major. You need help. No shame in that.'

Jim had nodded. He had asked for drugs to help him sleep, to get rid of the nightmares.

'Don't send me home,' he begged, and when it became clear that there was to be no option and that they'd been trying to get a hold of Mari-Rose to let her know that he wasn't dead after all, he begged them, saying, 'Let me get better first.' They sent him to Doctor Almara, a specialist and a military man who knew all about PTSD, living with it himself as he did.

'The mind, Lockhart, works like this.' And Doctor Almara had drawn on a whiteboard behind him, the two men sitting in an empty hall on the base while the other pilots were out flying. He drew a picture of the human brain. Jim didn't think it much looked like a brain, nor how he imagined a brain should look if it worked properly. He thought it resembled more a twisting snake curled and kinked in on itself and told the man so.

'We all see the same things, Jim,' he replied, 'but we all look at them differently.'

Jim nodded. He would listen to the man. He would do the exercises required of him, give it the time they stipulated, whatever – so long as they would let him go back up. He couldn't do anything else, wasn't trained for something else.

How would he ever explain to Mari-Rose? He wrote her letters that he tore up and scrunched into balls, aiming them at the garbage pail, trying to score, to hit the mark where his words had failed him.

'Excuses, Jim,' she would say, sounding like his mother, the same sad sigh behind her words. He could almost hear her voice already, could picture the look of disappointment. She would not care that he had loved the desert, had lain in the sands counting the stars, looking for constellations he knew from home, and she certainly wouldn't approve of Tayri nor of his yearning heart.

'You will experience some symptoms probably for a while. Memories, flashbacks, survivor's guilt, nightmares perhaps. The shaking ... that's part of it. Don't be frightened by this. It is the mind's way of healing itself, working through what you've experienced. Try not to judge yourself too harshly, nor expect too much, too quickly.'

'How long will it take to heal?' Jim asked him.

The man hesitated.

'For some men, it's a matter of months, a year or two – but for others, it can hang like a shadow for a long time. But ... in the main, those are the ones who don't seek help. Look, I'll have my colleague Doctor Stanilus check you out too. How's that sound? Second opinion? You don't believe me, maybe you'll listen to him.'

Jim blushed, ashamed that the man could see how he doubted him.

'Jim – the mind is an amazing thing. It can heal – given time. Give yourself time.'

'What if I was broken to start with?'

Jim muttered it, more to himself than the doctor. The man put his hand on Jim's shoulder.

'Just give it time.'

Jim waited, but it got worse; the shaking, the unravelling of the edges of his mind, nightmares that followed him into the day.

'Lockhart.'

'Yes, sir.'

'They tell me you've been here six weeks now.'

'Yes, sir.'

'Any chance you might be thinking of going home soon?'

The new doctor, Doctor Stanilus, less patient than the first, looked at him, narrowing his eyes, clear cold blue eyes that looked right through Jim, already focused on his next appointment, and the next and after that, a late lunch and an afternoon rendez-vous with a pretty waitress from a bar near the base.

Jim shrugged, seeing the man's lack of interest in him, his mind engaged elsewhere.

Jim's face was still bruised, his eyebrow cut where they'd hit him. *Funny way to get a man to have a conversation*, he'd said to them at the time. But he had understood. Man's just doing his job.

'Home, sir?' Jim's voice cracked.

'Yes, home. Says so here on your papers. Look son, we can't keep you here forever and, well … you won't fly again. Your tests, your leg, the way things went … I'm sorry, but it'll be a medical discharge.'

The man wasn't sorry at all. Jim could hear the indifference in his voice.

Jim had looked out of the window behind the doctor, its glass dirty around the frame, a dead bluebottle resting on its back on the windowsill. He looked out at the hangars beyond, at the planes ready for take-off. He had always loved the base, the smell of it, the energy of the place, the camaraderie, the constant hum of activity, the way just being a part of it all made him feel more alive. And he had let them all down, had blood on his hands, had lost his nerve.

Yet this place was home to Jim, or as close to home as he had ever known. Even more than Ireland had ever been to him as a child, a time which he just remembered now like a dream, the way you do about childhood memories, all polished with love and yearning. Here the sunshine and dust were real, the orders were clear. There were rules, a way of behaving, a code – all that Jim could work with, all that he needed.

'Don't send me back to Roseville, sir.'

The words escaped him.

'Why, your wife and son will want to see you, now they know you're alive, Lockhart. Haven't you spoken to them yet?'

Jim shook his head, ashamed.

The man shuffled the papers on his desk, keen to be rid of Jim's presence.

'Look, the memory lapses ... this is not uncommon. PTSD. The mind shuts down. It's a coping mechanism. Mind's way of protecting itself. Besides, Doctor Almara seemed to think maybe you remember more than you're letting on ...'

'I ...' Jim hesitated, not finding the words, knowing anything he would say would be a betrayal of sorts.

'You don't need to explain it to me. But you do need to go home.'

The man sighed. 'Look, I'll write you a prescription for something to take the edge off, help you sleep, deal with the nightmares. You still having them?'

Jim nodded.

'That'll pass with time.'

Time, these doctors doled it out like it came on prescription.

'What about the pain?'

The man looked at Jim, seeing a still young man, his face damaged but that would heal, the leg would improve with care and therapy, but the pain, he wasn't sure he could write a prescription that would work for that, that would do anything other than numb it. He had seen too many men like this – they would go off, whole and hopeful, excited even, and come back (if they did make it back) broken, like the heart had been ripped out of them and they couldn't be fixed up quite right anymore. He always knew the type when he would see men in the streets, some sleeping rough, others a glint in their eyes, people more alert to life, unable to let go of what they had seen or done.

'A man has to learn to carry his pain, Jim. I can write you a script for it – but it won't take it away for good for you. You understand what I'm saying? You have a wife and child – that's the best cure in the world, family.'

Jim had smiled weakly and taken the prescriptions from him, shaking the man's hand, thanking him anyway.

Soon he was back in Roseville, standing at the end of the street where the bus dropped him, just standing staring up the road at the lake, seeing two boys playing in the shade of the weeping willows by the water, and one of the boys turning and seeing him standing there, and then shouting, 'Pop!' and running towards him, shouting so loud even Mari-Rose came running out to the garden, and then the boy had thrown himself against him, was swinging on his waist, trying to clamber up him, squealing with happiness, and all Jim could feel were the tears running down his cheeks, the sadness pouring out of him, his body shaking, the little boy stopping shouting for a second, looking at him, quieting down now.

'It's okay, Lenny, it's okay.'

Jim pulled the boy's straw curls to his chest and smelt the top of his head, and squeezed the boy tight, the sobs shaking his body still but the boy letting him lean on him.

'It's okay, Pop, it's okay.' Lenny echoed back and stroked his head, touching the skin above his eye – the bruise still there, green now.

Down at the fence, he saw Mari-Rose watching them both, a look of disbelief on her face. She had not really expected to see him again, had given up on him long ago. Jim realised that now.

He took the boy's hand and together they had walked down to the house, nodding hello to Miss Julie, who had smiled to see him returned in his uniform, holding Lenny to him as they passed by her, sitting out on her back porch, watching the boys playing in the summer sunshine, watching the world go by.

Chapter Forty-Two

Roseville, 2012

Miss Julie heard the ringing at the door for a while before she got up to go answer it. Her hip had gone stiff again from sitting and it took her a while to move, and maybe if she just sat quiet, whoever it was would go away. It wasn't good news. That she was sure of. And it wasn't Lenny.

But the ringing persisted and by the time she was up on her feet, a pale moon-shaped face was peering in at the window, with a long, knitted scarf wrapped around the head, curls flying loose.

Miss Julie opened the screen to the porch carefully. You never knew with folks these days. Could be anything.

'Miss Julie?' The girl asked her, a strange, heavy purring sound coming from the bag she had hanging off her shoulder.

'What is it?'

Miss Julie held tight to the screen door handle. She wished she'd lifted something heavy, taken it with her, just in case. Anything would have done – even Stanley. He at least had sharp edges.

'What do you want?'

She peered at the woman's face.

'Is Lenny here?'

The woman hesitated.

'I'm Lucy, a … friend, a friend of Jim's and Lenny …'

She faltered now, no longer so certain. She took a step back.

'I'm sorry, it's just he talked about you – picked up cookery books for you … I just was worried, you see.'

Lucy sighed. It was all shaking loose from her now.

'The boy seems in a bad way and … and I know his father is having some difficulties, and well …'

Miss Julie looked at her through the screen. Seemed sincere enough. Probably not an axe-murderer. She opened the door an inch.

'And how do I know what you're saying is true?'

'I … I don't know,' said Lucy mulling it over, 'only I don't see why I would lie. I mean, I'm the librarian.'

'Ah,' said Miss Julie. 'Léonard mentioned you were kind to him.'

'He did?' Lucy brightened.

'Not in so many words,' replied Miss Julie, and then seeing the girl's face cloud over, 'but he has a way of letting you know things, and I could guess as much. He said you like his father.'

Lucy blushed.

'Well, don't stand there making us both cold. Come in.'

Miss Julie opened the door wide enough for Lucy to slide past. 'But the cat stays here.' She pointed to the screened-off porch. Lucy nodded, dropping her bag down to the floor, and edged into the room, perching gently against the back of a chair.

'So, is Lenny here?'

There was such hope in her voice that Miss Julie almost lied. Almost.

'No, and I don't think he will be either. I saw him earlier in the day. He was here, surely was …' she tutted, annoyed at herself again. 'I sent him out to buy some groceries. Boy loves to be helpful. He never came back, and I just …'

She didn't say anything more, didn't need to, for Lucy had the same sick feeling in the pit of her stomach.

Chapter Forty-Three

False River, 2012

When Jim woke up slumped on the damp boardwalk, the darkness and cold were seeping into his bones. His shirt sleeve was damp up to the elbow where he'd let it trail in the water. *Lucky a gator hadn't swum by*, he thought, shivering and standing up, his legs and back stiff from the slats of the boardwalk.

It was the nights before sleep that he feared most. It was then that everything flooded to the surface. If only he could drink. Then it was manageable, the pain ebbed away, and it became as if he was outside of himself. Some nights he would see villages burning, hear grown men screaming like children. More and more often he would waken, terrified, seeing Tayri or Izil next to him, saying nothing, just looking at him, disappointment or anger clouding their faces by turns.

Sometimes, he would feel lost for hours, whole days, weeks passing, so it felt to him as he slept, trapped amongst the dunes, dying of thirst, yet somehow always surviving, long enough to waken once more and realise that the nightmares had taken hold again and that he was here, by the river and trees, and the night sounds he heard were not those of the desert but the bayou, settling to sleep around him.

Most of all, he hated the nights when he would waken and find Lenny watching him, the boy looking frightened – whether for him, or of him, Jim could not tell.

'It's okay, Pop, it's okay.'

Lenny would try to reassure him, and inside Jim would fall apart a little more.

At the base, they had shown him ways to manage the nightmares.

'Be present,' the doctor had told him. 'Find something to focus your mind on, make something. A lot of the men find that helps.'

Making the origami helped. It required concentration, the folding of the paper this way and that, the order of things, no room for improvisation, just one paper fold after the next until the shape revealed itself and the figure took on its intended form. Lenny delighted in watching him, and for Jim the satisfaction of making something out of nothing, something beautiful for the day, and to see the delight on Lenny's face, it truly helped him.

'It's magic!'

Lenny had clapped his hands when Jim passed the fox to him.

'Show me how to make one, please.'

They had sat together, Lenny patiently copying his father, Jim taking his time over it – feeling useful again, like a father to the boy, letting go of the shadows. If only for a few moments – he felt alive.

There was something beautiful and wondrous too about sleep when he did not have the nightmares, he thought, being able to switch off from everything, close it all out, and surrender to something else. He had dreamt of lying on the mat in the desert, looking up at the night stars, holding Tayri's hand in his, but in his dream when he turned his head to smile at her, it was Lucy Albert there instead, smiling back at him.

It was times like this, when he would awaken and the truth of the day would hit him in the throat, and he'd realise the warmth he had felt, that he had blanketed himself in as he slept, did not exist, and it was then that Jim struggled hardest. He had not wanted to come back to Roseville, fearful as he was. It was only Lenny in the end who held him to the place, and he had failed Lenny, hadn't he?

That's what Mari-Rose would say if she saw him now.

Jim pulled at a clump of reeds and moss. *Lenny would be better off without me*, he thought, rolling the idea around in his mind like it was a possibility. Some days he wished he were back in the desert, that it was all lost to him once more so that he couldn't feel the pain of it, only the absence.

If he left and headed back to Texas, maybe he'd have more luck finding work. Though with his bust leg he wasn't quite sure what kind of job he'd find. Hadn't one of the first lieutenants, fresh out of Iraq, found a job doing some sort of clerical something or other, a desk job – a veteran organisation arranged it, Jim recalled. Then maybe he was more charming than Jim. And he'd lost a leg. That right there was reason enough to help the man.

Anyone looking at Jim could see he'd come off lightly. Of course, they couldn't see how he was doing inside, the way it had all cut him up and tangled everything for him – from the outside, there was no sense of any of that, the only hint of it the glint in his eye from time to time, a sort of madness seeping through.

Jim had wanted to talk to someone afterwards, when they made him pack and leave. He just didn't know who to burden with it all. Mari-Rose had seemed like the obvious choice, but she wasn't interested none, and he had no other family left to speak of except the boy and he couldn't bring this on Lenny. Things a child doesn't need to know about his father, about life – ever.

A dragonfly buzzed past his ear and down the boardwalk path amongst the rushes Jim could hear an egret calling out, settling to sleep for the night. *Birds closing up shop*, he thought, laughing to himself at the stupidity of it all: him, here as the darkness drew down, Lenny somewhere out there making his way back no doubt to the old house, or with any luck to Miss Julie. *She was a funny one*, Jim thought. Kind of her, how she'd given Lenny that sweater but let him keep his pride. Same for Jim with the pancakes, the way she'd handled that. Without his pride, a man's nothing. Jim felt this now that all he had to offer

Lenny was thieved gumbo mix and worn stories by the fire. But his mind was splintered, full of jagged thoughts, making it impossible for Jim to find a way through.

How can I help you Lenny, when I can't help myself?

He thought about going under, just letting the water take him. Wouldn't that be the kindest thing? Lenny would manage, wouldn't he? Jim loved the boy so much, though, it surprised him, this insistent tugging at his heart. Before he had left to travel far from home, without worrying about the boy, thinking he was better off with Mari-Rose, but now that he'd come to know him, that they'd spent so many nights together camping out under the stars, trying to find a way through it all, the boy never blaming him once, never turning on him – now he felt his heart tangled up with Lenny, and he knew he could not leave him.

Behind him, he heard a splosh as a gator dropped into the water and started coming towards him. Jim had half a mind to stay, wrestle the thing out of the water and thrash about with it on the boardwalk, let it take him if that was how his last moments on this earth should be. A second later and the gator would be snapping at his ankles. Was that what he wanted? What about Lenny? He had to choose. Right there and then, Jim chose.

Chapter Forty-Four

Roseville, 2012

Lucy Albert sat perched on the edge of Miss Julie's couch. The house had a woman's touch to it, and it was clean, too. Lucy looked down at her shoes, a rim of mud on the sole of the right one. She slipped them off and tiptoed with them back to the porch where she checked in on Hervey who, indignant at being made to wait neither inside nor out, was pacing around and scratching at the screen of the door.

'Behave, Hervey!' Lucy chided him before digging into her cardigan pocket and bringing out a small handful of cat biscuits, which she let him lick off her hand before wiping it down on her sleeve, and going back into the house, her socks slipping on the vinyl in the kitchen where she stood in the doorway.

Miss Julie lifted the cups and saucers onto the tray, placing them alongside the little teapot, as she turned. Catching sight of Lucy in the doorway startled her and the tray clattered in her hands.

'Here, help me.' She held out the tray to Lucy, who took it from her.

'You were like a ghost, standing there,' Miss Julie tutted, as if Lucy had disappointed her by being alive after all.

'Sorry, I didn't mean to frighten you.'

Miss Julie frowned at the suggestion that she was a woman who could be frightened so easily.

Lucy laid the tray down on the small table, next to the pile of letters Miss Julie had been working on.

'You write letters?'

Miss Julie just raised an eyebrow and held out her china cup for tea. Lucy served, then they both settled back, Miss Julie sitting now in her armchair and Lucy on the edge of the couch. Stanley kept a watchful eye on them both.

'I love letters,' Lucy said. The sentence hung there, apologetic and lonely in the air. Miss Julie pretended not to hear her at first, then looking at the girl, and thinking how it was this shadow of a girl was responsible for organising against the chemical companies, for bringing everyone together, she decided to give Lucy Albert a chance.

'That so?'

'Uh, huh. Though I never get any. Only bills, knitting catalogues, flyers for pet food, letters reminding me to write my will, that kind of one-sided correspondence.'

She sighed.

'But there's something magical about a letter. You know, someone sitting down to write to you, to share what they're feeling, thinking about. I ...'

Lucy's cheeks reddened. 'It's kind of romantic really.'

'There's nothing romantic about these letters, that's the Lord's honest truth.'

Miss Julie stifled a laugh, looking at the girl's hopeful moon-face. *Here was someone just bleeding for love, no wonder she had latched on to Lenny and Jim*, thought Miss Julie, though she saw the young woman was nervous too, her hands twitching in her lap.

'I write to companies, mainly, letters of complaint, a kind of reckoning or holding to account.'

Lucy nodded, the cup shaking a little in her hand.

'Someone has to keep them honest.'

The girl placed the cup down next to the stack of letters. Her eye had lighted on the name of the chemical company that most folk were blaming for the sinkhole.

'And this one?'

'Well, there's the sinkhole for starters, the reports of illness, the chemicals in the drinking water. Reckon there's a whole lot of account-taking to be done there.'

'I know!' said Lucy, excited now, the colour up in her cheeks. 'Folk said I was foolish, trying to take a stand against them, but if we don't all come together and say something, it'll be ...'

'... too late.'

'Exactly.'

'There's nothing so bad it can't be fixed,' said Miss Julie, her eyes lighting on Stanley a moment. Lucy looked at her, startled.

'Well, ain't that the truth. Nothing. That's why I came, if being honest, I just ... I feel that boy is like a responsibility. There's no rhyme or reason to it, I'm not kin, I don't have ... it's just,' and here she looked right at Miss Julie, 'it's just I *feel* it.' She put her hand on her heart, the long knitted sleeve trailing in the half-drunk cup of tea as she pulled it to her chest.

'I feel it too, dear.' Miss Julie looked at Lucy, and she saw the goodness in her and how the girl could be a help to the boy, to Jim.

'Things have been hard for Lenny, no use denying it. I've watched things change around here. Used to be he lived next door.'

Lucy looked uncomfortable and shifted on the leather of the couch a little.

'Can I ask ... Lenny told me that his mama was ill? I mean, is she gone?'

Miss Julie's eyes twinkled a little at the question. *Now, who is that for*, she thought – *you or the boy?* But she answered her anyway.

'Mari-Rose had a sickness of sorts, a kind of unhappiness, eats away at a soul and ain't no cure for it in particular. You have to get lost a bit more in living, that's all, but she wanted things to be ...'

'Different?'

'I guess so. She wasn't one much for mothering, that's for sure. Lenny is better off without her, even though it breaks my heart to say that of a child and his mother – it's true. She lost her way, got frightened, I suppose. Hard to forgive, though, a thing like that. Marks a child forever.'

Miss Julie supped on her tea, blowing gently on the liquid, careful not to burn the insides of her mouth.

'And his daddy?'

'Jim? Why Jim's all kinds of broken, like a tin of biscuits that's been shook up and kicked about the place.'

'Lenny said he was in the war?'

'He was, somewhere in the Middle East, couple of those wars in fact, or peacekeeping missions – isn't that what they call them these days? Though Mari-Rose always feared they had him working on ... what's it called ... covert? Special operations? Well, that. But you know ... who knows really?'

Here she leant forward towards Lucy.

'Jim was always a bit broken. Right from when he and Mari-Rose first moved in next door, before the baby came even, he had the look of a man that was haunted. I'm only guessing now, but I'd imagine he'd a difficult time as a boy – always seems as if he'd like to step away from himself. I think the war, the places they sent him, whatever it was happened there, just shook it all a bit looser in him, that's all. Some people get to be pretty expert at running, you know ...'

She gave Lucy a shrewd look.

'I don't think he's so broken that he can't be healed,' Lucy said.

'No? Well, that's a start. Probably what the man needs to hear.'

'Oh ...'

Lucy started to sob, her chest rising up, her hands flapping at her cheeks.

'There now, what did I say?'

Miss Julie wasn't one for grand displays of emotion, cluttering up the place. That sort of thing was best handled in private. She stared at the girl, not knowing what to say to comfort her.

'I ... it's all my fault,' Lucy sobbed, her eyes so wet now that they had gone a bit puffy, *and the girl not that pretty to start with*, sighed Miss Julie to herself, handing her a tissue to wipe her nose with.

'I'm sorry – I ... Sometimes it just all hurts a bit too much.'

Miss Julie nodded. Of course, it did. Wasn't that just a part of life, the hurt? No point crying over it, not really. But she felt for the girl too, and she felt for herself and how she'd sat on the floor sobbing only a few hours ago talking to Stanley, and so who was she to judge this Lucy Albert?

'You don't understand ... I kept him with me. I wanted him to stay – so much. I didn't care about Lenny, and now Lenny's gone.'

Lucy wailed, and in the porch Hervey set to echoing her mournful cries until Miss Julie's nerve snapped, and she got up out of the seat.

'Well, we must go find them then!'

Lucy looked at her from behind the tears and sniffed. The old lady was right. What was the point of sitting around waiting for something good to come to her? How long had she waited already like that? Patient, well-mannered, polite. Courteous to most folk, understanding, digging down for compassion even when people were ignorant or curt with her. It was time to stop waiting for life to come to her.

Lucy sniffed once more and stood up. It was time to take control.

'Here, put this on,' Miss Julie threw her the ski jacket from the hall cupboard, finally finding a purpose for it. It was too big for Lucy and Lucy didn't think the night – though sharp with chill – quite merited it.

'It's not for you – it's for the boy when we find him, he'll be cold.'

'Oh, okay.' *Not everything is about you, Lucy Albert*, she reminded herself, looking at her red-streaked face in the mirror above the hall table.

'Who's this?' she asked, her eyes moving to the photo of Stanley.

'That's Stanley.'

Miss Julie was busy now in the kitchen filling up a flask with hot water and juice, putting together sandwiches as supplies, and gathering some bits and pieces for their expedition out into the night.

'Should we call the sheriff's office?'

'No. That would be terrible. The boy's homeless. They'd only take him from his father. You want to make a bad situation worse?'

Lucy shook her head, horrified. She hadn't realised, hadn't understood how the boy was living. The old lady was right.

'Here, help me get my scooter out, it's round at the front, under the porch.'

Lucy obliged, picking up her bag and Hervey on the way out.

'What do I do with Hervey?'

'Bring him, leave him, up to you.'

Miss Julie stood on the sidewalk impatient now to be off, clambering into the mobility scooter, pulling up the collar on her coat.

'Just mind you keep up!'

Lucy decided to leave Hervey in the warmth, even if he didn't appreciate being left behind. She ran to the kitchen and came back, putting a dish of milk in front of him, bending down, whispering to him that she'd be back in a while. Hervey circled her legs a moment, then seeing she was going, leaving him behind, he turned from her, indignant.

Who knew where they were headed, how long they would be? Still, he would be fine. *Cats always are*, she thought.

By the time she caught up with Miss Julie, the old lady was already whizzing down the street, turning by the corner towards the jetties and heading for the boardwalk. She had the scooter lights switched on, casting a long beam along the slats of the boards, enabling her to see the edges that she bumped over as she went, the wood creaking under the weight of the scooter.

'I'm not sure the boardwalk is meant for this,' said Lucy, nervously keeping pace behind Miss Julie. 'Do you know where you're going?'

Miss Julie pushed on.

'We're going to the sinkhole.'

'The sinkhole?'

'Trouble follows trouble,' was all she would say, pressing down on the accelerator button and bumping on ahead of Lucy who stumbled about behind her in the dark, her shoes slipping on the mossy planks.

Apart from the light of the scooter lamps, the bayou was dark and lumpen, and Lucy, for just an instant, was wishing she had gone home instead. Right around now, she would have fed Hervey, made herself a cup of watery coffee and had a square of dark chocolate after her supper, and be sitting down to read and listen to the radio, some Philly soul or French music, depending on the show.

Instead, she was here, stumbling about in the dark, running after the scooter, wind whipping at her cheeks, her puffing, already out of breath, her life taking a new direction, and Lucy running to keep up with it.

Chapter Forty-Five

Bayou, 2012

Lenny had walked a long way along the boardwalk carrying the orange box, first in one hand, then swinging it to the other, before turning it upside down and wearing it like a hat on his head for a spell. He had never ventured this far alone in the bayou before. Times when he and Arturo had journeyed out, they had always stayed within an hour's walk back to Roseville. Anything more and they'd have been in trouble with Mari-Rose and Beatriz. Now he had been walking a long time. Somehow, he had missed the turn down to the lake where Jim liked to go and for a while he hadn't noticed, just kept going expecting to find him around the next corner or bend, or the one after that.

Lenny's head smarted badly from the fall and he felt light-headed and woozy – the cold and the illness still upon him. And the fear, for Lenny was convinced he would never see Jim again, that his father had gone for good this time.

He kicked out at the mossy branches that sometimes wound themselves around the slats and criss-crossed the boardwalk bends, the tree roots strangling the open spaces, clinging on to the path, sucking it back up into the bayou.

'Don't go getting lost in there, y'hear!' Mari-Rose had called after him and Arturo when they would sometimes venture in, but she had never stopped them either. 'And don't talk to any of the river folk, be polite but no stopping, and no going into any of the cabins or camps or boats. People there … well, who can tell?'

Truth was Mari-Rose didn't rightly know. She had never really ventured in far, had only heard stories. But her own childhood memories were of the swampland as being full of mystery and unknown and dangerous things – a place of nightmares, her mother had called it once. She didn't see the beauty of it either – the way the darkness sucked the light out of the day, the gloaming of the place … or the smell of the gators, with their yellow eyes, or the shadows dropping across the boardwalk paths – none of that touched her soul. Mari-Rose preferred the light, and to be able to see the sky clear above her head and to feel freedom – more freedom, it turned out, than Roseville could have ever offered her.

But Lenny liked the cool, the dark twists and turns of the bayou, the way the wooden slats floated above the water, the sense of everything slowing right down. Here it was seldom day, more a shaded version of things, the canopy of leaves overhead cutting out the sharp sunlight. Here he could drift.

Lenny found himself thinking about the angry man in the grocery store – he shivered, remembering the look of him, the tone of his voice. King of his own empty kingdom. Lenny hadn't cared for that. The other man, Mr Bertrand, had been kinder. Still, he had felt the loneliness seeping out from under him too. *Adults didn't realise*, he thought, *how heavy they could be, how they weighed you down with their sadness and unhappiness – how they couldn't just be.*

He looked down at the empty box – Miss Julie would be waiting for him, no doubt, but he didn't feel like going back. She weighed him down in a different kind of way, with some kind of love. It wasn't heavy exactly, but he had to carry it around, nonetheless.

It was a case of belonging and Lenny was no longer sure where – if indeed anywhere – he belonged. He didn't fit with Mari-Rose, she had made that abundantly clear, nor with Arturo, who had broken with him and left. What about Jim? Hadn't his own father left him alone to sleep outside, unloved, uncared for – just up and disappeared? And the worry it had caused Lenny

– the way his daddy could just change like that, leaving Lenny not knowing which direction the wind was blowing. Well, it was about time someone worried a little about him instead. He resolved not to go back.

But who would care? Miss Julie – a crazy old lady who sat talking to a dead photograph? Lucy Albert? Maybe. Yeah, Lucy and Miss Julie would care.

Lenny stopped a moment, unzipped his jeans and peed into the water, watching the surface break up and form in circles, rippling outwards. He heard animal sounds in the undergrowth and in the scrub by the path and watched a flock of pelicans pass by in formation overhead in search of shelter for the night. He heard fish jump in the water, and at one point he thought he saw a snake only to discover it was a tree root, hanging down from the branches. Lenny felt his heart beating fast in his chest and put his free hand to his head which ached now, duller than before but with a constant throbbing, nonetheless.

You have to keep your wits about you, Lenny – this was Mari-Rose's voice inside of him, always warning him. He pressed the stone in his hand and for an instant thought about throwing it out into the water. But he couldn't. He couldn't let go of the thing, so instead he pushed it down into the pocket of his jeans and walked on. Above his head, on a tree branch, a snake watched him as he went, but Lenny didn't see it, never knew it was there.

Chapter Forty-Six

Bayou, 2012

For the first time in a long while, Jim felt like he could see clearly. Lenny needed him. Nothing else mattered. No amount of fear or self-loathing or doubt.

It was true he had failed Izil. Jim's heart twisted at the thought of it, how he hadn't protected the boy. He flinched, thinking of Elliot's men pulling him away and into the helicopter, Izil left lying in the sand, Tayri screaming. It all felt like another life. If only he could go back, but what would that have changed? *No, you can't go back*, Jim thought. *You just have to keep going.*

Yet he had a second chance with Lenny.

'Look after that boy now,' wasn't that the gift Mari-Rose had left him? And it was a gift – Jim could see that now. If only he wasn't too late. He'd make things good with the boy. He was broken, sure, but not so bad it couldn't be fixed. Not if he really tried.

By now, Lenny would have gone to Miss Julie's – Jim was sure of it. *Boy's got more sense than any of us*, he thought, hopeful, and hurried along the wooden slats, heading towards home.

Chapter Forty-Seven

Bayou, 2012

Soon enough, it would be dark. Lenny could tell, both by the dying light but also by the cough in his throat that bubbled up, always worse at night. Anyone out would surely hear him and this disturbed him, for all he wanted to do was melt into the night. But he couldn't sleep on the boardwalk, and though feeling reckless, he was not stupid and knew the dangers of the bayou, and that he would have to find a safe spot to settle for the night.

Jim had taught him this too – from his own training. Time was Lenny had been proud of Jim. Wanted to be just like his dad. Not anymore. But he could have felt sorry for him, could have loved him (couldn't help that), would have stayed with him – *they could have lived a drifter life*, he thought. Jim had talked about that once, like it would be a great adventure, wandering out free under the stars. But now? Now he had been abandoned and forgotten about, cast off to fend for himself … Lenny felt the anger rise in him once more. Buried deep in his own thoughts, he almost walked past Wild River Sal's cabin without stopping, even though the thing had so many fairy lights hanging off it you could have seen it from outer space.

The front of the cabin was wreathed in little white lights that flashed on and off. Along the front by the water's edge were bright neon blue lights, and around the roof pink and green bulbs blinked. On the jetty post a fat Santa Claus perched, a miniature fishing rod in his hand. Even though it was only autumn, the cabin was ready for the holiday season all year round. Wild River Sal liked the lights, they made her feel less lonesome, and besides it was a whole bunch easier not to take them down and struggle to put them up each year – she didn't see any sense in that, not at her stage in life, her own light getting dimmer as it was. But what she did see was the little boy, trailing a box behind him, cussing and talking to himself like there was nothing else in the world but whatever was vexing his mind.

She had not seen another human being for over six days – last one being a tourist who had come upriver fishing and got lost in the river bends, and who had run off scared when she'd wished him good day. *Folks are so damn strange*, she thought.

Sal called out to Lenny, waving him over. The boy looked up an instant and screamed.

The old woman's skin was like that of an alligator, covered in lumps and bumps, her back hooked over some and she had wild wiry silver hair that flew out around her face. Her eyes were dark, small like raisins and lost in her face that looked like she was somewhere between 370 years old and eternal and everlasting. That's what Lenny thought. He had heard of her, the witch lady of the bayou, how she put hexes on people, practised voodoo, could smite you with the evil eye if you didn't do what she asked. Lenny and Arturo had often wondered what they would do if they ever came across her. Arturo said he would run – no point hanging around to get turned into stew or gator feed.

But Lenny had not been so sure. He was curious about anyone who would choose to live so far from everyone else, to be so different. That took a lot of nerve. *Most people too busy being all the same*, he thought, thinking of Beatriz, Arturo's mom, and how she would try and lighten her skin up even if the creams made her skin itch, and Mari-Rose warned her it would give her cancer.

'You don't understand,' Beatriz, whose skin was lighter than Lenny's even, had wailed at Mari-Rose, who gave her a look somewhere between disbelief and disgust.

But he saw it all over, people wearing the same clothes, talking the same way, buying the same stuff in the store – like it somehow protected them. This woman – whose face had so terrified Lenny on first glance – wasn't like any of them.

Once he recovered from his fright and took in the blinking lights and the woman's sad look on her face, for she hadn't meant to scare the boy, he went a bit closer.

'Hello there, *bonsoir petit,*' she called out to him, her voice like the croak of a bullfrog.

'*Bonsoir,*' Lenny replied, standing tall and purposeful, as if he knew right where he was headed, and that his night-time expedition had nothing of the peculiar or unusual to it.

'You lost, child?'

Lenny shook his head, gripping the agate stone tight in his pocket.

'Where you headed?'

'Just going to meet my dad – he's just up ahead a little.'

'That so? Ain't seen no one pass by today. You sure he went this way?'

Lenny wasn't sure at all. He knew in fact that the turning for the lake was a long way back now and that he had missed it, but he had hoped to double back to find it – lot of the paths out here just turned in circles and if you walked long enough, soon you'd get back to where you had started. For now, though, he was lost.

'Hungry?'

She could practically hear the rumble of the child's stomach from across the water, and his face was pinched and pale looking, a sickness and fever on him. *She had cures could help him with that,* she thought.

Lenny was starving. He hadn't eaten since lunchtime, nor had anything to drink since the soda Appleby Bertrand gave him earlier that afternoon, and he liked the lights twinkling onto the surface of the water and lighting the whole place up, and the old woman – though she looked terrifying – seemed kindly enough. Lenny could hear Mari-Rose's warning ringing in his ears as he walked across the rickety bridge to the cabin. *You can't trust anyone*, she had told him time and time again, but he was tired of that, tired of all the running away.

'Happen I am, been walking all afternoon.'

'Well, you settle here on the porch then, take that blanket – you cold, you shivering. Wrap up in that, I'll bring you something to lift that sickness off you.'

Lenny looked at her, surprised. How could she tell? But then she saw him in a way he could not see himself, so Lenny snuggled down in the wicker rocking chair, wrapped up warm in the blanket (which had once belonged to a Choctaw chief the woman had loved a long time ago, and she had taken it with her after he passed, so she had something to hold on to from a life now lost to her). It felt scratchy and warm and full of love, and it surprised Lenny, this place, this old lady and the Christmas lights deep in the heart of the bayou.

She brought him broth, the steam rising off the bowl, a strong herby taste to it.

'Sup that down child, it'll help you.'

Lenny sucked down the broth, even though it was so hot it burnt the sides of his tongue, he didn't care. He let it fill him up, and exhausted he fell asleep, the chair rocking gently back and forth under his weight. The old woman watched him, the rise and fall of his chest, the pale colour of his cheeks, and she saw the shadow over him.

Child needs help, she thought and went to fixing a cure. Couldn't hurt to call on the spirit world none. She clipped one of his curls, dropping the hair into the broth she mixed up on the hob just inside the front door to the cabin, adding in herbs and then straining it all, lighting smoke over it, and muttering to herself.

Inside the cabin was no more than one room, divided into two by a hanging curtain behind which she would sleep. To the front was a small, squashed couch and a lamp carved into the shape of an African mask, carried from a research trip to Mali, or French West Africa as it was called then, many years ago. The kitchen was no more than the rings, and she had three plates and glasses, and two mugs, a couple of chipped bowls – didn't need no more than that.

Sal remembered when she had been a young girl – very pretty back then, lots of young men calling to the house in Napoleonville where she grew up, asking if they could take her out – her mother chasing them away, telling her, *make your own path, girl, don't have men carve it out for you.*

She hadn't realised quite how unusual her mother had been, passing away early as she did so the girl never got to know her, nor her ambitions nor dreams, dreams that stretched far beyond Napoleonville. Instead, sent away to live first with an aunt in New Orleans and then going on to study anthropology at the Louisiana State University in Baton Rouge, which had begun not long before accepting African-American students, like it was some great favour, only then when she found herself alone on campus, did Sal realise the depth of her mother's feelings and the message she had been trying to share with her.

She had chosen to study anthropology for no particular reason, she felt, other than that she had the grades for it, the curiosity, the course had the places and there would be a period of time spent abroad – field studies. The idea of escape had grabbed a hold of her. That first trip to Africa was how she set her own course, only for it to end up here, far from everything else, just a cabin full of old history books and sad little memories. Still, the lights made it jolly and got her through now she was on her own again. She was not her mother. She had not chosen that half-life. Instead, she had loved and strived, and for that she was grateful every day.

From the man who she fell in love with, she had learnt about healing and spirituality and the way that nature and the soul collide, and how the stars and the sun heal, and all this learning she brought now to trying the mend the sick child.

This child's soul, she thought, sensing how time would splinter and bend around him soon enough. She wanted to protect him from what lay ahead yet knew that there was little she could do for him, her own life force dimmer each day.

Seeing him sleeping there, unaware of all before him, she decided she would do what she could – even if it took all she had left. She would help him. Wild River Sal stroked his curls and watched over him a while.

Lenny, drowsy from the broth, exhausted by living, slept deeply, unaware of the old woman chanting about him, wafting smoke out over the water, and then sitting by him as he slept, her hand on his head.

Chapter Forty-Eight

Bayou, 2012

'Look,' called out Miss Julie to Lucy Albert. The boardwalk forked in two ahead and coming along one side in the dark was a tall figure making a dragging sound on the wood. The two women stopped, Miss Julie tilting the scooter, training the lights on the figure who came towards them, one arm lifted up about his face to block out the lights.

As he came nearer, Lucy recognised his silhouette.

'Jim!'

It surprised her to say his name out loud, to call out to him like that in such a familiar way in front of someone else. He peered forward, trying to see who was there. The lights were blinding him.

Jim remembered the lights of the planes overhead, the cries of the Imuhar. He came towards the women, confused for a moment, lost far away, but he stopped from pushing the scooter off the boardwalk just in time, realising it was only Miss Julie and Lucy Albert.

'*Bonsoir*, Jim,' Miss Julie called out to steady him.

'*Bonsoir*,' he mumbled back, brushing past them, his mind stuck on Lenny.

'Jim!'

Lucy called after him. He stopped a moment, dazed.

'We're looking for Lenny,' said Miss Julie. 'Think he might be headed to the sinkhole.'

The man stopped and turned.

'The sinkhole? Why would he go there?'

'Just a notion, something happened earlier, made me think … he's not with you, is he?'

'No, no he's not.' Jim shook his head, his arms outstretched in exasperation, for surely they could see he had lost the boy. His eyes were focusing in the dark better now, seeing Lucy's wild curly hair and her eyes, plaintive, looking up at him.

'Well, you going to help us find him? Woman my age ought not to be out, cold night like tonight. It's a long time since I have been this far from home,' asked Miss Julie.

Jim's eyes clouded over an instant, then cleared. *It was like one moment he was there, the next gone*, thought Lucy, nervous of him and drawn towards him all the same.

'Sure, I'll come with you. Or better you both go back, wind's up. I'll find him.'

Jim wanted to be alone and find Lenny, apologise to the boy, let him know things would be different, yet there was Lucy, smiling at him, hopeful. If only he could quiet the noise in his head, see things straight, maybe then it would be okay.

'Lenny was mighty upset earlier. Just hope he doesn't do anything stupid before we catch up with him.' Miss Julie turned the steering wheels on her scooter and carried on along the boardwalk, lighting up the way.

For a time, Jim followed the women, his leg dragging on the wooden boards. Seeing Lucy turning, her pale face searching for him, he came up along beside her, not looking at her, just feeling her there – her presence soothing him from the worry over Lenny. That boy, why would he have made for the sinkhole? Jim wondered about this, thinking how little he really knew Lenny, knew the boy's heart, how the boy was still a mystery to him.

Then there was his part of it – deserting the boy like that, why? Why had he left him so alone? Jim cursed himself, his fists clenched tight, scowling into the darkness. Lucy's eyes calmed him, and slowly Jim and Lucy fell into step together behind Miss Julie, Lucy reaching out her hand for his, timid but searching.

Jim felt her grab a hold of him and something electric passed through him, just to be wanted. *Wasn't that something unexpected and beautiful*, he thought, squeezing her hand back, feeling the soft wool of her cardigan, the ends of the sleeves hanging low below the ski jacket, covering his hands now too.

He thought of Tayri without meaning to and flinched, but Lucy didn't let go. She – not seeing the wandering of his mind nor understanding the fear at the heart of him – was happy, happier than perhaps she had ever been, and even though she hardly knew him, she knew her heart was full with joy around him. If they could just find Lenny, then she knew it would all work out okay. It really would.

Chapter Forty-Nine

Bayou, 2012

Lenny had woken up feeling free and happy and rested. The dawn was beginning to press down on the bayou, the light changing from black to inky blue. He looked at the old lady beside him. She was snoring a little. Lenny guessed she was cold and took the blanket off his knees and wrapped it around her gently, so as not to waken her. She had been kind to him. Arturo and Mari-Rose, they had been wrong. Not everyone was beyond trusting. He felt in his pockets, wanting to leave her something in thanks. He took out the agate stone, looked at it a moment, but he couldn't part with it, not yet. In the other pocket, he had a crumpled paper eagle, the fox and a bear, made for him by Jim. They were precious to him, and he wondered about it, but then picked out the fox – for he liked it best – and he sat it down on the wicker rocking chair. He thought she would like that too, would appreciate the gesture, would know what he wanted to say.

Lenny slid down off the deck where the cabin sat. He turned and looked at the shack one last time, all lit up in the darkness, and then he carried on, one hand in his pocket for warmth, the other dragging the orange box, but it surprised him how clear-headed he felt. His cough had disappeared, and he went quickly, knowing now it could not be far.

Wild River Sal had fallen asleep next to the child. He had looked so perfect there, with his light curls and the gentle rise and fall of his breathing. The broth had cleared the cough from his chest, a little colour coming back into his cheeks, but it wasn't just the cough that she had wanted to clear from him, it was the shadow that had taken to following the boy, weighing him down.

For his was a soul close to the thin places – perhaps such a boy could even pass through, as a soul or spirit walker – wasn't that what she saw in him? Wasn't that what the shadow chased after too?

She believed that beyond this world was another, and another world after that, and on and on, all infinite realities, orbiting one another, all like this world yet different each time – and the child's soul seemed one of those few able to sense that, able to travel between worlds – for this, Wild River Sal was sure of it, was a child who could bend time. For that reason, the shadows chose to claim him for their own, chasing after him, seeking to drag him down into the belly of the earth.

It was that she had cast about for in the darkness, seeking to rid the boy of it. She knew some folk, like her Choctaw lover, had a belief in spirit walkers, in those blessed with gifts reason or logic struggled to understand. She had learned about this before, witnessed things others would call miracles, and she believed it too. Lot of things in this life we can't see, like these worlds beyond. Doesn't mean they don't exist.

The boy murmured in his sleep, holding the agate stone warm in his fist. She felt his fever drop, the rattling of his breathing easing out.

Wild River Sal had lived dozens and scores of years, most of them here in the swamp, alone. It would be a shame to see the boy leave. He was in need of a home, that much was clear. But she couldn't keep him. No, the stars had other plans for him. That she could feel in her bones, so she let sleep carry her off and when she awoke it was almost dawn.

The boy had placed the blanket over her. On the rocking chair, he had left behind a small, folded-over piece of paper. She picked it up and looked at it in the half-light, that murky time of between-worlds, neither day nor night. It was an origami fox.

The old woman began to laugh, a deep belly chuckle growing in her, rising up, running through her veins until she sat, her laughter spilling out across the bayou, seeping out into the arterial waterways criss-crossing the land. A gift for a gift. And she knew the shadow was gone.

All he had to do now was find his way home. She took the fox in the palm of her hand and looked at it a while, and although she was far from everything and everyone, she was close too, she was right at the heart of it all.

Chapter Fifty

Bayou, 2012

Jim, Lucy and Miss Julie had shouted themselves hoarse calling for the boy. It was plain useless. What if he had slipped in the water? Been snapped at by a gator? Taken perhaps by some of those fishing boats from upriver, the ones with the dark glass windows – who knew what they carried along the riverways? Every scenario, every possibility, Lucy had run through them all in her mind. *These things never end how you want them to*, she thought.

By now they had searched for hours, midnight long gone hours before, further and further into the bayou, circling back on themselves several times over, never finding any sign of Lenny, not finding the sinkhole either. They were lost, stumbling about in the dark, and exhausted. Jim had opened up his rucksack and taken out the hammocks, slinging them across the boardwalk in a sheltered corner, tying them to trees, making a little fire. He'd set up the little tent nearby too (though this, unlike the woods nearer to the town, was a poor place for bivouacking) and he hung canvas sheets over the hammocks as shelter, cutting out the cold night air as best he could. He'd given his blankets – which smelt of booze and forest nights – to Lucy and Miss Julie to share, and the three had huddled around the flames, Miss Julie pulling out a flask of whiskey from the pocket under her seat. She liked to think of it as a medicinal night-cap, and had brought it with her, just in case.

'Have some of that …'

She had passed it to Jim so he could warm by the flames. She saw the shaking of his hands, worse now than before, his face pale in the light, a mad look of desperation sinking in with him, him fearing the worst for Lenny, or perhaps it was everything else he was carrying around, unable to let go whatever it was he had done or seen.

'What?'

She just looked at him, at the sadness that rolled off him, not knowing where to start, what to say to make the man feel better. What advice could she give Jim – she had never been to war, hadn't seen the things he had seen, that Stanley would have seen. She shivered.

Jim passed the flask to Lucy who took it from him, gentle and slow as his hands shook, little tremors that he couldn't hold back or disguise now. She passed the flask back to Miss Julie and took his hand and held it a while. He let Lucy touch him, not flinching this time. Instead, letting her settle him, her fingers tracing the rough palm of his hand.

'My Stanley always loved a campfire.' Miss Julie sat looking up at the stars clustered overhead. There was a clearing in the sky just above them, and she could make out Polaris and falling below it, the Big Dipper. At least she thought it was. She squinted up her eyes and remembered Stanley showing her. The two of them, sitting with the telescope out on the back lawn. How they had loved to do that, on the warm summer nights, no need for blankets then, and she could almost feel Stanley's hand in hers, as she sat watching Jim and Lucy, and the way they calmed each other's spirits without meaning to – sometimes it just happened that way. You got lucky.

'Stanley loved the stars.'

'He did?' Jim asked, interested now. 'I ... I take an interest in them myself.'

He tried to make it sound like it didn't matter to him either way, but it did. It was the only good thing he held on to from his childhood, the only thing had made him feel safe, loved even – when his father had shown him the constellations, had

pointed out the Andromeda galaxy to him, almost clear enough
to see without binoculars, high above The Glens, on the edge of
the island, stars bleeding into the ink of the night. And Jim held
on to that, all those years growing up caught in the crossfire
between his parents, watching them argue until it felt like love.
He had hidden away, waiting for the shouting to stop, his
father's face red from drink, his mother's blank stare when she
caught him watching them. This was what Jim had known of
love. He had come ill-equipped to life with Mari-Rose and then
Lenny – finding himself unexpectedly in a life he did not recall
choosing, feeling that elsewhere were other lives waiting for
him. That feeling as a child, that fear of love and what it could
do to you, had stayed with him.

To protect himself, he had taken himself off; had learnt
more about the stars, for they soothed him, helped him feel
he had a place in the world, no matter how small. He studied
more, discovered an aptitude for learning, spent many nights
outside alone, just lying on his back in the heather, looking
up. Sometimes, you stay still long enough, you feel everything
move you forward, without you even trying, and he'd held
on to that too – how the stars had stilled him and carried him
when everything else was uncertain.

'Lenny says you know all the constellations,' Lucy's voice
whispered, like she was revealing a secret, giving it to him and
Miss Julie to hold.

'Did he?' Jim was surprised, wondered what else Lenny had
told these two women. *Damn Mari-Rose anyway, shouldn't
she be here doing that, listening to him. Boy needs his mother.*
Jim's teeth ground together as he bit a mouthful of cold cuts
from the sandwich Lucy handed him.

'He didn't mean any harm by it.' Lucy looked hurt. 'He's
proud of you, that's all.'

Jim gave her a fierce look, his eyes saying, *don't you pity me,
don't.*

'Lenny helped me today, to take Stanley's old telescope out
from the cellar, bring it up onto the back lawn. Thing hadn't

been used for years. I'm sure Lenny will come back. Don't give up on him. He's a brave little boy – like his daddy.'

Miss Julie gave Jim a look that said, *this is partly your fault and you need to fix it – no wallowing now*. And even though she only looked it at him, he heard her nonetheless just fine, every word of it, and he knew she wasn't wrong. He had let Lenny down for the last time. He had to hope that was true.

Jim remembered the day when Mari-Rose had put his hand on her belly, and let it rest there a moment before pulling him close to her, kissing him slowly for a long time, then taking his hand again, putting it back on her belly and her whispering in his ear, *baby*. It had taken him a while to understand, and it had surprised him, that they could bring a whole new person into the world, without him even realising.

'This is tasty, Miss Julie.' There was Lucy, holding up the cold sandwich, sucking up to her, Miss Julie felt. Girl is yearning for a peaceful life. Must be. Look how she's locked herself away from the world, all that time, and hiding out in the library, hoping it would save her. Some folk have church, some folk have books.

'Thank you, Lucy, kind of you to say so. You like to cook?'

She nodded in the direction of Jim as if to say, *because it would come in handy if you mean to look after the man – and the boy, if we ever find him.*

Lucy blushed.

'I like to make things. I knit. And well, with the sinkhole campaigning I've been a bit busy truth be told for much cooking, but I admire it, folks that can. Takes a lot of love to make a good meal. That's what my mother used to say.'

Lucy teared up a little at the thought of Delfy, and she felt quite alone in the world. Only Jim gave her some small, quiet hope that flickered inside her, and that she wouldn't see dimmed – not by old Julie Betterdine Valéry or anyone else. And who says you have to be able to cook anyway? *Lots of ways to love people*, Lucy thought, though she worried too, for she could see the old lady was right – Jim would need more looking after than just love and woollen sweaters.

'Lenny says you love to cook,' she said. 'He picked up a book of Jamaican cooking last time he was ...'

A little hiccup caught in her throat.

'He'll be fine!' Miss Julie practically shouted at her, an edge to her voice, the anger rising in her now that her bones were stiff from the cold and the sitting in one spot, and the seat of the scooter sticking to the fabric of her skirt, and all she wanted was to be at home, asleep with Stanley.

Nights were when she got to have Stanley to herself, didn't have to share him with the interruptions of the day. At night, she would turn to the pillow next to her and stroke it a little, and sink in under the covers, and she'd sigh and call his name, and most nights he would be there, would put his arm around her shoulder, or stroke her cheek and tell her he was sorry and that he'd be back one day, and that she was doing good, much better than she felt she was, and not to forget that.

But it would be better she didn't talk to him so much in the daytime – folks had got to noticing and remarking – and they couldn't ever understand, of course, but best not to give them reasons to misunderstand. She had looked at him, and he looked exactly as he had the day he had left, and he wasn't any older at all, even though by rights by now he should be an old man, older even than her, and she shuddered when she thought of it. How had it happened? How had she lived so long, alone, without him?

Miss Julie felt tired, bone tired. She pulled the blankets right up over her chin and around her head and let her eyes close, her head dropping forward gently, her chin to her chest, and she murmured, 'Well, Stanley, look at me now,' and she smiled and laughed a little, before drifting deep into sleep, the night air blanketed round her now.

'She's sleeping?' Jim looked over at Miss Julie who snored gently beside them.

'She must be exhausted. How old is she?' Lucy looked at her, wondering how someone who lived alone as Miss Julie did could look so happy and be at peace in the world. She looked almost like a young girl, one with wrinkles and grey hair, and yet like a girl all the same, just beginning in life.

'Miss Julie? She's ancient, as old as that bald cypress there. She's waiting for her husband to come back, that's what she's hanging on for.'

Jim shrugged. It felt odd to talk about the old lady when she was right there beside him, but he liked to hear Lucy's voice, liked that he could talk to her, felt there were things he could say if she only asked the right questions, and he would be honest and true with her, and not try to hide things – not like with Mari-Rose, who hadn't wanted the truth – but Lucy, she needed it, asked it of him. And he felt a letting go inside, a whole lot of unhappiness he had squeezed tight to him for so long now, and it just was dropping from him and it was because of her, this girl-woman who held his hand in hers and wouldn't let go.

'I'm sorry,' she whispered.

'What do you have to be sorry for?'

'If I hadn't been agitating about the sinkhole ... getting people riled up. Lenny was in the library, listening to it all. I didn't think – you know, you don't realise how children hear a thing is different, I didn't know he'd take it all to heart.'

'We don't know if that's where he went – that's just Miss Julie's *hunch*, isn't that what she called it? Lenny's mad alright, but it's me he's mad at – not the sinkhole. And besides, what could he do, he's just a boy?'

Lucy nodded.

'Where do you think he is, then?'

Her voice trembled, embracing all the possibilities that had swirled in her head as they had walked behind the scooter, lost for hours, walking around in circles in the bayou.

'Right now? Probably back at Miss Julie's wondering where we've all got to.' Jim's eyes shone watery in the light from the flames. He pushed a broken branch onto the fire and sparks spat out at him.

'Or ... I don't rightly know. But don't you be sorry. It's my fault. It's me that made him run off ...'

'I once ran away from home,' Lucy said it quietly and let it hang there in the air, this part of herself she wanted to share with him, even if the sharing would chase him from her, she had to test him, had to see.

Jim looked at her a moment but didn't ask any further.

'I mean, some kids do take off for a time, doesn't mean it's serious, that you can't get them back, get the love back ... I mean, I came back home pretty quick and my folks were so mad at me, my mother especially, and she was so happy, and so mad too, and as soon as I got back – even before I got back – I knew that I loved her and my daddy, and that it had been a moment, that's all, a moment.'

Jim nodded, thinking how Lenny had no home to come to and no mother that cared either, so it wasn't the same.

'Sometimes being a child is harder than we remember when we're grown up. I guess I wanted to feel free or something, didn't want to be someone else's version of me. You know what I mean?'

'Sure,' Jim said.

'Thing is, all these years later and I'm still not quite sure – what that version of me would be if I chose it, believed in it. Mostly, I just sit on the side. You ever do that?'

Jim put his arm around her shoulders and sat closer to her, letting Lucy Albert rest her head on his sweater.

'It's soft,' she murmured, wondering what kind of wool it was and if it was machine-stitched or made by hand. She whispered to him quiet so as not to disturb Miss Julie. Like this they talked long into the night, sharing their stories, leaning further into each other as the night wrapped around them.

Jim, feeling the wind rising once more, wheeled the sleeping Miss Julie into the tent, to keep her from the cold night air.

'You don't mind, do you?' He looked at the hammock and Lucy, checking she was happy.

She smiled up at him.

'I'm glad I found you,' she said, watching how gentle he was with Miss Julie, manoeuvring the old lady carefully, without disturbing her, lost in her dreams. Jim smiled, unable to say the same back even though he was glad too, for he didn't deserve to be happy, couldn't make space for it – yet how was it that he could just stumble upon something so right? He pushed a twisted branch into the flames, stoking them again. Around them, the bayou was full of noise and life. He would not sleep that night. He would keep watch.

Soon Lucy was asleep too, her breathing slowing, her head heavier on his shoulder, pressed in against his sweater.

Jim lifted her up into the hammock and put his coat over her and the ski-jacket hood up around her head so that only her nose poked out and he thought how cute she looked, and how she was a bit broken too, and the comfort that gave him, to know that maybe she might understand and he could stop running away, from himself, from Lenny, from living – that he could just trust happiness. Maybe here with Lucy Albert, he could just be still.

Overhead, he saw the night look down on him, and he thought of Lenny, the fierce little look the boy would give him when he was drunk and outside of himself and lost to the world, the look of sadness, and he knew right there that had to change, and if he could only get another chance, then he would hold tight to that little boy's love and never let go again as long as Lenny would have him. He made that silent prayer, and Jim was not one for prayers, but he was desperate, and he knew no other way. *Just bring him back*, he pleaded. He asked the heavens, the stars, and the beating heart of the universe around him.

And further along the bends of the river, beyond where a group of small gators lay banked up against the mud by the little cabin all lit up with lights, Lenny turned in his sleep and dreamt he heard his dad calling out for him, and that he would be going home. Soon.

The early dawn light, and the noise of birds come early to the day, woke them. The fire had died right down and the cold hung off the tent and hammocks.

Miss Julie, reversing out of the tent, muttering under her breath, was exhausted and bleary-eyed, shivering somewhat despite being heaped up with blankets, her bones too thin to be camping out at night now – though she wasn't for complaining. Beside her, Jim and Lucy took to whispering as Lucy woke up too, both of them wrapped up in each other in one of the hammocks, Lucy's fingers slipped into Jim's hand, holding on to him tight, even as she had slept.

Perhaps it was best they go back. Miss Julie wavered a moment and then thought of the boy, her gut telling her he was far from Roseville and he needed them, and she knew they would not give up.

They packed up, and she had Lucy lift her up out of the chair and take her over to the verge of the path, so she could pee in peace. She straightened up her skirt and went back over to the dying campfire.

Lucy looked pink-cheeked and happy, enjoying the grand adventure that was unfolding before her.

'Surely, we must be near to the sinkhole by now ...' Lucy had asked, wondering if Miss Julie's sense of direction wasn't perhaps helping them out any, and wouldn't it be better if Jim led the way instead.

'Well, you'd smell it for a start!' Miss Julie had snorted when Lucy had dared to ask if they had possibly taken a wrong turn.

'But it'll be here somewhere, mark my words, all these boardwalks, sooner or later the path will pass by it – that's if it hasn't swallowed the boardwalk whole already.'

Lucy swallowed hard. She had seen the video footage of the sinkhole. Willie and some of his friends had taken a boat upriver. It had taken them a while to get close enough, one of the men holding the camcorder steady, Willie talking to camera, describing what they saw. Willie had brought in the tape afterwards and showed it to her and a few of her library regulars. It had left a big impression on all of them, Lucy most of all. And Lenny. Lenny had been there, and he'd watched it open-mouthed as the sinkhole sucked up whole rows of trees, pulling them by the roots, upending them into the water.

'But we have to stop it from destroying everything, we just have to,' she had cried out, startling Lenny, who sat there listening, transfixed.

Lucy was alive to the injustice of everything. She felt it more keenly than most, and it was in Lenny and in Jim that she had recognised kindred spirits.

Jim too was fed up circling around, no sign of Lenny in sight. His bad leg ached from all the walking, struggling now to keep pace with the scooter.

'Maybe he wasn't heading for the sinkhole after all? Surely he'll be back at your house, or at the library maybe, waiting on us.'

Jim tried to sound certain, as if they were making a fuss for no good reason, but his voice cracked. If they didn't find the boy, soon he'd have to tell the sheriff that he had left his son alone and had gotten so drunk he'd forgotten all about him, then they'd take Lenny from him. That would be an end to it all.

'You know what date it is?' Miss Julie asked him.

'No, can't say I do.'

For Jim, the days and nights had merged into one, stretching out before him, and with no idea about how to get through the next day, or the one after that. He no longer cared about time. It meant nothing.

'It's the date Mari-Rose left.'

'What?'

'A year to the day.'

'That so ...'

Jim scratched his head and looked embarrassed, his cheeks flushing pink. Lucy squeezed his hand a little tighter, territorial all of a sudden.

'Lenny told me once that she'd be back before a year had passed, that he was sure of it, but if she couldn't ... well, then, she wouldn't ever be coming back. Funny that, how children think.'

'But why the sinkhole?'

'What does anyone do when things get bad, only go where they're worse.'

She hesitated.

'And besides, if I told you that it was Stanley who told me, you'd think me a crazy fool.'

A worried look passed between Jim and Lucy.

'Stanley?' Lucy asked. 'Stanley thought Lenny would be at the sinkhole?'

Miss Julie shrugged, thinking honestly Jim for all his warmongering was like a child himself, and Moonface with him no better, both of them dreamers. Who were they to judge her? *At least Mari-Rose had the gumption to get up and go make something else of her life*, thought Miss Julie, though she didn't really believe Mari-Rose would have been much happier anywhere else. It was the boy in the barn, all those years ago, that did for her. Heart never quite recovers from a thing like that.

But Moonface and Jim, they had a chance of something good maybe. She could see that.

'I need to stop!' She put the brakes on. Jim and Lucy nearly walked into the back of her, almost sending the scooter and Miss Julie overboard into the water.

'What's the matter?' Lucy asked her. She could smell something like sulphur now on the air, filling her nostrils, making her want to gag.

'Is it nearby?'

'I need ...' Miss Julie felt her bladder pressing down on her. Oh, the indignity of it but what was she to do, only stop? 'Another rest break.'

'Oh, of course.'

Jim made himself scarce and Lucy levered the old lady, whose bones had frozen again with the damp and the sitting and the constant rattling over the planks. If they weren't careful, the battery on that thing would die soon and she'd be stuck out here forever.

She hunkered down, next to a blackened tree, careful not to lean against it.

'Well, what you looking at?' She waved Lucy away, waiting until the girl was out of earshot. Then, pleased with herself,

Miss Julie straightened up, flattened down her clothes and stepped back up onto the boardwalk.

What a strange place it is, she thought, looking around her at the bayou, hearing the life of the place all around her, the smell of sulphur from the sinkhole drifting over everything.

If the boy was out here alone, with only Stanley's sweater for warmth, what would become of him? Miss Julie, even though all she wanted to do was go home and climb into her own bed and talk to Stanley, got back into the scooter and called out, 'Lockhart, Albert, *allons!*'

And she was off again. In the distance, she swore she could see Christmas lights shining. Like some sort of crazy mirage.

Chapter Fifty-One

The Sinkhole, 2012

Lenny had been thinking again about *The Little Prince*. It was such a strange book Lucy had given him. He was sure it was the story Mari-Rose had told him to settle him to sleep. Wasn't he her little prince? Wasn't that what she had said?

Lenny knew what day it was, he felt it, saw it in the way the leaves were turning, had even read it in the book, the date stamped by Lucy, and he knew – even though he couldn't say it out loud yet, not even to himself – he knew she was never coming home.

He rubbed the stone in his pocket, and he called out to her, but she didn't answer him.

By now Lenny was about ready to go back to Roseville. His thoughts of needing to find the sinkhole had driven him on, but what if it didn't exist? Was that possible even? Lenny wasn't sure. Hadn't he seen Willie's video, didn't that look like hereabouts? Each clump of bald cypress trees looked familiar to the boy – like he had wandered down this part of the boardwalk many times before and was still no closer to finding the sinkhole. And if he did, what then?

Surely Jim would be back in Roseville, searching for him maybe. Perhaps he would have sobered up and be cursing himself for treating Lenny the way he did. Lenny wondered what had happened at the war to make his daddy so sad. One night he had woken, out in the woods, and he had heard Jim muttering in his sleep. Mostly it was a foreign language, the sounds strange and otherworldly to Lenny, here and there were snatches in English, words he knew. Jim was twisting and turning, the flames of the fire, low now, flickering on his face. He was crying out, 'Izil! Tayri!' (words that meant nothing to Lenny) and wrestling with something he imagined he held in his hands, looked to Lenny like it was a snake, then shouting the strange words again over and over, and Lenny had looked at Jim and wondered who this man was who had returned to Roseville and what had the war done with his daddy. For a while he had held on to this theory – that Jim was in fact no longer Jim, but someone else – but then, when his pop was sober and telling him stories, or showing him the stars, making him the small paper animals to play with, then he knew Jim was Jim alright. *Perhaps this is the thing about adults*, he thought, *perhaps when they change, they can't help it.* He thought about Mari-Rose – she had changed too, become all bitter and hard and pushing him away. Why had she done that? Why had she stopped loving him? Why had she gone away?

Lenny felt the tears coming to his eyes and he wiped them away. *Imagine Arturo could see you now*, he thought, *big sissy girl*, he'd say. Lenny pushed on, the pungent smell of the sulphur growing stronger now, a thickness in the air that made him want to cover his face. He pulled up the neck of Stanley's sweater, right up over his nose. Well, he would show Arturo. He would find the sinkhole, and he would find a way to stop it. That was Lenny's plan. He had had enough taken from him already – but they would not get to take Roseville from him. And he thought about how proud Miss Julie and Lucy and Jim would be – and that was something too.

As to how exactly he was going to destroy the sinkhole, stop it from sucking up the bayou, that he had not yet figured out, but he was determined, and that would have to be enough.

Daylight was beginning to break through, and he looked about him at the shadows lifting, the Spanish moss hanging from the trees, a strange otherworldly beauty to it all. The bayou teemed with life – all sorts of creatures, one group feeding off another, and on and on it went, a whole world unto itself, hidden underneath the deep canopy of skyward trees. He heard a splash in the water to the far side of him and saw the long-ridged back of a gator cutting through the water towards him.

Lenny ran a while, quick to put distance between him and the creature.

He stumbled over a gnarly tree root that had welded itself to the slats, winding across the boardwalk, and he felt a rip in the knee of his jeans and a scratch on his skin where the fabric had torn. He stood up, and felt his knee, twisting it, standing on it, checking it was okay. He would survive.

He heard a woodpecker tapping in the branches of a tupelo and looked up. It sat there on its own – its red-bellied coat glinting in the light, its beady eye fixed on Lenny, or perhaps not on Lenny at all. *What do birds see? When they look at the world, do they see it like I do?* He didn't know.

Lenny wished he could fly. Jim could fly – how magical must that be, to be able to soar above the clouds and look down on everything, and how small and simple it would look from up there? Jim had taught Lenny about flying. He had sat beside him, with Lenny in the orange box, and had explained to the boy where all the controls were, how they worked, how it all connected together, and what you had to do to take off and to land. He had tried to explain to the boy what it felt like, to fly a plane, at speed, to shoot through the clouds, to feel the heft of the control stick in your hand, to know you could spiral down into nothing – the exhilaration of it, the way it caught his heart, and how when you're the pilot you have to shut everything else out, and you become focused and your mind clears, and you're thinking ahead, and you're looking at the world so closely now, so closely. Lenny had listened to him and he yearned to fly, he ached to feel free.

Lenny clambered back into the orange box. His legs were tired from running and his knee throbbed a little. He would rest for a while, imagine himself high above False River and the bayou. Then he would be able to find the sinkhole. Then it would not be able to hide from him any longer.

He took a hold of the controls, 'Major, sir, taking off now.'

The boardwalk became his runway and he zoomed forward, careful of his knee, accelerating, taking off, gently rising up higher and higher until he was above the canopy of the trees.

From above he could see the row of houses sitting on the edge of Roseville, the jetties backing out onto the lake, the boats of the fishermen along the waterfront, the outline of the library roof, and the spine of Main Street running all the way up to Vincent's bar at the top, and he saw the gardens full of dying roses and the egret perched on the water's edge. This was home, this was Roseville, and Lenny was not for leaving.

Chapter Fifty-Two

Bayou, 2012

'Look! Are those Christmas lights?' Lucy squealed, straining her eyes, peering into the gloomy half-light.

'Either that or the aliens are amongst us,' Jim offered, sounding half-serious.

'Aliens ... huh?'

She smiled.

He looked at her, searching, seeing her face lit up by the reflection of the lights on the water. Was she serious about him? He felt she was, that she had been from that first moment in the library. Some people it takes you a long time to get the measure of them, but Lucy had got him straight away. He could tell, and it scared him, and it made him happy too. With Mari-Rose, he had never had that, not even when they were first together. They had been strangers to each other, interested in how different the other one was, how unknowable. There had been no sharing of souls, no connecting, not much holding of hands even – yet this girl with her wild curls and her pale face with the skin you could almost see through, she saw Jim alright. She saw everything, and she loved him, and that he could feel. He gripped tight to her hand and pulled her towards him.

'It's okay, I'll protect you,' he said, 'those aliens won't stand a chance.'

Lucy smiled back, and for a moment Jim felt what it must feel like to be normal – not to be afraid all the time – just for a moment.

Miss Julie snorted. She knew what was going on. Just because they were walking behind her, didn't mean she couldn't see them in her rear-view mirror that stuck out from the side of the scooter.

'You must be exhausted, Miss Julie, we've been walking for hours.'

Lucy said this because she didn't want to say, *I'm tired, I need to sleep, I want to lie down with you Jim and never get up again, not for a long time, I just want to hold you, let the earth carry on spinning around us.*

She couldn't say that.

'Let's check out the lights then,' said Jim, tired too, his bad leg hurting now, his voice hoarse from calling out for Lenny.

The early-morning mist hung low, shrouding the Spanish moss and the trees and the edges of the boardwalk, giving the whole place a ghostly air – making it seem even more mysterious than at night.

'It's a cabin, look, a fishing Santa!' Lucy called out, delighted by the strange lights, the bobbing Santa Claus stuck out on the post.

'How strange,' sighed Miss Julie. Life was always doing this, she found – presenting her with unwanted gifts.

As they drew closer, Miss Julie's scooter struggling with the ramp up to the deck, they saw the old woman and stopped. She looked part human, part as if she grew from the bayou itself, her skin all bumped and gnarled, a wildness to her, even as she slept.

'Shush,' warned Lucy, reaching out to touch the old woman's arm and shake her gently. She would show Jim she was not afraid of anything, that he could rely on her, that nothing would scare her away.

She shook the old woman gently. And then she screamed, as the old woman's head dropped forward, and Lucy realised, too late, that she was dead.

'Oh, dear heavens,' Miss Julie tried to get up out of the scooter, the wheels slipping about on the damp moss.

'Stop screaming, child. Haven't you ever seen a dead person before?'

She was sorry as soon as the words came out, for she could see from the expression on Lucy's face that she had indeed seen people dead before, and at close range, and that her heart had still not healed from it.

'It's okay, let's see …' Jim lifted the old woman back, so her head rested back on the headrest of the seat. 'Skin's warm,' he said, 'must have only just passed. She looks …'

'… ancient,' said Lucy, who had managed to calm down, and now instead was just whimpering slightly, and skirted past, peering into the cabin.

'What a strange place to live,' she said, gathering herself, looking about, seeing the piles of books – interesting books from so many places. She eyed them like a magpie, thinking of the library. She saw the old blanket, a photograph of a Choctaw chief, a couple of bowls, a spoon, something burnt in one small bowl. No TV, no telephone, no radio.

'We'll have to get the sheriff to come,' said Miss Julie.

The other two nodded, reluctant, but knowing it was the right thing to do, though they doubted the old woman would want to be manhandled in death, tipped into a motorboat, taken upriver – no, none of that seemed to sit with this place, this home.

She would prefer something with dignity, Miss Julie felt, then blushed, wondering was it this stranger she was thinking of, or herself.

'What's this?'

Lucy picked up the tiny fox from the dead woman's lap and showed it to Jim.

'Lenny!' said Jim. 'It's Lenny.' He held up the fox on the palm of his hand, and his heart leapt.

Chapter Fifty-Three

Bayou, 2012

Seeing the old swamp woman, dead in her seat alone in the bayou, had struck at the heart of Miss Julie. In her pocket she gripped tight to the envelope, the paper crinkled and familiar against her clenched palm.

'Let's go,' she said, 'I can smell the sinkhole, Lenny can't be far.'

'What if he's here?' Lucy wailed, 'What if she did something to him?' She was eyeing up the pots and bits of burnt paper and saw the few blonde hairs in the bowl.

'Look! Isn't this Lenny's hair? Oh, God.'

Lucy covered her mouth, but it was too late, and she threw up over the side of the wooden railing.

Jim held her curls back and placed his hand on her back, soothing her.

'Looks like a broth, some sort of healing concoction maybe.' Miss Julie pried about inside.

'I don't think she meant any ill to Lenny.'

'How can you know that?'

Lucy wiped her mouth and looked at the old woman.

'Instinct,' said Miss Julie.

'Instinct?' Jim asked, terrified now at the possibilities, at what may have happened to Lenny and all because he had been wrapped up in his own selfishness.

'I think Lenny left the fox for her, look, aren't those his sneaker prints on the deck ... and that line, that'll be the orange box. He's okay, I'm sure of it, but we have to find him soon. We'll call Sheriff Lentement later for her. I don't think she'll mind waiting. Maybe best you lay her down on her bed, though. Let her spirit rest easy a while.'

She gestured at Jim, who picked up the dead woman gently, and did as instructed. Lucy bent down to the water and tried to wash her face, darting her hand in and out again quickly, fearful of gators, the jacket getting wet as she leant over the bank.

'Sorry,' she said to Miss Julie who looked on, but just shrugged.

Miss Julie didn't care about the jacket, never had, it was always more the idea of it she had liked, that one day she and Stanley would travel and go to places far away, they would do unexpected things, live a life full of adventure – but then she had never learnt to ski, he had never returned and it all seemed unlikely now. The girl could leave it there for all she cared. Then, seeing the look of pain on Lucy's face, Miss Julie softened and put her scrawny arm around the girl's shoulders.

'We'll find him soon and he'll be fine. You'll see.'

Lucy sniffed and tried to smile. Then Jim laid the old woman out on her bed and pulled shut the cabin door. Miss Julie told him to let Sheriff Lentement know as soon as they made it back to town, and the three of them continued on, following the trail of muddy prints, following Lenny, deep into the bayou.

Chapter Fifty-Four

The Sinkhole, 2012

As he rounded the corner, Lenny, who had been walking along squeezing the agate stone tight in his fist, telling himself he was not scared, almost stepped off the end of the boardwalk into thin air, for the wood had been pulled clean away – only a ripped wooden plank and a twisted thin metal band left hanging mid-air. Beyond the ripped edge of the boardwalk surged and gurgled and spat the sinkhole.

The sinkhole was as big as the public swimming pool over at Constan (the bigger pool, the one with the deep end that scared Lenny for he couldn't see the bottom, couldn't see how far down it all went, all that water underneath him without end). It was as long as two of Man March's fields, as wide as the bend in the river where the Mississippi used to join up with False River long ago ... Lenny whistled and stared out at it, watching the surface bubble and burp. He kept one sleeve wrapped over his mouth and nose, to try and dull the smell, and he looked up, noticing how quiet and still the swampland had become around him. There was no birdsong. All the birds had flown away.

Carefully, Lenny stepped back. He did not want to fall in. He had seen the way the sinkhole would, all of a sudden, grab chunks of land, pull the trees down, trees that had grown for over hundreds of years, swallowed in seconds.

Instead, he walked back a way and found the sturdiest tree he could spot – a tall majestic oak, one that rooted deep and wide where once long ago was land, and taking off Stanley's sweater he tied it above his head to the trunk of the tree, then grabbed a hold of one sleeve to lever himself up the trunk, his feet flat against it, then once above the sweater, he leant down and untied it and pulled it round again with one free hand, the other holding tight to the branches above him, and like this, he climbed up into the branches of the tree and kept climbing until he was high above everything, high above the canopy of leaves, and able to look down and see for himself the sinkhole gurgling, ready to suck everything into the belly of the earth.

Lenny had never climbed so far before. Up there he could smell the sulphur less, and a breeze caught the leaves. All around him the tops of the trees shone with reds and golds and greens. In the distance he could see the towns beyond Roseville, smoke belching from factory chimneys along the river, to the south and west stretched the bayou, further west the highway, and the woods and the swampland and river reached out to the east, towards Roseville, with its rows of houses snaking around the bend of the False River in the sunlight.

And everywhere the land was sinking. Whole villages and towns, graveyards and electricity pylons, submerged half under water – telephone wires sticking up showing the only sign of lives once lived, before the waters rose and claimed back the land. Salt drifting up water from the Gulf, killing the trees, destroying the marshes. Spits of land, disappearing so quickly now, some feared there would soon be nothing left, nothing to hold on to. Lenny looked down on it all, this watery destruction.

If only Arturo could see him now. He would never call Lenny a sissy again – that was certain.

Lenny felt he was almost close enough to touch the clouds. If he squinted in the distance, he told himself, he imagined he could see all the way over to Baton Rouge, and somewhere down there was Mari-Rose. He wished she could see him. *She would have been mad as all hell*, he thought. But she couldn't see him, and she had let him go, and he would let her go too – because that was what she wanted. He looked at the watch on his wrist. It had stopped somewhere along the journey.

It didn't matter whether the watch worked or not for it only told time one way, as if everything travels in one clear straight line. Hour after hour, day after day. But it doesn't. Lenny knew that. He knew that as he had circled, lost, deep in the bayou, too frightened to call out loud but inside he was calling out to Mari-Rose, over and over, rolling the agate stone in his pocket, until it grew warm in his fist, even though he knew that for all that time could stretch and bend, he could not make her come back.

Lenny often wondered what had become of Mari-Rose. Was she happy now? Where was she? He didn't allow himself to imagine that perhaps she was somewhere thinking about him, missing him, trying to figure out a way to come back, and if she did that, would it be okay? No, not that – there was too much hope and wishing in it, and then, hadn't things been better without her? Didn't Miss Julie look out for him, and Lucy Albert, and his daddy – when he was sober and in his right mind?

He polished the stone in his pocket and tried to hold on to all his memories of Mari-Rose and the happy times, for they had been happy – sometimes.

Lenny remembered watching old MGM musicals on TV, Mari-Rose singing along, her feet dancing on the floor, her pulling him about the room, laughing, looking over her shoulder, a nervousness about her like she was always meant for somewhere else.

It had shocked him, the first time he had realised this – that she and he were not one and the same, but different souls, each within their own separate worlds. It had shocked him to his core to see that and know it true.

'One of these Sundays, you won't need me at all,' she had said to him one night, pulling closed the voiles on the window, switching off his bedside lamp, and he had stayed awake a long time that night, fearful and sad at the thought of being apart from her.

She had been gone so long now, however, the weeks becoming months, one running on after the last, yet she had never called or written or cared to visit, and if she had she would have found them gone on their Great Adventure – living wild in the woods on the edge of town. Would she even know them anymore?

For a long time, he had thought she would come back – for wouldn't she miss her garden, the flowers, the trees, and Lenny – wouldn't she miss him too? Then, when she showed no sign of return, he grew angry. It was then he had stopped going to school, at first missing a day here and there, until seeing that Jim was preoccupied, he stayed away longer and longer each time, and as the letters went to the old house Jim was none the wiser, so what harm could it do? After all, it was his mother's fault. And she could be mad at him when she got back – if she ever returned.

'School's the best you can do, Lenny. Learning takes you places. Gives you options in life. You've got to get to class. Then you won't end up like me – stuck here.'

She had told him that so many times – especially when Miss Avery would call her up, back when the telephone was connected, calling to complain that Lenny had taken to daydreaming again during the school day.

'Seems like the boy's not here at all,' the teacher had chided Mari-Rose.

'It's his daddy. Misses his father, that's all.'

Mari-Rose would apologise and promise Lenny would do better, and Miss Avery would make sympathetic, understanding sounds down the telephone line while Mari-Rose would take to crying over Jim and the war, and how hard, how hard it was to be her. Then the women would forget all about Lenny for a while, and it would just be a shared sadness at the world and the distance it cast between people, until Mari-Rose would eventually hang up. Then her tears would switch to shouting and anger, her voice chasing Lenny around the house, until he took to hiding out at Miss Julie's, who sheltered him from enemy fire.

Lenny knew all this as he looked at the broken wristwatch, and out over the trees.

From the top of the silvered oak tree, Lenny could see everything.

He saw that he could travel time any number of directions: that the moments and memories knitted one into the other, in an infinite number of possibilities. In his mind, he travelled back to when Mari-Rose would tell him that story about the little boy with the golden curls, the fox, a planet far away and a broken plane lost in the desert.

'What happens next?' he had asked his mother, feeling immense sadness for the lost prince so far from home.

'A story can end all sorts of ways,' she had soothed him, stroking his forehead as he looked up at her, his dark eyes clouded. 'Happy, sad ... and sometimes it doesn't end at all, it's just beginning.' She had looked away from him then, blinking back tears. Perhaps she was already thinking of leaving him. Even then.

He tapped the broken wristwatch gently, careful with the cracked glass, but it was long dead. He had held on to it all the same, even though it had stopped working properly. He looked at it once more, then took it off his wrist. Underneath the skin was paler and sticky with sweat. He rubbed at his wrist a moment, and holding on to the tree with one hand as its cracked branches dipped and bobbed in the breeze, with the other hand he threw the watch far out into the sinkhole, as far as he could throw it, and watched it drop down and hit the surface, and then sink quickly under until it was gone from sight. He rubbed his empty wrist a moment, and for a second regretted getting rid of the watch even though it no longer served him, but then he was glad. He had said goodbye.

From where he sat, looking out over the glinting bayou rivers and waterways, one arm held tight around the trunk, the rough bark scratching against his thighs, Lenny felt a letting go deep inside of him.

At first in his spirit as he said goodbye to Mari-Rose, he felt himself shake loose a little of the hold she had on his heart, and then he heard the gurgles from the sinkhole growing, and felt the earth tugging underneath the oak tree.

For a moment, everything was still and then, with a sound like a sigh rising from the sinkhole, everything was jolted sideways – as if the earth had let go of gravity.

Lenny grabbed a hold of the tree trunk with both hands. He felt the agate stone slip out from his pocket, saw it bounce from branch to branch below, hurtling towards the earth. He cried out, his voice lost against the fury of the sinkhole as it swallowed up shoots of young trees below him. Lenny closed his eyes. He heard the roots being pulled from the earth below. He felt himself flying through the air, the giant tree shuddering against him. He let go, falling backwards, twisting as if swimming through air up to the surface. G-force. Lenny's world tipped upside down. He was flying.

He heard a voice call out: was it Mari-Rose? He did not know. He saw the world a blur of greens, everything falling, hurtling towards the sinkhole, yanked into its gravitational pull, his arms reaching out, trying to catch a hold or pushing the branches out of his way – he wasn't sure which, only that he was free. He was flying at last.

'Time is elastic.' Jim's voice came back to him in that moment. 'You can stretch it out, make it last longer.'

Sometimes, though, it speeds up, taking you with it. Lenny wanted to slow down time. Wanted to freeze the moment, the feeling of weightlessness, of letting go. Lenny took a hold of time. He let it wind backwards, he felt the tree tip back up towards the sky, felt the pull of the sinkhole surrender the oak tree, found his grip on the sturdy trunk once more, the agate stone back, warm and heavy, held in his palm.

He felt a million different moments flickering through him, like the universe was trying to tell him something. He heard the voice of a boy far away in a desert, as if calling out to him. He wanted to help him, but what could he do?

Time coursed backwards through his veins, splitting off in a multitude of directions and all the while he held tight to the stone, back now in his fist.

Lenny stretched time and held it taut.

Chapter Fifty-Five

Bayou

It was so lonely by the sinkhole, Lenny holding on to the trunk of the oak tree as best he could. How was it he had managed to take a hold of time? He had been falling, the tree pulled downwards, and yet – Lenny looked out over the treetops, wishing he were not alone. Somewhere, surely, Jim would be looking for him. And Lucy, and Miss Julie – didn't they care too? Lenny closed his eyes, willing them to find him before it was too late.

It was Lucy's voice Lenny heard first, coming along the boardwalk beneath him, then his father's, both calling for him, their voices hoarse, shouting in all directions. Then he heard Miss Julie saying, 'Quiet down, we'll never hear the boy, you keep that up!'

'I'm up here!' he shouted down to them, startling them all, so that Miss Julie almost tipped forwards out of the scooter.

'Don't go further – the sinkhole, it's around the corner. Watch out!' he yelled down to them, fearful they would fall in.

They stopped and looked up into the dense branches of the ancient oak, silvery with salt, that towered above them. They could not see Lenny but they could hear him.

'Come down, Léonard,' said Miss Julie, her voice rasping and rattling more than usual. Exhausted, all she wanted was to see the boy safe and get home – it had been too much excitement for one night, for one lifetime she felt.

'But I can't.'

Lenny gripped tighter to the trunk of the tree.

'Course you can,' said Jim, encouraging him. 'Haven't you managed to get all the way up?'

'That's the thing, Pop, if I come down now, it'll all be for nothing.' Lenny squeezed the stone in his fist.

'Lenny, should one of us come up?' Lucy asked, relief seeping out of her now the boy was found. She looked at Jim with his bad leg, Miss Julie in her mobility scooter and her in the cumbersome ski jacket. Lucy had a fear of heights. She was terrified of them. They made her freeze. If she tried to go up, she would get stuck. Then what would Jim think of her. Hadn't she embarrassed herself enough already?

'Or maybe you just need a moment, to think about it?' she offered, trying a different tack.

'Lenny, what are you doing?' Jim called up to him, exasperated.

'Don't you see? The sinkhole is destroying everything. We have to stop it!'

The boy's voice came shouting down the tree trunk.

'I know, Lenny, but staying stuck up a tree isn't going to do that,' Lucy said, wishing he would climb down.

'Unless ...' said Miss Julie.

'What?' Jim and Lucy stared at her, seeing an idea hatch in the old woman's mind.

'Well, what if we called the TV and radio folk? Told them Lenny is protesting the sinkhole, that it's one little boy's brave stand for what's right?'

Miss Julie looked at Lucy, gauging how serious the young woman was about taking a stand herself, how far would she go to put things right.

'Can't hurt none, can it?'

Lucy mulled it over.

'Better Lenny just comes down,' said Jim, resisting the mad glint he saw forming in Miss Julie's rheumy eyes.

'It's dangerous here, with the sinkhole so close and all, and the fumes. Lenny's in danger the longer we let him stay here.'

Lucy stood between the two of them, looking from one to the other. She turned her face upwards, 'Lenny, look it might come to nothing, but Miss Julie has a notion that we could try to interest the media folk, draw some attention to the sinkhole, if you're willing to stay put a while? But Lenny, it's up to you. You want to come down, that's just fine too. We just want you to be safe. We'd like to get you home. What do you think?'

She looked at Jim, who pushed his hands deep in his pockets, his bags at his feet, only wanting the boy to climb down and that be an end to it.

'Home?' Lenny called down, a sad questioning lilt to his voice.

'Oh Léonard,' said Miss Julie, feeling the boy's sadness.

'You know, staying up there won't bring her back!' Jim shouted up to his son, angry now. Lenny said nothing.

They huddled around the bottom of the tree, whispering, so that Lenny could no longer hear them.

Lenny grabbed tight to the trunk. He had been found and he would be safe. But he didn't want to explain about Mari-Rose, how it'd been a year she was gone and how he'd needed to say goodbye to her in his own way. Lenny rubbed his wrist where the watch strap had been. He didn't want to admit to any of that.

Wild River Sal had whispered to him as he'd drifted off to sleep. She'd talked about spirit walkers and having a gift – being able to see things ways most ordinary folk would miss – but that he'd have to sacrifice a lot for that, and would it be worth it for him, was he ready?

Lenny hadn't understood, flat-out exhausted and ill as he had been at that moment, but now, having managed to bend time once – to stop the tree from being sucked into the water, his letting go of Mari-Rose, the watch surrendered, now being found by Jim and Lucy and Miss Julie just at the moment when he'd wished for it and imagined it – he was beginning to understand what the old woman had meant.

Could he stop the sinkhole? Was that what she was trying to tell him, or was it even something bigger than that? Lenny was uncertain, straining to make out what the adults were discussing below. He was glad they had found him, but mad too, angry that his daddy didn't even apologise for abandoning him as he had, just expecting everything to go back to normal when they were long past that.

'Léonard?' Miss Julie croaked up at him.

'Yes, Miss Julie ...'

'You figure you could hold on up there a little longer?'

For a moment, he feared that they all planned to leave him there alone once more.

'Why?' he hesitated.

'Well, like Lucy says, I reckon you've found a way to catch the attention of the chemical companies.'

Lenny thought about this. He remembered sitting in the library watching Lucy's little group, wishing to be a part of it all – now here was his chance. He could feel the tug of the sinkhole, testing the roots of the tree below. How long would he have? How long could he steady time before the world would tip on its side once more?

'I don't know,' he called down, sounding nervous now.

'Maybe he'll climb down after all,' he heard Lucy muttering below. Lenny clenched his jaw and squeezed the stone tight in his fist.

'What should we do?' Lucy looked to Miss Julie for guidance.

The breeze was growing stronger, bending the trees over, and from his eyrie, looking out over the swampland and the woods and the charred, empty fields beyond, Lenny thought about the times he had taken off into space, had set off on a mission of discovery, never knowing if he would return safely to earth or not. And now, here was a real mission. Not one imagined, but one that might do something good and true. He smiled to himself. Why not stay on longer – wait it out. If Miss Julie thought it would make a difference, wasn't it worth at least trying?

'Okay,' he shouted down, 'but hurry up.'

He didn't tell them about how time wanted to go one way, then another, nor how hard it was just to hold on, nor that the pull of the sinkhole was growing stronger. He didn't want to frighten them. And for once, if his daddy could just be proud of him, wouldn't that be something too?

'Lenny, think about this,' pleaded Jim. He had no way to force the boy down, and he could tell that this was not a job for Lucy, and that she and Miss Julie had their minds fixed on the bigger picture.

'I have, Pop. We need to stop the sinkhole. Miss Julie's right. We need to make them stop. If you bring the TV folk ... then they'll have to listen. The path to the left comes out by the crossroads. That's what it looks like anyway from here. I can see everywhere – right across the woods and the river and the fields. It's amazing, Pop, like flying.'

'We'll call the TV folk, Léonard, you just hold on now.' Miss Julie sat up in her seat, looking invigorated all of a sudden.

'Jim, Lucy, you both go – call the TV stations, all the locals, and the papers. Tell them a child abandoned by his poorly mama who was made ill by the sinkhole, son of a returned war hero, is waging a one-boy protest to protect the people of Roseville from the sinkhole and the pollution that is making folk sick and driving them away – and he won't come down until the companies causing it put it right. Tell them that.'

'But it's not right, Miss Julie, not how you're telling it ...' Jim hesitated, doubtful, looking at the old woman and the mad way her eyes shone.

'It's right enough, Jim – it's enough. Sometimes things need fixing – it's just a matter of finding out how. And Lenny has more figured out than all of us together. Go on, I can't wait here all day – and bring back food, and clothes, and water. Here, take my keys – and don't forget to check on that damn cat, it'll have destroyed my porch by now.'

'One of us should stay with you.' Lucy looked at her, worried by the glint in the old woman's eyes.

'*Pas du tout!* You know these people, Lucy Albert – show them what you're made of! You wanted to do something. So, go on, make a difference. Here's your chance.'

Miss Julie settled back into her mobility chair, her back to Jim and Lucy now who saw nothing for it but to do what she asked.

'Lenny?' Jim called up to him. 'You going to be okay a while, until we come back?'

'Sure, Pop.'

'You feel dizzy, you come down now. And keep an eye on Miss Julie, will you? She's exhausted, needs her rest. She needs to get home to her own bed. She's been up all night, searching for you, so don't you worry her none now.'

Miss Julie waved them away.

As soon as they were gone, she called up once more to Lenny.

'Léonard, I'm so glad I found you.'

'Miss Julie, how did you know where to look?'

'Stanley, Léonard, Stanley told me.'

Up in the branches of the ancient oak, Lenny, stretching time, picturing Jim and Lucy walking back to Roseville and Miss Julie waiting down below, sat back against the trunk and looked up at the blue of the sky, wrapping Stanley's old sweater around his chest and settling to sleep. He could sleep now a while. Down below, Miss Julie closed her eyes too and pulled the blanket around her knees and feet, and listened to the gurgling of the sinkhole nearby, before quickly falling asleep, her snoring reminding Lenny that he was not alone.

Chapter Fifty-Six

Roseville

'Do you think she's crazy?' Jim asked Lucy as they walked out of the bayou, following the route Lenny had sent them on, as he'd looked out over the treetops seeing where the path led, until they found the road back to Roseville.

'No, Miss Julie's not crazy, no more than any of us. Lenny's right too – we need some sort of direct action, something to make them do *something*.'

She looked solemn as she said this, the weight landing on her words. They stood a while on the verge of the road by the crossroads, eyes averted, nervous now they were alone, and there they remained, shy of each other, until they flagged down a truck passing by, asking the driver to drop them off, the man smiling at Lucy, patting the seat next to him for her to sit down, then on seeing Jim's darkening eyes, turning his own eyes back to the dusty road, soon dropping them off near the water's edge outside of town, Jim and Lucy walking the last of it together along the banks of False River, their hands held tight, Lucy turning and waving in thanks to the driver as clouds of dust rose up around them on the roadside.

'I mean, we're not really going to call anyone, though, are we? Lenny will come down, soon enough. Even if we did talk to them, who would listen?' Jim walked away from her a moment, trying to hear the thoughts in his head, feeling waves of panic rising again.

'I would listen,' said Lucy, quiet. 'If I saw that little boy on the news fighting for the place he's grown up in, fighting for it to be safe, I'd listen. And you know what, Jim Lockhart? I think other folk will too. Miss Julie's definitely not crazy.'

Jim puzzled it out for a moment. Maybe they were right. Maybe sometimes you had to get a little bit crazy, do something unexpected.

'Okay then, if you think …'

'I do.'

She took his hand again and put it in her pocket to warm it up, his skin cold to the touch.

'Thank you.'

'What for?'

'For this.'

Lucy leant over and kissed him gently on the cheek. Jim could feel his life turning, rotating towards her, drawn in whether he wished it or not. He was afraid. Afraid for Lenny, for himself, for Lucy. If she knew the truth of him, would she still smile at him? He doubted it, but he could not be sure. And that was enough. He squeezed her hand tight and worried about the TV folk and bringing all that on Lenny and what it would do to them. Surely it was a bad idea.

Jim felt his worries surfacing again, the world of the bayou blurring with the desert in his mind, seeing Izil speaking to him, reaching out, hearing Lenny's voice. Beads of sweat trickled down his cheeks. He just wasn't sure, but Lucy seemed so certain. She at least was real. He clung on to that.

Back at Miss Julie's house, Hervey had scratched deep marks into the boards of the porch – a cry for help, of some sort, perhaps. He gave Lucy a withering look as she opened the screen door and refused to engage in the hugs that she foisted on him almost immediately, before she noticed the damage to the floorboards.

'Oh no, Hervey, what have you done? Miss Julie will be furious.'

Lucy set to trying to fix the mess, then feeding the cat, all while instructing Jim on the people to call, the numbers to look up.

'And we'll call my group from the library, Willie and Appleby, Lionel and Betsy, the new girl Alma-Mae ... they'll all come and show support. We'll talk to the TV folk. Get a bit of community spirit going.'

Then while Lucy was busy calling everyone, coaxing, cajoling, making them see that this right here was a piece of news they wouldn't want to miss out on, Jim put together a bundle of blankets and sweaters (a mothball smell clinging to them), along with food and drinks taken from the ice-box and pantry, and put it all into the orange box Lenny had left at the bottom of the tree and that he'd taken with him.

Hervey watched him, one eye closed, then clambered up into the box, snuggling down amongst the blankets. This time he would not be left behind.

'You'll come then? Can you pick us up? Yes, down near the end ... Meet you there. Give me half an hour to finish the rest of the calls.'

Lucy gestured at Jim as she spoke to Willie. 'And ask Callie to come, will you? Ask anyone you can to come. It's important!'

Jim smiled back at her, watching the way she lit up, how she was good at getting people to do things, how she made it matter. He felt himself growing stronger around her. His hands shook less, and his heart didn't beat as if it wanted to break free of his chest. There was something about her that brought him back to himself. She believed in him and when he was with her, he no longer felt like a ghost.

Soon he had the box packed, ready to go, with Hervey buried happily inside, one ear peeking out from under the blanket.

'Mornin'. Is that Mike Sumners? Hi Mike, there's a story I think you'll be interested in? You have a minute?'

Lucy talked to the man at the TV station in a friendly way, quick and confident, winking at Jim as she spoke, explaining the rival stations were already on their way and the radio folk, and the papers, it was a story they didn't want to miss. The morning had been taken up with ringing round, getting hold of the right people, persuading them, assuring them that here was a big story, an important story, if they just knew where to look.

After a few minutes, she gave Jim a thumbs-up sign, then hung up the phone. They were going to come. It was after all a Tuesday, and nothing much was happening, and the thing with newspaper, TV and radio folk is that they do love a story, and one with a young boy alone, stuck up in the sky, hanging on the perilous edge of a poisonous sinkhole – sure, that they could use on a quiet Tuesday.

Then Lucy rang and insisted on being put through to the director of the big chemical company near the sinkhole, explaining to his assistant that it was an emergency, a media emergency, that he would want to take the call, that she was doing him a favour.

The man actually listened to her, thanked her even for letting him know, a note of frustration in his voice. In the background, Lucy could hear another phone, then two ringing insistently, the receptionist picking up, asking the callers – journalists perhaps – to hold the line.

'Hold the line, Jim!'

That's what Lucy said when she came off the call.

'That's what we have to do. Hold the line against them, then we'll have done all we can.'

Her eyes shone brightly as Lucy felt alive at last.

'Let's go.'

Chapter Fifty-Seven

Bayou

By late morning, there were three different TV crews gathered by Lenny's tree, along with Lucy's group of local activists, including Callie who was wrapped up in a turquoise kaftan and had Willie find her summer shades, for she wasn't used to being outside none nor in company, along with the library regulars and a few hangers-on from town, wanting to be a part of things. And there was Miss Julie, Jim and a handful of folk from roundabouts who had heard about what was going on and came down out of curiosity and for the cameras.

By lunchtime the crowd had grown in numbers and the local police were on the scene. Sheriff Lentement, back from the cabin with the Christmas lights, his face ashen, jaw set tight, was trying to keep everyone in order.

He was sure, when they had lifted Wild River Sal from her bed, that the old woman's hand had reached out to him, that she had whispered something about the sinkhole, yet how could that be for her body was long cold, and yet he had felt the spirit of her, lingering on. *World's full of things we can't explain*, he thought to himself, seeing his day turn even stranger now with the boy stuck up the tree, TV crews clambering all about him, the smell of the sinkhole making him feel sick.

Someone had called the fire brigade, but they couldn't get the truck anywhere near the sinkhole and would have to send a team with ropes and a harness and tarpaulin to try to bring the boy down.

Jim had given the journalists a photograph of Lenny, the only one Mari-Rose had ever sent him, with his blonde curls and his wide smile. The news-anchor lady had almost snatched it out of his hand.

'Amazing, what an incredibly brave little boy,' she purred. 'Must take after his father.'

Lucy had pulled Jim away, warning him to be careful of what he would say, fearful of what they might ask him.

'Let Lenny do the talking,' she said, cross at the woman with her swooshy hair and big white teeth.

Miss Julie, meanwhile, had brushed her hair and spritzed herself with the cologne Jim had picked up from the bathroom for her as per her instructions.

'Helps dull the smell of this fetid place,' she had said, before turning to the cameraman for her interview about the sinkhole. She had plenty to say about the shocking environmental and social disaster that was destroying the local communities along the riverbanks, tearing families apart, ripping up the bayou and taking with it a way of life they could never hope to replace. A small group gathered around her, waiting to hear the old woman speak.

There was a sense of being on the edge of something big, that something was happening.

'Young Léonard Lockhart, *Lenny*, is nine years old – but he's taking a stand to save Roseville. What a brave little boy.'

The woman reporter spoke to camera, her large blue eyes damp limpid pools as the camera operator zoomed in on her pointing up the tree.

The cameras had started rolling and the reporters were clustered around the base of the tree, all fighting to get shots of the sinkhole in the background, all covering their faces between takes to try and get rid of the smell that filled the air as behind them the sinkhole burped and bubbled, as if it too were waiting for something big to happen. All of them struggling to see Lenny up in his eyrie.

Overhead, Lenny could hear the sound of a helicopter hovering in the distance.

Jim heard it too. The whirr of the helicopter blades. And the sound of it did something to him. Something terrible. He took himself off, walking away fast from the crowd. Fear rising up in his chest, he clamped his hands over his ears to block out the sound.

Closing his eyes, Jim saw Tayri screaming at him, saw the camels fallen in the dunes, the ground turned dark, blood sucked into the sand. Izil was lying there, the women gathered around him, the helicopter overhead – a shadow against the stars.

And then he was running, running as fast as he could, dragging his bad leg, pulling it over the uneven earth next to the bayou, fighting his way out from the gloom of the swamp and the canopy of trees overhead. Once he reached the clearing and could see the road ahead of him, he bent over double, throwing up, watching the helicopter coming down to land in an empty field, its blades slicing through the air.

It was too late. Jim knew, it was already too late.

Lucy had called after Jim, seeing him sprinting away, wondering what he was doing, wondering if it was the fear that had got to him again. Miss Julie, watching it happen, seeing Jim run off, just shook her head and pursed her lips. Another question came from the journalist, the microphone pushed up near her face; she looked up and smiled for the camera, thinking *funny how we can feel one thing, show another.*

The man from the nearby chemical company had arrived and her interview was hastily cut short as the journalists, sensing blood, raced forward to interview him instead.

'You need to go, go get Jim,' Miss Julie hissed at Lucy, tilting her head in the direction he had run.

'But he was fine. Honestly. He seems so much better.'

'The man's in pieces. This is his boy. All this attention, it's more than he's fit to take.'

'I ...' Lucy stared at Miss Julie, knowing the old lady was right. She had thought they were doing something good. Doing what Lenny wanted. She hadn't thought about Jim, what it might do to him. She hadn't understood all he was carrying inside. She went after him now, calling out, chasing after him through the bayou for he had run back out towards the light and dust of the day.

'Lenny, how you doing up there, *sha?*'

Miss Julie called up the tree. For a moment, she heard nothing, only the din of the protestors and the questions to the man and the clatter of Lucy's shoes on the boardwalk.

'I'm tired Miss Julie, bone tired.'

She heard the boy sob and saw the agate stone dropping down branch to branch until it landed on the ground near her scooter. She bent over, stiff, reaching out to pick it up off the moss.

'You dropped your *gris-gris*.'

From up in the tree came only the sound of silence.

Over in the crowd, clustered around the director of the chemical company (a mild-mannered man from Utah who had decided he would hand in his notice on the Monday, head for Florida, go take up golf instead), everyone listened as he made promises and assurances to shut down all works and bring in specialists to help, for in truth it was beyond them, no one had expected nor planned for the sinkhole – it just happened. It was a phenomenon, something of nature, not man's doing, but nonetheless, they didn't wish to be associated with it, nor with damaging the fragile ecosystem of the bayou – and yes, seeing this little boy, hearing his story, his determination, his plea, seeing the sinkhole at close range – all that had made them think on ways in which they could help the local community, how they could all face this, and fix it together.

Overhead a few golden leaves drifted down and swirled gently about the man's head as he spoke, giving a strange otherworldly glow to his words. There were murmurs from the crowd, a majority choosing to believe him, to see sorrow on the man's face, a willingness at last to listen. A few, Willie and Callie among them, were unrepentant, continuing to shout at him.

'Sounds like you've done it, Léonard,' Miss Julie shouted up to him, on hearing the man's promises. 'You can come down now.'

'You sure, Miss Julie?' His voice wavered, sounding fainter and far away.

'I'm sure, Léonard. Truly sure.'

Lenny started to make his way down the trunk of the oak tree, going carefully from branch to branch, the bark rubbing hard against the palms of his hands, him feeling lightheaded now with his victory. It had mattered. He had mattered. Just for once.

For an instant, he forgot how to climb down and he held on, still looking out over the sinkhole and down at the gathered reporters, the cameramen, the firemen with their tarpaulin, and the local people all come to cheer him on. The crowd, on seeing the boy's sneakers finally peeking from the canopy of leaves, began to chant, 'Lenny! Lenny!' and there, in the midst of it all, he could see Jim and Lucy walking back arm in arm, Lucy soothing Jim, and Miss Julie smiling at Lenny – all with their faces turned up to him, all willing him back to safety.

But he held on to the tree an instant longer, his arms wrapped around the trunk. He held his breath and felt his heart beating fast in his chest. Lenny held on to time. All this – the protest, the promises, the rescue efforts – this was what he saw unfolding when he looked north, time stretching and twisting before him, showing how things could be.

And what, he wondered, would happen next? Would he clamber down? Would they want to talk to him? Would he look at the camera and say to Mari-Rose that he loved her and missed her but that he knew she was never coming back and that, somehow, he would be okay? He reckoned on Beatriz at least seeing it, prone as she was to watching television. Beatriz could tell Mari-Rose if she missed it.

The wind caught at the back of his neck, the sinkhole sighing, the smell stronger now. Lenny put his hand over his mouth and twisted a little towards the west. He could feel time pulling at him once more. He closed his eyes, closed out the sound of the crowd he pictured below. He felt his spirit lifting away from him, as if circling above him.

As he looked down, he saw himself climbing.

Letting time begin once more.

As Lenny made his way down, careful of where he placed his feet, testing each branch as he went, there was a strange, sucking noise and the group of onlookers started to panic below. Something was happening to the earth, something was pulling at it, the boardwalk was rising up at the end that had been ripped in half by the sinkhole.

Everyone started moving back, hurrying, panicking, Sheriff Lentement and emergency services folk were calling for calm but being ignored.

In the centre of the sinkhole, Lenny saw it. A large hole opening up, swirling in the centre, pulsing and spinning the mud and the water around, fast and faster still, and then the riverbank being pulled into it, unable to resist.

'It's the sinkhole! Lenny, get down.'

He heard Jim shout out to him, saw him arguing with one of the firemen at the bottom of the tree. Lucy was wheeling Miss Julie away at speed, chasing after the crowd that was making its way back towards the fields, hurtling from the bayou now. But Jim wouldn't leave him. Not this time. He didn't care what Lentement said, or anyone else.

'Sir, it's not safe, we have to ask you to stand back.' The firemen, all local men, looked at him, nervous, watching the trees shake behind them, everyone wanting to run but knowing the boy was still up there, needing help.

'Can you get to him?' Jim was asking them.

The man in charge shook his head, pushing Jim before him.

'It's too late. We've got to get back, please, it's too dangerous.'

The sucking noise was coming stronger now, and Lenny watched as it pulled up bald cypress trees and whole swathes of Spanish moss, swirling them round in the dark water before swallowing them whole into the belly of the earth. Huge clumps of the swamp were just being ripped up from the earth and taken. Lenny whimpered.

He had not planned for this, had not pictured it in this way. Where was the agate stone? Terrified, he couldn't move, even though Jim was calling for him, screaming at him to get down. He put his hand in his pocket and imagined it there, the *gris-gris* Mari-Rose had given him. He held on to it tight in his mind, even though it was gone. Lenny thought about a little prince far from home and a snake and a sad, lonely rose, and he thought of Miss Julie never getting to see Stanley, and of looking at the stars through the telescope on her lawn, and he thought of Hervey the cat giving him the stink-eye. Lenny looked down. Jim was pushing, shouting, fighting three firemen who were trying to drag him away.

'I'm going to jump,' Lenny shouted down to them.

For a moment, the men stopped. A tarpaulin lay on the ground where they had been readying it to catch the boy.

'Quick then!' The men ran back, grabbed it, each taking a corner, and the third caught his and pulled it taut, Jim grabbing the fourth.

'Jump, Lenny, jump!' Behind them came the crack of wood being ripped apart.

Lenny closed his eyes, imagined the stone in his fist and spread out his arms, teetering on the branch. He could see all the way down to the sinkhole, the tree twisting now, tilting towards the earth, shaking him upside down, the squashed paper animals tumbling from the pockets of his upturned jeans. The world spun on its axis. But if he just held his nerve. He could feel the oak tree shaking, the pull of the sinkhole having reached it at last.

Lenny felt the water swirling beneath him, ready to take him.

'Major, sir, can you hear me ...' Lenny's voice called out and he flew, pushing away from the falling tree, the wide sleeves of Stanley's old sweater rippling out in the breeze around him, then branches scratching his face, him shielding his eyes and turning in mid-air, flying free, then righting himself just before landing on the tarpaulin the firemen held below.

Then he was rolled up in it, the men running, carrying him along the boardwalk, Jim too, running, only focused on getting the boy to safety, as behind them the sinkhole sucked clean the trees, the great oak's roots ripped from the earth as the men ran. Jim looked back, only for a second, and he felt his hands begin to shake, and everything coming back to him again in waves.

He couldn't move and froze there until a voice screamed at him, 'What are you stopping for? Keep going, we've got to get clear. Come on!'

'Pop!' Jim heard Lenny cry out, his voice muffled from within the tarpaulin as they tried to pull him and Jim along. It was enough, that cry. Jim was able to move again, the men dragging him and the boy to safety, running back out into the open land where they laid down the tarpaulin on the grass, opening it up, unwrapping it like a present, the journalists turning to film Lenny as he stepped unsteady onto the flattened grass, with the helicopter waiting behind him.

Lucy ran over.

'Oh Lenny!'

She hugged him, a big warm scratchy woollen hug, and she put the orange ski jacket on his shoulders and made sure the medical folk were checking him for broken bones. Then she hugged Jim, kissed him, not caring what anyone would think. She claimed him, claimed them both.

'Time and place, Lucy Albert,' called out Miss Julie, tutting at her gently, but Lucy, tears streaming down her cheeks, didn't care. She truly didn't. She didn't care if the reporters filmed it, she didn't care what people would say. Lucy was done caring.

The boy was standing there, dazed. Jim hugged Lenny close.

'That was some flight, Lenny.' Jim looked at his son, and Lenny could see he wasn't in trouble, and that his daddy was proud of him. It was the way Jim looked at him, really looked at him properly – for the first time in a long time, and Lenny could see his daddy was finally there, not lost somewhere far away, not so sad anymore.

As he looked to the west, picturing all that, how they would find him, save him if he could just hold on, catch him if he would jump, and remembering Wild River Sal chanting about him, this was how Lenny bent time.

Chapter Fifty-Eight

The Sinkhole

Lenny had pictured how it would be, to be returned safely to earth, gathered up in the tarpaulin, carried away by the men from the sinkhole, Jim's face looking at him with relief and pride. A whole new beginning. He had seen this new future unfurl as they opened the tarp, a future in which his daddy was happy and normal, in which the sinkhole shrank away to almost nothing, and the people of Roseville got their happy ending.

It all felt so real to him.

He saw Lucy Albert moving out of her apartment above Eddie's Fish & Bait, moving in with Jim, Lenny and Miss Julie, for the old woman flat out refused to live on her own any longer.

'What is the point,' Miss Julie said, 'what is the point of having all this space, if I can't share it?'

He saw how at first they were careful to tiptoe around her but after a while she got annoyed with that and so Lucy knitted some new cushion covers for the couch, and Jim hung up his hammock under one of the magnolia trees in the back yard. Lenny got to paint his new room sky blue, then they all stuck those glow-in-the-dark stars over the ceiling so at night it was like sleeping outside – just without the cold night air and the risk of snapping gators. Lucy and Jim took the back room and she decorated it with blankets and throws she knitted, though Hervey didn't much care for the new arrangements and sulked in the porch, more often than not.

Lenny pictured all this – even seeing how he went back to school. Miss Avery wanted him to repeat a year, to stay with her a little longer she said, 'given all the time you've missed'.

Lenny felt he was okay with that.

The chemical company stayed good to their word, closing up operations, and a team from out of state came in and figured out how to shrink the sinkhole, which was still there, but smaller now, and shrinking more every day.

Lucy became secretive for a while, taking herself off on trips, not letting Jim go with her, and he hung about looking hangdog, until Miss Julie found him jobs to do about the house, building a swing seat in the garden, and a small platform for the telescope, fixing a new basket onto her scooter so she could get out more often. Jim became useful once more.

When Lucy came back one afternoon, with a crazy glint in her eye as she picked up Lenny from the bus after class, she took them all down to the jetty near to the house with a picnic hamper. They laid out the crawfish pies and a salad bowl along with drinks of lemonade and apple juice – an egret perched on the jetty post watching them, waiting for leftovers.

'What you up to, Lucy Albert?' Miss Julie chuckled, as if she knew quite well enough.

'Just you wait,' said Lucy, her eyes smiling in her pale face at Jim's.

And then, when they had almost finished eating and the light was falling in the sky, it came, the sound of a small plane overhead, the plane coming into sight, all of them looking up at it. Jim tensed a little. Lucy stroked his hand, soothing him quietly. Then, with a graceful turn, the biplane came lower over the surface of the wide river, slowing down, balancing up until it landed with a gentle flurry of bumps on the surface of the water and came sliding across to the jetty, stopping right by them.

It was a handsome-looking little plane, painted white with a blue stripe.

'Well, what you all waiting for?' Lucy got up, laughing.

'What's this?' Jim's eyes shone as the plane bobbed up and down on the water.

'She's a gift, Jim. For you. From me and Miss Julie.'

He stared at the women, his eyes damp and his throat swollen.

'I can't ... I can't take something like this.' He stammered at them.

'You can, Jim. Anyways it's an investment. A business opportunity. Charters, along the river. Bring folk down for the fishing. Bring tourism back. Do something good.'

'I ...'

Jim's eyes shone. Lenny squeezed him tight in a bear hug, almost knocking him over.

'Can we fly? *Pleeeeeease.*' The boy looked up at him, his curls dancing in the breeze.

'Not sure I can remember how.' Jim looked nervous now, his face pale once more, feeling he had no right to this second chance, this unexpected happiness.

'Course you will.' Lucy pulled him up off the grass, and took him over to meet the man who had piloted it down and who promised to stay on, to settle Jim back in.

'Go up with the pilot, give her a try, see what you think.' Lucy practically shoved Jim into the seat of the waiting plane.

Jim clambered in, turning to Miss Julie and Lenny, a wide smile breaking on his face.

'I don't know what to say.'

'Take her up, let's see what you can do!' Miss Julie waved him off.

Lenny danced from one foot to the next wishing he could go up, but Lucy held on to him, whispering in his ear, 'Next time, Lenny, this is for your dad, he needs to remember he can do this, that he's going to be okay. Then, when he's properly organised, he can take you up, okay?'

Lenny saw how they all watched as Jim pulled shut the door, and talked a moment with the pilot, and then the engines spluttered back into life, and the biplane backed away from the jetty out into the water, until they had a long clear stretch ahead of them, and she bumped along the water rising up, climbing gently into the sky.

When Jim came back an hour later, his cheeks flushed pink, his eyes shining clear, he pulled the women and Lenny to him, kissing them all on their foreheads, laughter bubbling out of him, out of all of them.

Lenny saw too how Lucy decided to take the rest of the inheritance and house money she had left, and with some help from Miss Julie who had been saving up now for years, she bought an old empty store on Main Street, and turned it into a bookstore with a café and a shop, selling the sweaters, scarves and hats she knitted, along with things for tourists to buy. On Thursdays they had local bands play and as the months passed, folk got to hearing about the place and would come down for the accordion and fiddle music and to browse the books and sometimes buy a few. The café business thrived, mainly thanks to Lucy's determination and helped by Appleby who did the bookkeeping for her and minded the place when she was down at the library, training up young Alma-Mae to be the new librarian.

It was Miss Julie who decided they should buy Lenny's old house back from the bank – quickly, for a bargain price, for people would want to stay in Roseville again soon. Lucy and Jim talked about it a lot, whether they could accept the old woman's help, whether it was the right thing to do or not – in hushed whispers late at night time – and decided they didn't want to leave Miss Julie alone again, nor live with the ghosts of the past, so the old house would be best put to use as a guesthouse for the tourists who Jim would fly down for the fishing and river tours – and Lucy would look after them, along with Callie who offered to help out. Things really began to change.

Jim stopped drinking, shaved and cleaned himself up, and started to let go of that hunched-over look he'd carried about for so long. Miss Julie kept up her letter-writing, and still had

Lenny help her with it, or let him mow the lawn on occasion, or had him sit with her to talk about the woodpeckers and ants in the garden.

Lenny saw all this, as he looked out west from the top of the oak tree – how his life could be, how Roseville could be home again. He began to cry. The tree was pulling sideways once more, and he was so tired now. He twisted a little, clinging on to a branch that was hanging down towards the sinkhole. He looked south, scanning the horizon, listening for sounds of voices. Surely, they would find him soon.

Chapter Fifty-Nine

Roseville

On the breeze, he thought he heard the faraway voice of a boy and his mother. She was calling out to him, in a language Lenny did not know and could not understand. She was asking him something or warning him – he wasn't sure which. Lenny would have liked to be a help to her, but he didn't know how.

He whimpered, the sleeves of the sweater catching on the sharp ends of the branches.

'It's okay, Léonard, it's okay.'

Now he could hear Miss Julie, could feel the old woman's veiny hand on his, her soothing him. They were in her garden, together in the sun. Lenny pictured this, time spinning around him. He felt her close to him.

Lenny saw Miss Julie taking a creased envelope out of the pocket of her dress, a look of momentary panic crossing her face.

'What's that?' he asked her, seeing how she was trying to hide it away again.

'What?' She looked at him, defiant.

'That envelope. You carry it all the time. Must be something special.' He shrugged. If she didn't want to tell him, he wouldn't pry. He'd learnt with grown-ups often it's better not to ask. But she looked at him, tipping her head to the side.

'I don't know what's in it, truly I don't, Léonard,' she sighed. 'I don't know.'

Tears tracked down her wrinkled cheeks and she pushed the wetness back, her hair getting damp at the ears.

'Come with me.'

He followed her, startled, over to the new swing seat. She gestured at Lenny to sit next to her.

'I've had this letter a long, long time, Léonard. I've always been too afraid to open it. It's from Stanley, you see.'

She held the envelope, folded over so many times, so many different ways, its edges frayed over time, the handwriting on the front faint from so much holding. Lenny wanted to give the old lady a hug. He didn't like seeing her crying like this, looking so lost.

'Wouldn't Stanley want you to read it?'

He looked up at her a moment, then down at his sneakers kicking gently against the bench.

'He would. I think he would.'

'Then why don't you read it?'

'What if I don't like what it says? What if ...' Her voice broke.

Lenny thought about this. He knew exactly what she meant. He thought about Mari-Rose, and how she had just gone without saying goodbye, and how for the longest time he had wished she would write to him, even though she never did, and that if she did, whatever she would say, it would make him feel even sadder, and he knew that. So, he understood Miss Julie.

'Sometimes it's better not to know.'

She looked at him, surprised.

'But what if it's something important?'

Lenny thought about that too.

'Then you should read it.'

He looked at the tops of his sneakers, all scuffed and pinching his toes now. He needed new shoes.

'Those sneakers getting a bit worn out,' Miss Julie said, looking down at his feet as they swung to and fro, as if she could read his mind. She'd often surprised him like that, just knowing what it was he was feeling before he said anything at all.

'Take some money from the jar in the kitchen, Lenny, go buy yourself a new pair.' She patted him on the head, gently pushing him away from her.

Lenny pictured himself wandering down the garden to the fence at the back and climbing up into Jim's hammock in the sunshine where he swung back and forth in the warm late spring afternoon, drifting into sleep, dreaming about a cabin decorated in Christmas lights, and an old woman talking to him about shadows and spirit walkers and how life is more than we can ever see or know, and a Santa Claus fishing in the bayou. These images jumbled in his mind accompanied by the sound of the woodpecker tapping in the garden.

On the shaded swing seat, Miss Julie, seeing Lenny drifting off to sleep in the sun, and hearing Callie busy cleaning and fixing next door, and knowing Lucy was away up at the library or over at the new store and Jim out for the morning with folk keen on flying over the bayou, took the envelope and slowly opened it, her strong nails slicing open the edge of the paper, and there it was – Stanley's letter. The one she had always said she had never received. There it was.

Chapter Sixty

Korea, 1953

My darling Julie,

I write this quickly to you. Forgive me, my love.

You remember my old telescope and how we would sit out nights, trying to see into the heart of the universe? I look up now at the sky here, it's full of stars. Even with all this chaos around us – the stars still come out for their nightly show. And I watch them, but all I see is you.

Perhaps when you look up at the sky, you'll see me too, for my darling, if you are reading this then you will know, I will not be coming home.

I've asked Captain Arnold to make sure this reaches you when they write to you, as they must, and in it, I send all my love. It is yours, always.

Don't be sad, ma petite. Time will bring us back to one another, somehow. Of that I feel certain.

Promise me this – that you will live a big life. Fill it full of joy and love. And know how lucky I have been to hold your heart to mine.

Forever I am here. Forever you are with me.

Toujours, ma petite, toujours,

Stanley

Chapter Sixty-One

Roseville

Miss Julie rocked back and forth on the swing seat. The page was creased and worn thin, but the writing was his, and his voice came to her, clear from the page. With it was another note, this a brief one, detailing his bravery, expressions of sympathy, a finality of tone. She folded up both pieces of paper and put them back in the envelope, placing it back in her pocket, having closed it once more.

Almost immediately she regretted having opened the letter, but then to hear his voice like that, to be sure of his love for her, that too was something. She looked down at her hands, lined and stained with sunspots now, at how they trembled on her lap and she felt her heart tighten in her chest.

Should she call out to Léonard for help? Miss Julie wasn't sure. At the bottom of the garden Lenny swung half-asleep, gently in the hammock, oblivious to the old lady's pain. On the tree above her, she heard Frederik tap. Across the lawn, the sun glinted off Stanley's telescope, which stood proud on the grass, pointing up at the heavens.

For the first time, she felt alone. Had she lived a life full of joy and love? How to measure a life? She wasn't sure, though she knew this – she had lived. All those years, she had lived and in her heart Stanley had lived too.

And now, she would have to say goodbye to him. But how?

She looked again at the telescope and remembered those nights when she had sat with him out on the lawn, the grass newly seeded, the flowers only starting to grow up the fence to the back.

If only I could go back, she thought.

She looked over at the hammock that had stopped blowing back and forth in the breeze. She could no longer see the boy.

It was as if Lenny was not there, for he had disappeared in the sunlight.

Chapter Sixty-Two

Roseville

The smell from the sinkhole was growing stronger and Lenny felt himself growing weaker. If he could just hold on, they would find him, wouldn't they? Time came more quickly now. Whole worlds danced through his mind. In some, Miss Julie was happy, in some Jim and Lucy and he had become a family, in one Mari-Rose was there, standing in front of him, holding out her arms, pulling him to her. One world blurred into another so quickly that Lenny no longer knew which world was true, which to choose. He had not expected this – to see as he did. Hadn't Wild River Sal called it a gift? Lenny squeezed his fist tight, holding on to time, unwilling to let go. Then he was back in Miss Julie's back yard, time flickering before him once more, as he saw them all together one last time. It was that half-light time between day and night, the sun setting, before it would rise again to the east.

On the evening that they had decided to say goodbye to Stanley, Lucy brought warm blankets out to the lawn and laid them in a patchwork around the telescope. Miss Julie cooked callaloo fritters, using the recipe from the library book. Jim lit a barbecue and was busy fanning the flames into life. Appleby and Alma-Mae, Willie and Callie, Betsy and Lionel would all come along later to wish Stanley well.

Lenny was helping Miss Julie down the steps as he carried the basket full of food over to the blankets. Lucy lit a couple of citronella candles to keep the biters away. From further up the street came the sound of music playing – a new family had moved into Arturo's old house and the two girls, one slightly older than Lenny, one a little younger, were curious about the boy who lived four doors along, and kept popping their heads over the fence, then would run giggling and swooping around their back yard, until called in for supper, and the music would be muffled as the back door swung shut. The girls, Joni and Charlie, had moved with their parents from California, their father having a job with the new farming company over by what used to be Alma. They were different girls; Charlie was very pretty and shy, Joni was wilder, more of a tomboy. Lenny liked them both, the way they smiled at him at the bus stop when they'd all wait for the bus to go to school. And it was nice to have other kids to play with again. The street no longer felt so empty and lonely. It felt like home.

Some days he found he didn't even think about Mari-Rose and that made him both happy and sad. But Miss Julie, she could make him laugh, lift the sadness from about him.

'Pass me that plate,' Miss Julie asked Lenny, reaching forward in her deck chair. Lucy offered her a space on the blankets next to them.

'*Pas du tout!* If I sit on those blankets, Lucy, the only way you'll get me up is to roll me up in one,' she said, preferring to sit in her deck chair, a tray across the arms of it. Lucy laughed.

Lenny passed the filled plate to Miss Julie as Lucy served up, then he jumped up to welcome their guests.

Willie called out to them from the side of the house, '*Bonsoir*, folks 'bout?'

Callie came along behind him carrying more food, not wanting to turn up empty-handed. Shortly after came the others, all kicking off their shoes by the porch, letting the damp grass spring up underfoot as they carved a path down to where the barbecue smoked out, the smell of it wafting towards the lake.

'*Bonsoir*,' Miss Julie waved at them all from her deck chair. It was a long time since the house had been so full of folk and even though she felt bone tired, with it all weighing heavy on her heart, with the loss of Stanley fresh in her mind, she still managed to welcome them all in, these people like stray cats that Lucy Albert had gathered to her who, on hearing that Stanley would not be coming home after all, came to be there for the old woman, Lucy only having to mention it to them. And she was glad of that.

After everyone was fed and full to bursting, they all sat back, on rugs and deck chairs, watching the sky dip orange and gold and then turn an inky blue-black as the day disappeared. But the friends stayed on in the darkness, talking and laughing, no one wanting to leave, Lenny casting a giant shadow against the back of the house when he'd stand in front of the jam jar with its candle flame flickering in the breeze.

'That was a fine feast, Lucy,' said Appleby, averting his gaze, reluctant now to stare at Lucy, given as she belonged with Jim and he could no longer hope of catching her eye.

As the sky darkened, they could make out the night stars, and they all, save Miss Julie, lay back on the blankets, staring up at the sky.

Jim held Lucy's hand in his, a sad faraway look crossing his face. She squeezed him close to her, feeling him fighting off the sadness that would still descend upon him every so often, though these days it happened less frequently and for shorter bursts, and she was hopeful that, given time, he would heal and the sadness would leave.

'I ever tell you the story of Fionn mac Cumhaill?' he asked. Lenny laughed. It had been such a long time since Jim had told him this story, back when they were camping out in the woods, and Lenny found he had missed it – his dad telling him stories in the night air. Miss Julie's chin had dropped, and she was snoring gently but as everyone else hushed, Jim carried on regardless, pulling Lucy and Lenny closer to him.

'Well ...'

Lenny laughed as Jim mimicked the thuds of the giant, crossing the sea, ready to fight his opponent, and Lucy listened wide-eyed, happy to discover a story of Jim's she did not already know. Everyone clapped as Jim finished and he looked at them, dazed.

Then Lenny was on his feet and peering through the telescope, scanning the night sky for constellations, searching for stories in the heavens.

'You know,' Lucy whispered to Jim, 'I once dreamed of that story I think, of the giants and the baby. I dreamt it without knowing what it was. But I remember it …'

Jim pulled her to him, warm in the large woollen sweater she had knitted for him, one sleeve a little shorter than the other, though he didn't mind. It was the thought that counted.

How had she come to find him, and him her? After Mari-Rose, and his impossible yearning for Tayri, he had given up on love, considered it something for other folk. But Lucy had put him back together. Slowly. Despite everything. She had never let go.

'Stanley …' mumbled Miss Julie in her sleep, deep in conversation with her absent husband. In her pocket was the letter in the envelope – closed over once more with sticky tape.

Lenny saw all this.

Through the telescope lens, Lenny could make out Orion – the Hunter, as Jim called it, or the Warrior of the Desert – shining in the distance. In his pocket, he felt the agate stone rub against his hip, as if he had never lost it. As if it had never dropped.

When he looked through the lens again, he felt as if he were looking up at himself, somehow, and a shiver passed down his spine.

The telescope was tilted up to the stars, this small boy with white-blond curls turning it, his face looking upwards. Beyond the fence of the house, the path led down to the wooden jetties that stepped out into False River as it hugged the banks of Roseville, the water glinting silver in the night, and the biplane resting by the jetty. The little boy could make out a multitude of constellations through the lens of the telescope – it amazed him how the stars connected in these ways. *Are the shapes there because we see them, or do we see them because they are there?*

He wondered at it all. Always.

Lenny's eyes flickered open an instant. He saw it all before him.

But the stone was gone, and he could no longer hold on to time. It twisted from him, the boy letting go of the oak tree as the earth tipped.

Finally, the tree was bent double, bowed over to the sinkhole, the crack of the wood ringing out, the trees and plants around it sucked forth and down, and Lenny was flying through the air.

There was no one there to watch him fall.

Chapter Sixty-Three

Roseville

There on the small patch of green wrapped in white magnolias and bordered by deep beds of roses next door, lay Jim with his arms around Lucy Albert. Beside Lucy were Lionel and Betsy, Appleby next to Alma-Mae, Willie and Callie, all staring up at the stars. Next to them sat Miss Julie in her striped deck chair, head nodding in sleep, her crocheted blanket over her knees. For this was how Lenny wished to hold on to Roseville.

Up in the stars, where light pulsed and space rock hurtled, Lenny looked down on the houses next to the river. *Time enough*, he heard Mari-Rose's words once more. He saw Wild River Sal, remembered her muttering, warning him of the sacrifice he would make, soothing him, lifting something dark from about him. A shadow.

He was so very high up now. All the way to the edge of things. Stretching time all around him. He had a mission and he would be gone a while.

From up there he could see everything growing smaller, Roseville peeling away from him, the earth growing into a ball of light and blues and greens. And around him, he could see other planets, some like his own. On one he imagined Mari-Rose, kneeling in the grass, Jim with his arms around her, Lenny and Miss Julie chatting over the fence, Lucy Albert and Appleby Bertrand strolling past. Arturo calling around to play spaceships. *If only Arturo could see me now*, he laughed.

On another planet, one spinning very much like our own, he saw Stanley coming home to Miss Julie, her looking a lot younger, Stanley taking out the telescope to the back yard, the two of them sitting there gazing up at the stars, a young couple starting out on an adventure, making a life together. Miss Julie smiling back at Stanley. Her looking pretty and happy. A smile passing between the two of them. The red-bellied woodpecker, Frederik, singing in the background.

On another, he saw Jim and Lucy and Miss Julie, all crying, all holding on to each other, swaying by the water, as if the light had been sucked out of the day and he just wanted to reach out to them all and let them know it was all okay. Lenny called out to them, but this planet was too far away, and it turned from him before they could hear him.

Then another, this last one, where Jim – having never left Roseville – was coming back from the lumberyard up at the edge of town, calling out to Mari-Rose, taking something made at work from his pocket – a fox, carved out of scraps of wood, made in the quiet moments of the day, made with love.

As he fell, flying through the air, Lenny saw these worlds one by one.

Chapter Sixty-Four

Ubari Sand Sea

Somewhere, far below, is a young boy in the desert, wearing a *California Dreamin'* T-shirt, with an amulet, made of yellow desert glass, tied around his neck to protect him from *djinns*. The boy is also looking up at the stars.

In the desert, you can see the stars so clearly. There is no light pollution to dim them. Each night is a front-row seat into the infinite. That's what Izil thinks as he watches a fighter jet stream past high overhead, until, almost as quickly, it is gone. He wonders what it would be like to fly one of those planes – to travel faster than the speed of light, to feel G-force pressing down upon you, to see the whole world tilt upside down, then right itself.

If he ever meets one of those sky devils, he will ask him. He will ask him what it is like, and he will tell him about the stars, and point out the constellations to him.

On a clear night – when you can watch them all streaming into infinity.

Nearby, Izil hears the camels settle to rest, their humps silhouetted against the night sky as they sit huddled together.

'Izil!' His mother Tayri, anxious, calls for him. For a moment, there is a tremor, the earth shaking, the tents sucked down tightly into the sand. It lasts only an instant, then is gone, as a star shoots across the heavens.

The boy, reluctant to leave, pulls himself up, dusting the sand from his trousers.

'I'm coming,' he calls back to her, his voice lifted by the warm air caressing the sand sea, the sounds pulled upwards, up towards the heavens, until his words become an echo, reverberating in the night sky.

Chapter Sixty-Five

And Lenny, although he is already so very far away – from Roseville, from home – hears the boy and his mother in the desert and feels happiness without knowing why.

Acknowledgements

Lenny has had the support and encouragement of many individuals since the earliest drafts of the manuscript. I am deeply grateful to all the readers and those who have kindly supported me in this endeavour.

An earlier version of the novel was shortlisted on both Hollywood's ScreenCraft and The Tracking Board platforms for manuscripts with the best book-to-film potential. I found the reading reports and the feedback from both organisations very useful in shaping the story, and I am thankful for their support and enthusiasm for my writing.

On the editorial side, many thanks as ever to Amber Burlinson for her skilled guidance and wisdom on the early drafts – much appreciated.

My thanks to all the wonderful folk at New Island Books, especially Aoife K. Walsh, for your unending passion for books and your love for *Lenny*. It is a joy to work with such a talented team. Thanks also to Meg Walker for doing a brilliant job on the final edits of the manuscript. and to Anna Morrison for the gorgeous book cover design that beautifully captures the spirit of *Lenny*.

The novel in part pays homage to the writing and spirit of Antoine de Saint-Exupéry, who helped guide the way.

Roseville, the story's characters and many of the places within the novel are imagined and a work of fiction, but the concerns the novel explores are real – and so I am grateful to all those who work to raise awareness of the impacts of both conflict and environmental damage on our planet.

Finally, to Howard and Riley, thank you for your love, your encouragement, and for always being the stars in my night sky.

Readers' Guide

1. Reading and the imagination help transport Lenny far from the harsh reality of his circumstances. For Lenny, the library becomes his safe space where he can journey to other worlds through the power of story. What are some of the childhood stories you loved and that transported you elsewhere?

2. The novel examines notions of time, space and reality. Can you identify the different ways in which this is done? How is the novel as a form particularly suited to this kind of exploration of ideas?

3. Environmental issues feature throughout the novel – from the flooding, rapid land loss and ever-expanding sinkhole in Louisiana to the drought in the desert in North Africa. What are the connections between these different settings? How can we, as individuals, make a difference?

4. In the novel Lenny is reading the classic *The Little Prince*, and Jim also shares the mythical stories from his childhood with his son. What is the role of a story nested within a story? Can you identify narrative echoes for both in the novel?

5. The novel explores the notion of what makes 'home'. Lenny is homeless, sleeping rough in the bayou. Jim is 'uprooted', feeling disconnected from place and from himself. Miss Julie insists on remaining in Roseville for Stanley, for 'that is home'. Yet for Izil and his family in the desert, home is

not limited to one exact place because the Ubari Sand Sea itself is their home. What makes 'home' for you? Is it place, people, memories?

6. One of the themes of the novel is war and conflict and their impact on individual lives. What are some of the connections and impacts explored in the story and how?

7. In a world where it can increasingly seem like empathy and love in the face of human vulnerability are in short supply, what transformative role do both play in the novel?

8. Although Lenny is the novel's protagonist, the novel is written as an ensemble of voices, swapping between the perspectives of all the key characters. Do you have a favourite character in the novel and if so, who and why? What is it that makes us care deeply about a character in a story?